AN
IMPOSSIBLE
PROMISE

Also by Jude Deveraux and Tara Sheets

CHANCE OF A LIFETIME

Look for Jude Deveraux and Tara Sheets's next novel
in the Providence Falls series
available soon from MIRA.

For additional books by
New York Times bestselling author Jude Deveraux,
visit her website, www.judedeveraux.com.

For additional books by Tara Sheets,
visit her website, www.tarasheets.com.

JUDE DEVERAUX

AND TARA SHEETS

AN IMPOSSIBLE PROMISE

mira

ISBN-13: 978-0-7783-1212-3

An Impossible Promise

Mira
22 Adelaide St. West, 40th Floor
Toronto, Ontario M5H 4E3, Canada
BookClubbish.com

Printed in U.S.A.

For those who can't be together

AN
IMPOSSIBLE
PROMISE

PROLOGUE

THE CELESTIAL CHAMBER OF JUDGMENT WAS not cozy by any stretch of the imagination. Most of the time it appeared to be nothing more than white roiling walls of mist, which the angel Agon found downright dreary. But his associate Samael deemed it necessary, believing that human souls facing judgment were better off with no distractions. This was probably why Samael's face was now scrunched in open disapproval—an expression Agon had grown used to over the centuries.

"What," Samael demanded, pointing an elegant finger at the object against the chamber wall, "is *that*?" With his blond ringlets and cherub cheeks, he looked like a Renaissance painting of a frazzled choir boy.

It made Agon want to smile, but he refrained. For an angel as old as himself, he'd learned a thing or two. Instead, he drew up to his full height, impressive even by angelic standards, and stretched his snowy wings wide. "It's called a recliner," he said cheerfully. "For sitting and resting. Very comforting to humans, from what I gather."

Samael looked incredulous. "I've told you before, this is no place of solace. Human souls are summoned here to face judgment, and not all of them are headed to a comfortable destination."

"True." Agon sat on the edge of the overstuffed chair, swiveling left, then right. "But I see no harm in offering them a place to rest while we review their lives. If nothing else, it will provide an alternative to their usual pacing and wringing of hands and stumbling about in distress. It is pitiable when they do that, you must admit."

Samael sighed, shook his head and turned toward the wall of mist. A good sign, Agon decided. For now, it seemed the new chair could stay. Perhaps later he could bring in a few other earthly things to liven up the place, but what was that human expression? Ah, yes. *Baby steps.*

"We haven't time for your antics," Samael muttered, waving a hand at the wall of mist. "Our wayward rogue is about to learn a valuable lesson."

The mist cleared, revealing a city street at night. A swarthy stranger in a black leather jacket and designer jeans pulled his motorcycle to a stop outside a sports bar.

Agon rose from the chair and went to stand beside Samael as they watched the scene unfold. "You're sure this man is just like Liam O'Connor?"

"He has all the same traits as the rogue," Samael said. "The arrogance, the selfish motives, the questionable morals. He wasn't originally scheduled to cross paths with Liam, but it was easy enough to arrange."

Agon tilted his dark head, studying the man who was now sauntering toward the entrance of the bar. A neon sign that read ROOKIES blinked above the door. "And you're certain introducing this man to Liam will serve a useful purpose?"

Samael crossed his arms. "It will be good for Liam to see his own personality traits reflected in someone else. Perhaps then, through serious introspection, the rogue will realize his many faults and be at peace with the task we've given him."

"Perhaps," Agon said, though he wasn't so sure. Liam O'Connor and peace did not seem to mix. The man was hell-bent on winning Cora McLeod for himself, no matter how much he assured the angels he was trying to help Cora achieve her true destiny by marrying Finley Walsh. Agon knew what desperation looked like in a man's eyes, and paired with determination, it could be a dangerous combination. Liam had both in abundance. "I hope it works. He only has two months left to achieve his task."

Samael let out a huff. "It has to work. We can't interfere with his free will, and this is the last thing I could think of to help steer him in the right direction. We've already agreed to some of the 'boosts' he's asked for. Rudimentary computer knowledge. Fair warning when we plan to visit. We've even made it so he'd no longer feel pain whenever he and Cora touch." He gave Agon a stern look. "That last one was only because you advocated so strongly on his behalf."

"I think we can trust him to make the right decisions," Agon said. "I know he seems like a lost cause, but let us have faith that he will prevail."

"Mmm, faith," Samael said as they watched the tall man disappear into the bar. "In a rogue. What could possibly go wrong?"

1

LIAM O'CONNOR WRAPPED HIS ARM AROUND Cora McLeod, shifting her body so she was exactly where he wanted her, flush against his. "Now, don't overthink it. Just let it happen."

"I can't believe I'm doing this." Cora's voice was like a whisper of silk against his skin.

He closed his eyes, savoring the exquisite nearness of her. He'd waited lifetimes to hold her in his arms again.

"You can go now, Liam." Cora stuck her tongue between her teeth, squinted one eye and aimed at the dartboard on the wall. "I've got this."

Liam stepped back, already missing her warmth and the sweet herbal scent of her hair. It had been several days since he'd learned he could touch her without that initial snap of pain, and he'd been elated the angels had granted him that. There weren't many reasons to like those two, but that was a big one.

It was her friend Suzette Wilson's idea for them to all come to Rookies, a sports bar near the Providence Falls university district. Suzette had insisted Cora and Liam needed to spend Saturday night doing something fun with "normal people," and she wasn't wrong. They'd been wrapped up in police work ever since the murder of John Brady, a respected businessman in the community who also happened to be the husband of Liam's ex-mistress. It had been a complicated month, and if it wasn't for the kindhearted Cora and the well-meaning street kid Billy Mac intervening on his behalf, Liam might've lost his only chance at redemption. Now he had two months left to save his immortal soul, but he could focus on that tomorrow. Tonight it was nice to get out and do something carefree.

"You can do it, Cora," a man's deep voice said from the bar.

Liam hid his grimace with a swig of beer. Suzette had also taken it upon herself to invite the world's greatest bore, Finley Walsh. Unfortunately, Finn was Cora's destined soul mate, and as much as Liam hated the task the angels had given him, he had to somehow find a way to make Cora fall in love with the man. If he didn't succeed, well... Best not to think about the alternative.

Cora drew her hand back and let the dart fly. It missed the entire board by a good eighteen inches, landing with a *thunk* against the wood-paneled wall. She gave a frustrated growl and stomped her foot, which made Liam smile. Cora was adorable. Standing before him in blue jeans, a fitted cream sweater and heeled boots, the top of her head barely reached his chin, but she had enough feisty spirit to rival anyone. A blond curl fell across her sun-kissed face, and Liam struggled with the urge to reach out and smooth it back. She had no idea how beautiful she was to him. No idea how much he wanted her.

"Wow, Cora," Suzette called over the blaring music. "You're doing so much better!" Perched on a bar stool, Suzette raised her margarita glass in tribute. Her red hair was loose around her face, and her laugh was contagious. She jerked a thumb at a girl dressed in a referee shirt. "Last time you almost took out that server's eye."

The server made a wide berth around Cora and Liam, hefting a tray of drinks above her head. She hurried toward a group of college guys watching a boxing match on one of the flat-screen TVs. In another corner of the bar, a loud cheer erupted over a baseball game, and a boisterous group of fans gave each other high fives and slaps on the back. The air was thick with a mixture of booze and fried chicken wings and cheap cologne. Rookies was one of those relaxed hangouts where everyone talked a little too loud and drank a little too much. Liam loved it.

"It's official. I suck at darts," Cora said in defeat. She placed her last dart in Liam's hand. "I think it's safer if I quit now before I maim someone."

"Don't give up yet," Finn said. "You're making progress." He was sitting next to Suzette, and he'd been nursing the same beer for the past hour, the lightweight. He looked out of place in his pressed slacks and collared shirt, and for the millionth time, Liam wondered how on earth he was supposed to get Cora to fall in love with someone so painfully dull.

"No, I'm not making progress," Cora said with a sigh. "But thank you for pretending."

"I bet you'll even hit the board next time," Finn encouraged.

Cora laughed. "I'm afraid that's a bet you'd lose."

"He's not much of a betting man, anyway," someone said from the doorway. "Are you, Finn?"

They all turned as a tall, broad-shouldered man approached. He wore a leather motorcycle jacket the same dark shade as his hair, and he walked slowly, almost arrogantly, as if he had all the time in the world. There was a day's worth of stubble on his jaw, and a devil-may-care glint in his eye, and he seemed to know Finn, which Liam found surprising. This man appeared to be Finn's polar opposite, and therefore, somewhat interesting.

"Magnus," Finn said. He turned to the group and made introductions, explaining, "This is my colleague Magnus Black-well. He's an attorney at Johnston and Knight, too."

"I'm surprised to see you here, Finn," Magnus drawled. "Didn't think this place was your speed."

"I like it just fine."

"Really?" Magnus's polite smile was so genuine that Liam almost missed the skepticism behind it. The only reason he caught it at all was because he, himself, was an expert at subterfuge. Growing up thieving in nineteenth-century Ireland during the potato famine had given Liam plenty of opportunities to practice.

"Then maybe you should come out to the racetrack sometime," Magnus said to Finn. "Bring your Porsche and put it through its paces, for once."

Finn shook his head. "Not my thing."

"No?" Magnus didn't look surprised. He addressed Liam and the girls with a conspiratorial smile. "I never could understand why some people own fast cars but never bother to let them loose."

"You race cars?" Liam stared at him with a mixture of admiration and envy. His own car couldn't win a race against his elderly neighbor Mrs. Gilmore, and she walked with a cane. Why the angels stuck him with such an outdated heap of junk for an automobile, he'd never understand. It was probably some kind of lesson in humility, the bastards.

Magnus sized up Liam. "Sometimes, though not as much as I used to."

"Wow, racing cars. That sounds so—" Suzette's voice dipped to a sultry purr "—*dangerous.*"

Magnus gave a cocky smile. "Not if you know how to handle them. I teach stunt driving at the track once a month. There's a class this weekend, if any of you want to check it out."

Cora and Suzette laughed and gave their excuses, but Liam was already making plans to look up the class with his newfound computer skills. He wasn't going to pass up an opportunity to get behind the wheel of a sports car and just *go* for it. The thrill of racing in such a powerful machine! Who wouldn't want to fly like the wind, if they had the chance? Oh, right. Liam flicked a glance at Finn. The world's biggest bore.

Finn was scrolling through emails on his phone, ignoring Magnus. His expression remained carefully neutral, but Liam had the distinct feeling he was struggling with a negative emotion.

"So…" Magnus slapped his hands, rubbing them together. "Did I walk in on a bet over a game of darts?"

"Oh, no." Cora waved a hand. "I'm terrible at darts, and Finn was just teasing me."

"I wasn't teasing, Cora," Finn said, looking up from his phone. "I think you were really improving."

"How about you and me, man?" Magnus jerked his chin at Finn, a challenging glint in his eye. "A friendly game of darts. Say, twenty dollars to the winner?"

"No, thanks." Finn drank the last of his beer and signaled the bartender for another.

"Come on," Magnus said. "Darts isn't even my game, so you'll probably win. It'll be fun. What do you say, ladies? Want to see me fail miserably?"

"I do," Suzette sang out, eyeing Magnus like he was a prime cut of beef. "And if darts isn't your game, I want to know what is."

He gave her a slow smile and winked. "Tell you later."

Suzette's eyes sparkled with interest, and she gave a fluttery sigh. She was so visibly impressed by the man, Liam wouldn't have been surprised if she melted into a puddle on the floor.

He almost laughed. Magnus was a smooth talker, but Liam knew a hustler when he saw one. Magnus had all the moves—the charm, the easy smile, the casual wager. In fact, Liam would bet good money Magnus was great at darts and was trying to swindle Finn. Liam was beginning to like the guy, just on principle.

Suzette giggled then whispered something in Cora's ear. The two of them wandered into the crowd with their heads together, talking about whatever it was women talked about.

"So," Magnus said, turning to Finn, "you in?"

"No," Finn said flatly. He appeared cool on the surface, but Liam could tell he was bothered. How marvelous. This night was getting more entertaining by the second.

"I'll play," Liam offered with a shrug. "Though darts isn't really my game, either." He gave Magnus a vacuous smile. It had been a long time since he'd had a chance to cheat someone out of their money. Though Liam hadn't grown up playing darts, years of hunting, target practice and other varying games of skill—not to mention the manual dexterity involved in thieving and occasionally running for his life—made darts look like child's play. This was going to be fun.

Magnus gave an amiable nod. "Let's do it."

The match was ridiculous. Magnus was clearly throwing the game. Liam knew all the rules in the hustler's handbook. Magnus's score was always one or negative one when he busted out, but Liam wasn't fooled. He could tell Magnus had considerable skill and was holding back. So Liam went along for the ride, enjoying every second as Magnus played poorly on purpose. Liam matched him with terrible moves of his own, and they continued to bust out over and over until, finally, Liam made a "lucky" toss and won the game.

Magnus shook his head in defeat. "Told you I wasn't any good."

"I'm sure you'll do better next time," Liam said, playing his part.

Magnus started to hand over a twenty then stopped, as if a thought had just occurred to him. "How about one more game?"

And there it was. The hook. Liam's grin was genuine. People never changed, no matter the century. "Nah, I'm good."

"You sure?" Magnus asked. "We could make it more interesting. Say, one hundred dollars to the winner this time?"

Liam chuckled. This was the part where a clueless man would eagerly accept, then get fleeced for all his money. He hadn't had this much fun since he'd arrived in Providence Falls. As tempting as it would be to swindle Magnus out of a hundred dollars, Liam wasn't sure he'd actually win. Magnus was the kind of guy who always had a few tricks up his sleeve. He reminded Liam of his thieving friends back in Ireland. Liam suddenly felt a strange sense of camaraderie toward Magnus, and a sharp twinge of nostalgia for those times long gone.

"It was pure luck I won," Liam announced, slapping Magnus on the back. "I don't want to tempt fate."

"Come on, man," Magnus cajoled. "Live on the edge."

Been there, done that, already paying the price. "Some other time."

Magnus seemed disappointed for a split second, then let it go as a tall, curvy brunette breezed by on a cloud of cotton candy perfume.

She peeked over her shoulder at Magnus, gave a haughty toss of her hair and kept walking.

"Ah, Lola," he murmured with appreciation. "I think she's still mad at me for standing her up the other night."

"That's too bad," Liam said, watching her go. The woman's spiked red heels could double as lethal weapons in a street fight, but the deliberate sway of her hips suggested more enjoyable activities.

"Nah. I'll just buy her a drink, tell her what she wants to hear and she'll get over herself." Magnus gave Liam a knowing smile. "It's all how you play the game, right, man?"

"Not everything's a game," Finn said in irritation. He'd been so quiet throughout the match that Liam had almost forgotten he was there. Not surprising. If only Liam could forget the man forever. Cora deserved so much better.

Magnus narrowed his eyes and stared down his nose at Finn. "All of life's a game. Anyone who says otherwise is just no good at playing." With a nod to Liam, Magnus followed the woman into the crowd.

Finn looked pissed. What had Magnus done to get on Finn's

bad side? Liam didn't even know Finn had a bad side. Mostly, he just made calf eyes at Cora, smiled too much and bent over backward to do any little thing for her. He was a complete push-over. Magnus must've somehow pushed him all the way over.

Ever one to poke a hornet's nest, Liam leaned against the bar and said brightly, "Well, Magnus seems like a great guy. How long have you two been friends?"

"We're just business associates," Finn corrected. His jaw was set, and his mouth was pressed into a hard line. "We work at the same firm, but we don't work the same cases. Not unless there are special circumstances."

Liam watched Magnus across the bar as he sweet-talked the brunette. She'd gone from giving Magnus the cold shoulder to giving him a warm one. She was now pressed into his side, toying with the zipper on his leather jacket as he whispered in her ear. Impressive. The man worked fast. Maybe Finn was just jealous because Magnus knew how to have fun. He seemed like the type of man who took what he wanted from life, consequences be damned. An admirable trait, to be sure. He reminded Liam of… Well, himself.

Later that evening Liam discovered a new form of modern-day torture called karaoke. Cora and Suzette were flipping through a songbook while someone in the corner of the bar wailed into a microphone about a devil in a blue dress, or some such non-sense. Sweet Christ, at least in the past when a drunkard sang at the top of his lungs, there were no machines to amplify the noise. The singer's voice sounded like two cats fighting in a burlap sack, but even that was preferable to talking to Finn, so Liam couldn't complain too much.

Finishing the last of his beer, Liam noticed Magnus leaving arm in arm with the brunette and another woman who appeared to be her friend. Magnus gave Liam a cocky wink on his way out the door. *All how you play the game, indeed.*

Liam raised his glass to Magnus, then turned back to Cora,

who was now in a playful argument with Suzette over their song choices.

"Let's let Liam decide." Cora pushed the book toward him. "Which one?"

He looked over the list of titles, choosing the first one that resonated. "'Never Gonna Give You Up.'"

Suzette groaned and dragged the book back. "That's it. Your roommate is officially trashed, Cora. It's the only explanation for such a lapse in judgment."

Cora grinned at Liam, her blue eyes sparkling with laughter. Her smile was as bright and carefree as the Cora he remembered from another lifetime ago. *His* Cora. The girl who'd welcomed him with honest kindness the night he'd climbed into her bedroom window to rob her house. She'd been open and inquisitive and genuinely happy to meet him, and she'd never looked at him like the filthy, thieving peasant he was. Cora McLeod, daughter of the village squire, had made Liam believe he could someday be worthy of a woman like her.

His heart beat with that familiar sense of desperate, reckless hope. The kind of hope that promised impossible things. He remembered it so clearly, he could practically taste it like ambrosia on his tongue, their sweet dream of a future together, in spite of all the odds stacked against them. But according to the angels, he'd messed up Cora's destiny by crawling through her window that night so long ago. Getting her to fall in love with Finn, now, was the only way he could save himself from eternal damnation.

And yet… He glanced at Cora, warm and beautiful as sunlight, with her golden head tipped back, laughing at something her friend said. What if Magnus was right, and it was all how you played the game?

Liam's mind began to spin with dangerous possibilities. Maybe he just needed to find a way to bend the rules.

2

"YOU'RE WORKING," CORA SAID OVER A CUP OF coffee on Wednesday morning. She stood in front of Liam's desk at the Providence Falls police station, unable to hide the surprise in her voice. "At your actual desk. On your computer and everything."

"Mmm." Liam barely spared her a glance.

"I was beginning to think you were computer illiterate," she teased. Not once had she seen him do anything at his workstation. He was always fiddling with the mouse, pressing buttons on the keyboard, studying them like they were alien objects. But this morning he was treating his computer the way everyone else did—like it was just a tool.

"Whatever gave you that idea?" he asked without looking up.

Cora nodded to the growing stack of paperwork on his desk. "All that, for one. You haven't made a dent in it since you got here. And you're always coming to my desk, letting me do the research while you watch. So I figured either you didn't know how to use a computer, or you're just really lazy." She gave him a cheeky grin. "Now I know."

"Lazy?" Liam arched a dark brow, still focused on his screen.

Whatever he was working on, it had his full attention. "I'll have you know I took your advice and tried running around the neighborhood this morning, for no reason other than to *exercise*."

"I did notice that." He'd left his running shoes in the hallway, and she'd almost tripped over them. Not surprising, since he was proving to be a messy roommate, as well as an opinionated one. When he'd first moved into her house last month, he'd gone all fire and brimstone on her when she'd tried to do her morning exercise routine. He'd insisted her clothes were too revealing, which was ludicrous because they were just basic spandex workout shorts and a tank top. Later, he'd admonished her for running without a reason because, according to him, it was a waste of time and energy. "And how did you like it?"

He frowned. "It made me hungry."

"Yes, I noticed all my Pop Tarts were gone, too," she said drily. Liam was always hungry. He ate like a fraternity guy on a junk food bender. Just last weekend she'd watched him go through an entire box of frozen waffles in one sitting, yet he still had the lean, chiseled body of an athlete. Men and their metabolisms. It wasn't fair. "You mow through that stuff like it's candy."

"Sublime," he whispered, still staring at his monitor.

"I wouldn't go that far."

He made a purring sound of appreciation in the back of his throat.

Cora narrowed her eyes. "What exactly are you working on?" It was past ten in the morning, and they were about to go into the field to question a potential lead about the John Brady case. So far it was at a standstill, and they had nothing new to report. They were trying to track down Lindsey Albright, a college student who'd taken a selfie outside the Brady house on the night of the murder. According to Lindsey, she'd caught two figures in the window behind her in the picture. Captain Thompson said the photo was useless because it was too grainy and dark to show anything definitive. But Cora was hoping to interview the girl herself, in case she remembered anything else from that night.

Cora rounded Liam's desk and peered over his shoulder. "What the heck is this?" Photos of brightly colored sports cars were splashed across the screen. One car was weaving through a setup of orange cones. Another was caught in a tailspin, a wave of gravel arcing into the air behind it.

Liam finally dragged his gaze from the monitor. "I'm signing up for a two-day course in speed and stunt driving this weekend."

"With *your* car?" His poor sedan wouldn't make it around the first cone without blowing a tire. It reminded Cora of something her grandfather would've driven back in his heyday. She often wondered why Liam hadn't upgraded. Maybe he held on to it for sentimental reasons.

"Of course not. It says right here I'll get to drive one of theirs." He pointed to the web page, grinning up at her like a pirate who'd just discovered a hidden stash of gold doubloons. With his glossy hair waving rakishly over one eye, and the dark stubble on his strong jawline, he looked like the ultimate Hollywood bad boy. Though Cora hadn't wanted to admit it, she'd been overwhelmed the first time they'd met. Liam was the kind of attractive that made a woman feel simultaneously giddy and wary. It was an unsettling combination. Everything about him— the powerful physique, the deep velvet voice, the dark eyes that promised deliciously wicked things if a woman was willing— had thrown her off balance. It had been so unexpected, she'd actually stumbled when he'd first grasped her hand. But that was then, and now... Now she was much better. Totally fine.

She took a fortifying sip of coffee. They were roommates, and that was all they were. He'd made it pretty clear he wasn't into her, anyway. In fact, sometimes when they accidentally touched, he jerked away. Heat scorched across her face at the thought. It pricked her pride a bit, knowing he found her that undesirable, but honestly, it was a blessing in disguise. She didn't want him, either. Her friend Suzette was forever getting into trouble dating men who weren't right for her, and Cora didn't need that kind of stress.

She read the website title out loud. "Extreme Precision and Stunt Driving."

"Look at them," Liam breathed, scrolling through the car photos. "Aren't they glorious?"

"Happy Fourth of July, everyone!" Otto Simpson ambled into the office, holding a plastic container of frosted cupcakes with American flags and candy sprinkles. "I picked these up at Sugar Pie's on the way here." Otto was a heavyset man with a balding head and a deep love of God and country and baked goods. With his round face and ready smile, he reminded Cora of a Campbell's soup kid from one of those old-fashioned advertisements.

"No time for your snacks, Otto." Happy Blankenship rose from his desk across the room, eyeing the cupcakes with distaste. Though he was younger than Otto by several years, his wiry frame and pinched expression always made him seem older. "And don't bother sitting down, either. We just got another call from the Greenfield Country Club."

Otto plunked the cupcakes on his desk with a heavy sigh. "Those kids setting off bottle rockets in the street again?"

Happy gave a curt nod. "And this time they've been drinking. Apparently, they got their hands on some M80s, too. The big ones. They're lighting them in the cul-de-sac near the dog park."

"Every year," Otto grumbled, following Happy out of the pen. "It's like clockwork with those teenagers."

"I'll tell you what's clockwork." Rob Hopper hung up his phone and dropped his head to his desk, banging it a couple of times for emphasis. "Mrs. Wilson and her weekly complaints."

"What's wrong this time?" Cora asked. "Raccoons in her garbage cans? Someone trampled on her flower bed?" Mrs.

Wilson was the old widow of a retired police officer who had died several years ago. The Providence Falls police were kind and attentive to her because they wanted to honor her husband's good name, but it wasn't always easy. She was as bored and as crotchety as a shrew. Mrs. Wilson's kids were grown and gone, and judging by her personality, Cora guessed they didn't often visit. It was probably the reason Mrs. Wilson kept filing formal complaints about the neighborhood with the local PD. It gave her something to do.

"She wants me to arrest her neighbor because his dog won't stop barking," Rob said with a groan. "Says if we don't put a stop to it, she's going to lace one of her fruitcakes with rat poison and feed it to him."

"The dog or the neighbor?" Cora asked.

"Exactly. With that woman, you just never know." Rob's face filled with hope. "I don't suppose you and Liam want to take this one?"

"Not a chance. We're off to the university district."

Rob gave her a long-suffering look. His boyishly handsome face was a little sunburned, reminding Cora of the way he'd looked back in high school when he ran track. Sometimes she couldn't believe she'd briefly dated him, but teenagers weren't exactly known for their stellar decision making. Luckily, she'd wised up fast, and they'd never gotten serious. Rob was a nice enough guy, but he was an outrageous flirt and had a reputation for charming the socks—and other articles of clothing—off scores of women. Cora suspected her friend Suzette had a secret thing for him, but to Cora he was just like an annoying brother.

"Hey, look on the bright side," Cora teased. "Maybe Mrs. Wilson will save you a piece of fruitcake."

He threw her a look equivalent to a rude hand gesture and stalked out.

Cora turned to Liam, who was back to salivating over sports cars on the website. The look on his face was downright indecent.

"Come on, *Fast and Furious.*" She slapped the back of his chair and went to grab her purse off her desk. "I want to catch Lindsey Albright at her apartment before she goes to work."

"I'm not angry," Liam said, taking one last look at his computer screen.

"What?"

He stood and stretched like a lazy lion. "You called me fast and—"

"Oh, no way." Cora gaped at the blank look on his face. "Don't tell me you've never seen *Fast and Furious.* With the racing cars and all that?"

He shook his head.

"Jeez, Liam, you must've been living in a bubble before we met. I guess we'll have to have another movie marathon this weekend." For someone who loved fast cars as much as he did, she was surprised he'd never heard of the films. But then there were a lot of things Liam seemed to have missed, like roller coasters and ice-skating and senior prom. Just the other day he asked her if she'd ever seen the ocean. Weirdo. It was only a few hours away. Did he expect that she'd never traveled outside the town where she'd grown up? Cora smiled at the memory because, whether she wanted to admit it or not, his quirkiness was growing on her.

"Tootaloo, y'all!" Mavis sang out as they left the police station. The receptionist was wearing one of her trademark sweatshirts with a quilted birdhouse on the front and dangly feathered earrings in patriotic colors. As usual, her heavy perfume wafted through the air around her desk like an invisible force field.

"Don't get into any trouble while we're away," Liam said, snagging a butterscotch candy from her dish. "Wait until I get back, so I can join you."

Mavis gave a high-pitched giggle that ended on a snort.

Cora shook her head as she pushed through the front door. It seemed no woman was immune to Liam O'Connor's charm. Except herself, of course. Thank goodness.

★ ★ ★

The university district was a fascinating melting pot of humanity, with people of all ages and walks of life bustling from one activity to another. There were modern offices next to quaint independent bookstores, and dusty music shops selling old vinyl records. People lounging on wrought-iron bistro chairs sat outside street cafés, chatting over lattes while their dogs snuffled for breadcrumbs under the tables. Quirky art galleries lined the avenue along with a pipe shop, a tattoo parlor and consignment stores with racks of retro clothing spilling onto the sidewalks.

"This place is amazing," Liam said, staring at a group of impressively limber women doing yoga on a grassy lawn. Posters advertising the night's Fourth of July celebration were pasted against the brick wall behind them. He knew about the American holiday from the basic knowledge the angels had given him. The fireworks were sure to be outstanding, but Liam found the idea of celebrating freedom from the British even more fascinating. He'd never been one of those rebels who called themselves Fenians, or anything like that. Politics didn't mean much to a hungry man, but the idea of wresting independence from the Crown tickled the imagination.

"Lindsey's apartment is on the other side of those dorms," Cora said, pointing to a redbrick building in the distance. She swerved just in time to dodge a bicyclist weaving through traffic. "This place is a zoo today. This part of the city's always like this on holidays."

Liam had often heard people remark that Providence Falls was small, but to him it seemed as vast and ever changing as the sea. Every part of the city was so unique; you could drive four blocks and be in what felt like a whole different world. He thought he'd grown used to it, the constant commotion and traffic and noise, but today he was reminded again how far from home he truly was.

Home. The thought always left a hollow ache in his chest, because he knew it no longer existed. Everything and everyone from his old life was dead and gone.

He looked at Cora as she turned the car onto a residential, tree-lined street. Her delicate profile was so familiar and dear to him, it helped lighten the heaviness in his heart.

A few minutes later they pulled into Summerwalk Apartments. It was a two-story complex with indistinguishable units in varying shades of beige. Many of the people coming and going appeared to be college students or young professionals, and everything about the place screamed "temporary."

Lindsey's apartment was on the second floor. Loud, thumping music boomed from inside, and a girl's high-pitched giggle could be heard over the bass.

Cora rang the doorbell. When no one answered, Liam raised his hand and knocked. Still no answer. He made a fist and pounded hard on the door.

The music lowered, and the door swung open to reveal a flush-faced young woman chomping on a wad of chewing gum. She looked annoyed and slightly out of breath, wearing nothing but an oversize T-shirt that barely covered the important bits. "Can I help you?"

Cora flashed her badge and introduced herself and Liam. "Are you Zoe?"

The girl nodded, eyeing them like they were door-to-door snake oil salesmen. Liam was familiar with that look. He'd been on the receiving end of it countless times in his past life—usually for good reason. It was oddly comforting to know the world might appear different, but people didn't change much.

"I spoke to you on the phone last week," Cora said, putting her badge back in her pocket. "We're looking for your roommate, Lindsey Albright. Is she here?"

"Nuh-uh." Zoe blew a small bubble, then popped it in her mouth.

"Do you know where we can find her?"

Zoe scoffed. "Probably in The Doghouse with the rest of the freaks."

"Doghouse?" Liam asked.

"Yeah, that motorcycle compound on the north side. She's dating one of the Booze Dogs but keeping it on the down low because her parents are crazy conservative. Her dad's a pastor, if that tells you anything."

"Zo!" a young man's voice called from inside the apartment. "Bring the pizza and get your fine ass in here, girl."

Zoe gave an impatient flip of her hair, revealing a purple love bite on her neck. "I gotta get back to my study group."

Liam raised a brow. Was that what they were calling it these days?

"Can you tell us Lindsey's boyfriend's name?" Cora pressed. "Or anything else that might help us find her? It's important that we talk to her."

"Look, she doesn't hang out here much, okay? Me and Lindsey don't run in the same crowd. We're just roommates, and we stay out of each other's business. Don't ask, don't tell. All I know is her boyfriend rides with the Booze Dogs." *Snap* went the gum. "And he likes K-pop music."

"He…" Cora looked skeptical.

"I know, right?" Zoe gave a derisive snort. "You'd think he'd be into death metal or something more eighties-hair-bandy, but nope. Lindsey wears his BTS shirt to bed at night."

"Anything else?" Liam asked.

Zoe leaned against the door frame and gave him a coy smile. "Underwear, I guess. But like I said, I don't ask."

"Anything else you can tell us to help *find* her," Cora explained in a voice filled with infinite patience. Liam had no idea how she managed to deal with the public on a daily basis and still remain calm and collected. It was a true gift. One he didn't possess.

"That's all I've got. Why? Is she in trouble?"

"Not at all," Cora assured her. "We just wanted to ask her some questions."

Zoe jammed a hand onto her hip. "Well, when you find her, tell her she needs to get her ass back here because rent's due, and I don't have the money to spot her again like last time."

"Babe!" The music volume increased, and the man inside made a sound like a great jungle cat. "Don't make me come haul you over my shoulder!"

Zoe rolled her eyes and said, "Later." Then she shut the door in their faces.

Cora blinked at the wood paneling. "Thanks."

"She was a treat." Liam turned to go.

"No wonder Lindsey's never home."

"Yes. I imagine it's difficult to live with someone who has such...vigorous study habits."

Zoe's piercing giggle and a deep male growl could still be heard over the music as they walked away.

Cora drove north toward The Doghouse with a growing sense of unease. While she hoped they'd find Lindsey there, she couldn't help being a little concerned. The Booze Dogs were notorious for their rowdy parties and borderline-legal activities, and they weren't keen on unexpected visitors. The founder's family were moonshiners during the Prohibition era, and the club was known for having their own code of justice that didn't always correspond with the law. Cora had never been to their clubhouse on the outskirts of town, but she'd heard about the place from other officers. It was down a long dirt road off the main highway, and the whole compound was surrounded by a chain-link fence with barbed wire. Not exactly a welcoming place.

"Can you not drive a bit faster?" Liam asked, shifting in his seat. "I'm going to grow white hair by the time we get there."

Cora checked the speedometer. "We're going exactly seventy, the speed limit."

"Aye, but we're law enforcers. I'd say that gives us leave to bend the rules a bit."

"Which is why I'm driving, and you're not."

He leaned back in his seat and mumbled, "My class this weekend can't come fast enough."

"Is this the driving class taught by Finn's friend Magnus?"

"It is, but they're not friends," Liam said with a chuckle. "Finn doesn't like the man. He was so cold to Magnus at the bar the other night, I got frostbite just standing next to them."

Cora frowned. "That doesn't sound like Finn at all."

"No? Maybe you don't know him as well as you think."

"Sure, I do." Even though Finn was only a few years older than she was, he'd been golfing buddies with her father. For years Cora had always thought of Finn as being on the stuffy side with his polished manners and meticulous way of dressing, but she'd recently learned he wasn't stuffy at all. There was a quiet strength in him she hadn't noticed before, and he was steadfast and reliable, which was refreshing.

"Believe me, Cora, there's a lot you don't know." There was a smug undercurrent in Liam's voice that grated on her nerves.

She shook her head. "Your arrogance never ceases to amaze me, you know that?"

"I'm just speaking the truth," Liam said with a shrug.

"I've known Finn a lot longer than I've known you," Cora pointed out. "And since you've already proven yourself to be a hothead who's prone to impulsive actions, forgive me if I'm more inclined to assume you misjudged the situation. Finn is a really nice person." She gave him a sideways glance. "The jury's still out on you."

"Ah, the illustrious Finley Walsh." Liam's tone was laced with mock sincerity. "Ever the perfect gentleman."

"What is your deal?" Cora spit out. "Finn's been nothing but nice to you, so there's no need for the sarcasm. Anyway, better a gentleman than a playboy like that Magnus guy."

"Playboy?" Liam had the gall to look offended. "Just because a man likes to have fun and enjoy life doesn't mean he's insincere or flippant with his feelings. Some people may look a certain way on the outside, but inside they feel just as deeply as… Never mind. It doesn't even matter." His voice trailed away on a whisper of regret, the words sounding sad and vulnerable. It was impossible to miss the haunted look in his eyes.

All Cora's annoyance suddenly evaporated. "What is it?"

He swallowed visibly, then looked out the window in silence.

If Cora didn't know any better, she'd say Liam was grieving. His shoulders were slumped, and his gaze seemed a million miles away. Maybe he was hurting because of his recently ended affair with the widow Margaret Brady. Liam and Margaret's secret relationship was discovered after her husband was mysteriously murdered. For a while Liam had been a suspect in the investigation, and he'd almost lost his job with the Providence Falls Police Department because he'd kept his affair with Margaret a secret. Once his alibi had been confirmed and his name was cleared, everything seemed to go back to normal, but Cora suspected there was more to Liam than he pretended. Maybe all his arrogant swagger was just a facade, and he was really dealing with a broken heart.

"You might be surprised to find some men want the same things you do, Cora," he finally said. "And they just need the chance to prove it."

Cora sighed. "Suzette said the same thing to me last Saturday night."

"Well, there you go. If you don't want to listen to me, then listen to your very wise friend."

"I don't usually equate wisdom on dating with Suzette, but maybe she's right." Cora shrugged. "I guess I'll consider it."

"Good." He paused. "Wait, what?"

"I mean, she did give him my number." Cora took the next exit toward the road leading to the motorcycle compound.

Liam's head whipped around. "Who?"

"And he was sort of charming," she mused, switching lanes as they approached the intersection. "In a whole my-what-big-eyes-you-have type of way. He's really more Suzette's type, and she even said as much, but since she's dating someone else right now—"

Her phone rang, the shrill sound filling the car.

Liam sat up straighter. "Who are you talking about?"

She flicked a glance at him. "Magnus. Who else?" Then she pushed the button on her audio speaker. "McLeod."

"Get out to the jogging trail behind Wilson's house." Captain Thompson's voice blared through the car speakers.

"But we're almost to Lindsey's—"

"She won't be there," the captain said curtly. "Lindsey Albright was found in the woods thirty minutes ago. Dead."

Cora gasped. "Are you—"

"We're sure. Just get out here," he barked, before hanging up.

Cora looked at Liam in disbelief.

His eyes were filled with storm clouds and a thousand dark emotions.

She felt the same way. *Another* murder. In all the years she'd worked on the Providence Falls police force, they'd never had two so close together. This morning Cora had hoped Lindsey would help them get one step closer to solving the murder of John Brady, but now the poor girl was dead, too. Were their deaths connected? If so, how?

Punching the gas with enough speed to impress even Liam, Cora made a screeching U-turn at the intersection. Her mind boomeranged back and forth between every possible explanation, but no matter how she spun it, only one fact remained clear. Everything just got a hell of a lot more complicated, and she had a feeling it was only going to get worse.

3

MRS. WILSON'S HOUSE WAS PART OF AN OLD BED-room community called Glen Acres, built back when JELL-O molds were the ultimate party food and automobiles came standard with built-in ashtrays. Ramblers and split-level homes lined the narrow streets like retired railway cars in shades of rust and moss. The postage stamp–size yards were varied, some surrounded by low, chain-link fences and potted plants, others with overgrown weeds and random bits of furniture lurking in the tall grass. Cora never liked lingering in this part of town if she could help it. The neighborhood always felt so stale and forgotten, as if time had swept through the world like a giant broom, but somehow missed this one spot, leaving it to roll into obscurity like a dust mote under the couch.

"I told you it was an emergency, young man." Mrs. Wilson's cranky voice could be heard from her front yard as Cora and Liam approached. There were three police cars and an ambulance parked at angles along the street, and a few neighbors milling on the sidewalk. "That dog's been barking all night. Why it took y'all so long to get out here, I'm sure I don't know."

Rob Hopper nodded politely at the old woman as she ranted.

From the slump of his shoulders and the tight lines around his mouth, Cora could tell Rob had been there for a while.

"It's like I always say, this neighborhood has gone to the birds." Mrs. Wilson's head shook, threatening to dislodge the three rollers clinging to the wisps of hair near her ears. Hands on hips, she stared at Rob through crinkled, watery eyes. Even though she was wearing a floral housedress and velour slippers, she still somehow managed to look like a stern school principal reprimanding a wayward student. "When my Ansel was alive, people here were decent, God-fearing folks. Now there's nothing left but a bunch of no-good rabble-rousers. And what do we get for it? *Murder!*" Her shrill voice rose, and she threw her hands in the air. "Murder, that's what!"

An audible gasp followed by hushed, frantic voices came from the neighbors across the street.

Mrs. Wilson's face had turned an alarming shade of red, and her mouth kept opening and closing as if she was at a loss for words, but Cora knew they weren't going to be that lucky.

Rob gently ushered the old woman toward her front door. "Why don't we go back into the house, and you can tell me more." He caught sight of Cora and Liam and threw them an exasperated look before jerking his head toward the backyard. "The jogging trail's just beyond those trees," he told them, pointing into the woods.

Liam barreled through the yard and into the greenbelt behind the house, his back ramrod straight. He clenched and unclenched his hands at his sides, and he seemed deeply agitated.

Cora hurried to catch up with him. "You all right?" He hadn't said much since Captain Thompson's phone call.

"Fine." He didn't seem fine, but maybe the news of Lindsey's murder was just hitting him hard. It was understandable. Cora was fiercely protective of her beloved town and the people in it. It was the reason she'd joined the police force in the first place. Anytime a tragedy like this happened, it pierced through her mental armor, but it was something she'd learned to compartmentalize. Years of growing up with her police captain father had taught her how important it was to stay focused on the job, even when a wave of emotional turmoil threatened to pull her under. But not everyone was good at it, and even Cora struggled sometimes. Maybe Liam just needed a breather.

"Listen, if you want to go back and help Hopper with Mrs. Wilson, I can take it from here," she offered.

Liam didn't answer. Instead, he charged down the jogging trail in big, ground-eating strides, muttering under his breath. In the distance police officers stood near a taped-off area of dense foliage. A man who appeared to be the coroner was crouched near the ground with the glowering Captain Thompson standing over him.

Cora reached out and caught Liam's forearm.

He turned, blinking like she'd just pulled him from a dark room into daylight. "What?"

"It's not a problem if you don't want to see this right now," she said quietly. "I get it. We've all been there. Why don't you head back, and I'll fill you in later?"

Liam's stormy expression smoothed into one of mild amusement. "If you're suggesting I'm better off dealing with that old lady and her poisoned fruitcake, I'd prefer to take my chances out here with the murderer, thanks."

Okay. Apparently, he could compartmentalize just fine. Cora pushed past him. "I was only trying to help."

His large hand caught hers, and he pulled her back to face him. "I know you were, and I thank you for it. It's in your nature to help others. You've always been that way, *macushla*." There was deep admiration and warmth in his gaze, almost startling in its intensity. His thumb brushed lightly across the back of her hand, sending tiny ripples of awareness over her skin.

Cora's lips parted on a tiny exhale, her mind skipping like a needle on an old-fashioned record player. It was happening again. That odd sense of déjà vu that ebbed and swelled around her like it often did when Liam got this close. Everything felt infinitely familiar. The way he stood against the backdrop of trees, enveloping her in the scents of rain and wood smoke and leather. The way he smiled down at her as if he knew her deepest secrets. Even the roughness of his calloused hand against hers... All of it felt like something she'd experienced before.

He gave her hand a squeeze and turned away, breaking the spell. "I've no problem looking at dead bodies, if that's what you're on about," he said over his shoulder. "Where I come from, it's a familiar enough occurrence."

Cora frowned as she followed him toward the crime scene. Before he moved to Providence Falls, he'd been stationed in Raleigh, but the murder count wasn't that high there. Unless he was talking about the place in Ireland where he grew up, but just how dangerous could a small, rural town in Ireland be? She'd heard him refer to it as a village once or twice, which brought to mind the flowering cottages and cobblestone streets from those Thomas Kinkade paintings. They didn't exactly scream Murder Capital of the World.

She smiled wryly and shook her head. Liam was a bit of an enigma. It was strange how she could feel so connected to him in one moment and light-years apart in another. There was so much about him she really didn't know. *Macushla*, for example. She kept meaning to ask him what it meant. Whenever he used that word, it did strange, swoopy things to her insides and made her limbs go all soft and melty. But that was probably because his Irish accent grew thicker when he said it. Her reaction had nothing to do with *him*, of course. Every woman on the planet knew that a deep Irish brogue packed a heavyweight punch to the libido. Common knowledge.

A gruff voice cut through the hushed silence. "McLeod. O'Connor." Captain Thompson waved them over, his face as dark and brooding as a thundercloud. He wasn't a warm and fuzzy person, even on his best day, but today there was an angry tension emanating from him that surpassed his usual stoic demeanor.

Lindsey Albright's body lay on the ground in a shallow ditch, partially covered in mud and damp leaves. She wore a blue T-shirt, denim shorts and canvas tennis shoes with ankle socks speckled with cartoon narwhals. Cora's stomach churned. They were too cheerful, those socks. Too sweet and carefree for such a somber scene, and it threatened her composure. She swallowed hard, ignoring the smiling narwhals to focus on the evidence. The only thing that stood out was the angry marks around the woman's slender neck. Her face was bone white, the soft features devoid of the sunny cheerfulness Cora remembered when the girl had entered the station just days ago.

"Strangled," Liam said in a low voice. "Just like John Brady."

"Looks like it," Captain Thompson said. "Couldn't have happened more than forty-eight hours ago, but we'll know more after we send for the specialists from Raleigh."

"Has anyone interviewed the residents?" Cora asked.

"Yes, and so far no one's seen or heard anything out of the ordinary," Thompson said. "Aside from Mrs. Wilson's complaint about her neighbor's barking dog. Seems the neighbor finally went to go fetch his dog, and that's when the body was discovered."

"This greenbelt isn't that deep," Cora observed. About a hundred yards from the jogging trail, traffic was visible from a street on the other side. "If the killer assaulted her while she was on the trail, he could've come from that direction. There'd be less chance of being noticed."

"It's possible," Thompson said. "Would be more difficult to trace, if that were the case. That street's hidden from the main road. Anyone could've gotten in and out without being seen."

"Whoever did this, it was likely someone she knew," Liam said as he crouched to view the body. "No apparent signs of struggle, and aside from the marks on her neck, the rest of her looks untouched. No rips or tears in her clothing. No visible abrasions on her hands or knees. Even her hair is still neatly braided. It almost seems as if…she was killed somewhere else, and then dumped here." He stood, scanning the area around them.

"Elaborate," Captain Thompson said through narrowed eyes.

"If the attack happened on the jogging trail, there'd be mud scuffs on her shoes, or something noticeable in the surrounding foliage, at least," Liam said. "But everything appears intact, and the ground is undisturbed. No signs of dragging in any direction."

"It rained some last night," Cora said.

"Even still, the forest tells stories, if you know how to look," Liam continued. "There'd be a broken branch or a crushed shrub. There'd be some evidence of a scuffle. A body doesn't just go limp all of a sudden if someone cuts off your air. You *fight* to breathe. At least for a minute or so, until your brain begins to shut down from lack of oxygen, and your limbs go numb and your vision goes dark."

Cora frowned, wondering how Liam knew that.

He peered through the trees to the road beyond the greenbelt, then stared down at Lindsey's body. "It would've had to be someone strong enough to carry her deadweight quickly through the woods. If this was planned, the killer would've hidden Lindsey's body better, not just tossed her in a ditch like this." He lowered his head, deep in thought. "Must've been in a hurry. Perhaps her death was an accident."

"Maybe it was a lover's quarrel gone bad," Cora said to Captain Thompson. "We just found out Lindsey was seeing a guy who rides with the Booze Dogs. We were on our way to their compound to question him when you called us."

"All right," Thompson said with a nod. "Track him down, and bring him in."

4

IT WAS LATE AFTERNOON WHEN LIAM FOUND himself in a staring contest with a mountain of a man named Bear. The man stood on the other side of a chain-link fence at the motorcycle club compound known as The Doghouse. He was muscular to the point that it appeared uncomfortable, with huge, swollen biceps and legs the size of tree trunks. A bandanna held his hair flat against his boulder-shaped head, and tattoos snaked around his neck and forearms. With a huge hand resting on a faded sign that read TRESPASSERS WILL BE SHOT, he made an imposing gatekeeper. Behind him a long line of motorcycles was parked in front of a two-story building, and a party was in full swing on the lawn outside.

Cora flashed her badge with her usual professional politeness, but after initial introductions, Bear seemed less interested in her words and more interested in her lips, her chest, her legs and then her chest again. His grisly mouth lifted, and he let out a hum of pure male appreciation.

Liam stared daggers at him, shifting his weight to maneuver his shoulder in front of Cora. Bear sized him up, and for several long moments they had one of those silent male conversations that, in Liam's experience, women often missed.

Don't even think about it. She's off-limits.

Sure about that?

Aye, so watch yourself or we'll have a problem.

Bear scoffed, then turned his attention back to Cora.

"So we'd like to speak with one of your club members named Slice," Cora was saying. "We were told he might be here."

"Who?" Bear asked her chest.

"Slice," Cora repeated. "We heard—"

"Who told you he'd be here?"

"That's not your concern," Liam said sharply. He was getting tired of the man's wandering eyes. "Just go get him and be quick about it."

Bear glared at Liam and turned to go. "Can't help you."

"We understand Slice has been seeing a woman named Lindsey Albright," Cora said.

"Never heard of her, sweet cheeks."

Liam hooked his fingers through the chain links, bristling at the man's blatant disrespect. He'd never taken down a bear, but there was always a first time.

Cora tried again. "We believe she's been coming here with Slice sometimes. We need to get some more information about her and—"

Bear let out a sound that almost passed for a laugh. He swung around and pointed to the party. "See those chicks?"

Scantily clad women danced to loud music thumping from car speakers in an open garage. Some were lounging with guys on fold-out chairs around a central fire pit, while others drank from red plastic cups as men hauled beer kegs off a flatbed pickup truck. A few women in wet T-shirts and cutoff shorts ran screeching and laughing from a man chasing them with a garden hose.

"We got girls coming and going here all the time," Bear said.

"Some new, some repeats, but all in it for the same reason. All looking to party and have fun, no questions asked. That's how we like it. Ain't got time to learn every chick's name when it don't matter in the long run."

"Not even if she's been murdered?" Cora called out.

Bear slowed to a stop. The ropey muscles on his neck and arms flexed like a wild animal bracing to defend its turf. His expression was downright feral. "What's that got to do with the Booze Dogs?"

"Nothing, yet." Liam kept his tone mild, but there was an unmistakable edge to it. "We're not here to make trouble with you or your club. We only want to talk to Slice."

"He ain't here," Bear said. "The kid only hangs on the weekends, so you're out of luck."

"Do you know where we can find him?" Cora asked.

Bear gave a half shrug. "Maybe his mama's house."

"Where does she—" Liam began.

"I don't know, man. Do I look like I got Google Maps stamped on my forehead?"

"Sorry we interrupted your party," Cora said politely. "Thanks for your time, Mr. Bear."

"It's just Bear," he said to Cora, letting his gaze roam over her one last time. The appreciative leer was back, and Liam wanted to stamp the man's forehead with his fist. "Shame you're a cop, or I'd invite you to come party." He looked at Liam and growled, "Not you."

Before Liam could react, Cora grabbed his arm and pulled him toward the car. The loud pop of fireworks started from somewhere inside the compound as they drove away.

"That man was an idiot," Liam grumbled as they left billows of dust in their wake.

Cora grinned. "You're just jealous he didn't invite you to the wet T-shirt party."

"What kind of a name is Bear, anyway?"

"A very appropriate one."

"I didn't like the way he spoke to you."

"That was nothing," Cora said with a laugh. "You should've heard Crack Rock Cecil going off on me when I had to interrogate him. He makes Bear sound like the butler from Downton Abbey."

Liam grimaced, sinking into the car seat. Cecil was a former drug dealer who'd committed many other crimes, one of which was a mugging incident involving Liam. If it wasn't for Cora's dragging Cecil in for questioning, Liam wouldn't have had an alibi during the time of John Brady's murder. Liam could've lost his job, and even worse, his chance at redemption. He rubbed his face and gave a heavy sigh. After Cora's musing about dating Magnus earlier, he'd been in a foul mood, which only grew worse with the death of Lindsey Albright. At times like this he felt like he was careening out of control. There were too many distractions and problems, when all he really needed to be worrying about was getting Cora to fall for Finn. As unsavory as that may be, it was priority one.

"You're not really thinking about dating Magnus, are you?" he asked suddenly.

"No." Cora looked at him like he was crazy. "After the week we've had, I can't even think about dating. There's too much going on, and all my energy needs to go into focusing on work. Right now all I want to do is go home, take a hot shower, drink a cold beer and zone out."

"I'll drink to that," Liam said.

"I don't want to go to the Fourth of July party tonight, either," Cora added wearily. Earlier in the week they'd made plans to spend the evening with Suzette and some of her friends. "I'm just too tired. But last year I discovered there's a pretty good view of the fireworks from the roof of my house, if you're interested. That's where I'm going to be tonight. Want to join me?" Her grin was so warm and bright, Liam felt it in his bones.

Later that night they climbed onto the rooftop and huddled under fuzzy blankets sipping cold beer with a sliver of a moon winking down at them.

"Beautiful," Liam breathed, staring up at the starry sky. It was a shining reminder that the universe was vast and mysterious and inexplicable. Even though the mere thought could be enough to cause anyone to feel small, Liam felt a sense of peace. When he looked up, there was no marked passage of time, no change in the order of the heavens that he could see. Without having to try too hard, he could almost believe he was back in Ireland in eighteen forty-four with his beloved Cora.

"What are you thinking?" she asked softly.

He dragged his gaze from the heavens and looked at her. She was all at once his, but unattainable. Close, but worlds away. If he reached out to touch her, would she shy away? Or would she welcome him with open arms like she once had? Sometimes his old life felt like a fading dream, like wisps of fog through his fingers when he tried to hold on to the memories. But this version of Cora was so vibrant and alive and utterly magnificent, he couldn't grieve for his lost life. He was here now, with her, and that had to be enough.

"Earth to Liam," Cora teased. "I never know where you go when you get that look on your face."

"Old memories," he said, taking a sip of his beer.

"Good ones?"

"Aye." His smile was a little sad. "But not as good as the ones we're making now."

Cora nudged his shoulder playfully. "You can save that lethal charm for the ladies, Officer O'Connor, because I'm already invested here. See this?" She held up her half-empty beer bottle. "I'm going to drink another, and maybe even another after that. And I'm going to stay right here and watch the fireworks. So you're stuck with me tonight."

"And I wouldn't have it any other way," he said, clinking his beer bottle against hers.

They laughed and talked about nothing and everything, just like they used to in that cold field in Ireland in a different lifetime. This was a stolen moment; Liam knew that, but with Cora's soft voice and the evening breeze ruffling his hair, he remembered what it felt like to be truly happy. And when brilliant fireworks began to splash across the night sky, one after the other cascading in a glorious spectacle of shimmering color and light, all he really saw was her.

5

Kinsley, Ireland
1844

"HOLY MARY, MOTHER OF GOD," LIAM WHISPERED, sitting on the stone wall beyond his brother's cottage. "Pray for us sinners." Though he realized it was sacrilegious to pray for help when he was actively planning to defy one of the Ten Commandments, he figured it couldn't hurt. Saint Mary was supposed to be merciful. If she wouldn't bother with his sorry sack of bones, he couldn't blame her, but maybe she'd have mercy on him for Cora's sake. He needed a lot of money, and he was going to need it soon. In his experience, stealing from the wealthy seemed like the most logical plan.

It was early morning, and the sun had yet to rise, but Liam couldn't sleep. He'd left Cora's house hours ago. In between sweet kisses and whispered secrets, they'd talked about running away together. Now Liam felt as if he could fly. Cora *loved* him. It was everything he'd never dared hope for. Only in his wildest fantasies had he imagined Cora could care for a poor peasant like himself. He'd been elated when she told him her feelings, but also downright terrified. By choosing to love him, she was placing her life and future in his hands.

He stared down at his dirt-smudged fingers, rough and calloused from years of physical labor. What was he going to do? All his life, he'd scraped and scrabbled just to eat. Just to help put food on the table for his brother and family. With his friend Boyd, Liam had carved out a life as a thief, which had never bothered him until now. The extra money had allowed them to survive when crops failed and food grew scarce, but that was before Liam met Cora. Now he wanted to be the type of man she deserved.

One last time, he vowed, hopping off the low stone wall to cross the field. He'd track down Boyd, and they'd target someone rich who could afford to part with a bit of their fortune. If they managed to steal enough, then Liam and Cora could leave within the month. They could travel to Cork and buy passage on a ship to America. There were clergymen who could be bribed to perform last-minute marriages in those coastal towns. Anything could be bought for the right price. Heart leaping at the thought of making Cora his wife, Liam set off in search of his fellow thief.

That afternoon Liam and Boyd sat on the muddy riverbank in the woods, skipping stones and discussing their next target. The Bricks had joined them, but they rarely spoke when it came to figuring out logistics. The twin brothers were huge, sturdy as boulders, and just as dense. Luckily, they had just enough wits to understand their talents did not include complex scheming, so they left that up to Liam and Boyd.

"I'm telling you, the man's had it coming for a long time," Boyd said bitterly, as he tossed a rock into the shallow river. "John Brady's as rich as a king, but stingier than a starving mongrel with a bone. Did you know he threw old widow Murphy out of the house because she came down with the lung sickness? Thirty-four years she worked for his family, and just like that, she's dumped out like a chamber pot because she's too weak to serve. John Brady has no love or loyalty to anything except his money. He even ignores his lovely wife." Boyd's sly, all-knowing gaze slid to Liam. "But you'd know all about that, wouldn't you?"

Liam ignored him, never one to boast about his affair with Margaret Brady. They weren't together anymore, and it had been a well-kept secret between them, but Boyd was shrewd, and he'd known Liam since they were boys.

"Why'd you end it?" Boyd asked, baffled. "Any woman who looks like Margaret, with all that money at her disposal, would be a solid catch if you ask me. Only a crazy man would give up a romp like that."

Liam *was* crazy—for a kindhearted girl with a rosebud mouth who spoke to him and smiled at him like he was the most important person in the world. The moment he'd laid eyes on Cora McLeod was the moment he'd lost his heart to her. No other woman would do.

"Think Margaret would toss you a bit of money if you asked her sweetly?" Boyd wiggled his eyebrows.

"I'd never ask. What do you take me for?" Liam frowned at Boyd. "John Brady's a stingy man. Margaret may dress the part of a wealthy, pampered woman, but he controls all aspects of her life, even down to her spending." Liam remembered Margaret complaining that she never had freedom to do anything unless her husband approved. She was like a pretty bird in a gilded cage. "The jewels and carriage and fancy clothes are all for show— John Brady dressing up his prized possession to make himself look good. Margaret's as trapped in her life as the rest of us."

"Well, lucky she had you for comfort, then, when her cold husband was away on business," Boyd said with a hint of jealousy. Even though Boyd was married to Alice, it wasn't an easy union. Alice was forever complaining to Boyd about their lack of money.

"John Brady's due home tonight," one of the Bricks said in a voice like gravel. "Heard it from the butcher's boy. John's cook was in this morning for a side of mutton and said the master would be back before sundown."

"His carriage comes through on the main road, like everyone else," Boyd said with a spark of greed in his eyes. "I'd say this is fortunate for us."

"John has two footmen and a brawny coachman," Liam pointed out.

"Milksops, the lot of them," one of the Bricks said.

His brother grunted in agreement. "No bigger than saplings. Easy to break." He snapped a stick between his fingers for emphasis.

"There you have it," Boyd said, as if it was a done deal. "The Bricks can take the men, and you and I will deal with the rest."

"His coachman will be armed," Liam said.

"Aye, and so will we." One of the Bricks pulled a pistol from his coat and held it up. His brother did the same. Together, they looked like grinning madmen.

"Where did you get those?" Liam asked uneasily. Over the years he and Boyd had sometimes used a pistol to hold up the occasional carriage, but it was only for show. Liam preferred stealth over brute force, and he only got into fights when there was no other way out. He and Boyd had always been schemers, quick on their feet and quick to improvise, but they'd never gone so far as shooting anyone. The Bricks were a different story. Liam didn't actually know them very well, but Boyd had always vouched for them.

"Last week's loot," one of the twins said. "Lifted them off a traveling merchant."

"Lifted?" Liam asked.

"More like pounded his face until he kindly offered them up," the other twin said with a grin that revealed more gaps than teeth.

"You won't need them," Liam said lightly. He didn't like the idea of the Bricks carrying weapons, but he knew it would be no use appealing to their logic. He targeted their pride instead. "Two strapping fighters such as yourselves. It would almost be a shame if you had to resort to using those against three spindly men. I've seen you take on five men apiece and walk away with hardly a scratch between the two of you. You're that strong."

The Bricks looked smugly satisfied. One of them grunted in acknowledgment.

"Right, well, there's no need to get your wheel in a rut over pistols," Boyd said to Liam. "The boys will hold up the men, while you and I relieve John Brady of his purse. We'll meet at the bend in the road near the river."

While they hashed out the details of the plan, Liam let the usual thrill of the hunt override his earlier unease. Robbing John Brady was a risky endeavor, but Liam's urgency was greater now than ever because he had to think about Cora. He'd risk robbing heaven itself to keep her.

Several hours later, when the sun dipped low in the sky, Liam crouched in the branches of a tree near the bend in the road. From his vantage point he had a clear view of John Brady's carriage approaching. Liam adjusted the cloth around his nose and mouth to obscure his face, then whistled to alert Boyd, who was hiding on the other side of the lane. The Bricks were at their posts a few yards away, and when the carriage rolled into view, they sprang into action.

Liam swung from the branch to land lightly on the balls of his feet, just as Boyd stepped from his hiding place on the opposite side of the road. Side by side, in an act they'd done dozens of times before, Liam and Boyd faced the oncoming carriage.

The horses reared, and the coachman yanked on the reins. "Who goes there?" The coachman pulled a pistol from his coat and cocked it. "Speak up, or be gone, the both of ye."

"We're here to do business with your master," Liam said politely. "Won't be but a moment." He hadn't even finished his sentence before one of the Bricks hauled the coachmen from his seat and tossed him into the bushes. The other Brick was already fighting the two footmen.

Liam yanked open the carriage door.

"Back away, you lowlife scum." Spittle flew from John Brady's wrinkled mouth. He sat with his back ramrod straight, glaring at Liam with murderous intent. His sagging face was a picture of bitter disdain, and in his gnarled hand he held a pistol aimed directly at Liam's head.

The carriage door behind him jerked open, and John startled.

Boyd swung in, catching him in a chokehold as he struggled for the gun.

The pistol suddenly fired, missing Liam by a hair's breadth as it cracked through the side of the carriage.

Boyd snatched the pistol from John Brady's grip and tossed it to the floor. "Now, that's no way for a gentleman to behave. And here we were planning on keeping things civil. Don't move, or I'll have to choke you until you pass out, and we wouldn't want that, would we?"

John winced, his face growing redder by the second. "Just take the money and go."

"How kind of you to offer." Boyd dug through the old man's pockets, withdrawing a fat purse of coins.

Remembering something Margaret had once told him, Liam stepped into the carriage and began running his fingers along the wood paneling. She'd once complained how her husband always carried stashes of gold with him on trips. He hid them in secret compartments in his carriages, but she was never allowed to touch any of it unless he approved.

"What are you doing?" the old man hissed. "You got what you came for. Now, go."

Liam ignored him, sliding his hands over the seats and underneath, until his fingers caught on a lever. He lifted it, and a section of the seat opened to reveal a small wooden chest.

"What's this, then?" Boyd asked the man, jamming the pistol harder into his head. "You were holding out on us?"

"That's none of your concern," John Brady said furiously. "Leave it be!"

Liam lifted the small but heavy chest and set it on the opposite seat. He opened the lid, and Boyd let out a whistle of pure satisfaction. A small fortune in gold coins gleamed from within.

Boyd grinned. "Why, Granddad. Is all this for us? You really shouldn't have."

"Filthy, thieving swine!" John Brady shook with rage, struggling in Boyd's hold. "You're not fit to wipe the dirt from my boots, let alone—"

A shot rang out in the woods, followed by another. The horses startled, and the carriage lurched forward.

Liam grabbed the small chest and leaped to the ground with Boyd on his heels. The old man's angry curses could be heard as the carriage disappeared around the bend.

The Bricks came lumbering up a few moments later, snorting like winded bulls.

"What happened?" Liam looked from one to the other, dreading the answer.

"One of the footmen decided to play the hero. Pulled a knife and tried to threaten me with it." The twin glanced at his brother, and their faces broke into craggy smiles. "Shot him in the arm, I did."

"And I got the other one in the shoulder," said his brother proudly.

Liam's stomach grew queasy. "Are you mad? You could've *killed* them." Even with those injuries, the footmen were ruined. They'd never be able to keep their jobs, especially with a master like John Brady.

"Aye, that was the goal," one of the twins said in annoyance. "I was aiming for his heart, but I missed."

"We just need a bit more practice," his brother explained. Neither of them seemed to understand the magnitude of what could've happened. Liam had always known the Bricks were savage and mercenary, but he never thought they'd go so far as to try to kill someone. It was one thing to steal from the rich, but murder was another thing entirely. In all his years as a thief, Liam had never even considered it. Some lines you just didn't cross.

"Imbeciles, the both of you," Liam said, gripping the chest of gold tightly so he wouldn't be tempted to knock their heads together. They wouldn't make it easy for him, but he'd give it a good try. "Thieving's one thing, but murdering people in cold blood has never been my game."

"Maybe you've gone soft, then," one of the Bricks said smugly.

Liam closed the distance between them until he was right in his face. "It's you who's gone soft. In the *head*. I'll tell you right here and now, you're only a part of this because Boyd's always vouched for you, but this goes too far. We don't kill people, do you hear me? Not now, not ever."

"Oh, I don't know." The other brother moved to stand shoulder to shoulder with his twin. "Seems like sometimes it's the best way to make a point."

"Enough," Liam said in disgust. "Both of you toss those pistols in the woods before the night is through."

One of the brothers crossed his arms in challenge. "Not even if you paid us, O'Connor."

"You insist on keeping them, then take your cut of the loot tonight and leave this village. You'll have enough to take you anywhere else," Liam said coldly. "Go, and never step foot in Kinsley again."

One of the Bricks snorted in derision. "Who died and made you king?"

"Nobody," his brother answered. "Liam here is just as dirty as the rest of us, even though he likes to put on airs."

"I mean it," Liam said icily. "I never want to see your faces again." They were too dangerous with firearms, and too unpredictable. Even though he was running away with Cora, he couldn't leave these murderous thieves in his wake to wreak havoc on the village. Liam and Boyd had always targeted the rich, but the Bricks had no code of honor. He hated thinking of what they might do in the future, and if he had a chance to stop it, he'd take it.

"You wound me," one of the Bricks said, slapping a hand dramatically over his heart. "And here I thought we were friends."

"You're no friends of mine," Liam said grimly. "Never have been."

"Where are the footmen now?" Boyd changed the subject. He'd been strangely quiet through the whole confrontation.

"Ran off together," one of the Bricks said.

"And the coachman?"

"Out cold in the bushes. Maybe we should finish him off." The brute's expression lacked all traces of empathy when he looked directly at Liam. "I could use the target practice."

"I'm finished with the both of you," Liam said furiously. "Leave now, or I'll—"

"Come, let's not fight," Boyd said in a placating tone. "We've just landed our biggest haul yet. We should all be celebrating. Let it go for tonight, Liam. The lads didn't do any real harm."

Liam clutched the box of gold coins, staring at Boyd as if he'd never seen him before. Boyd was slapping the twins on the back, visibly thrilled with the treasure they'd just acquired. For the first time Liam felt like an outsider as he watched them. Had Cora changed him so much that he could see just how far they'd all fallen?

"Let's get out of here before anyone else comes along," Boyd said.

Later, they'd divided the treasure among them in tense silence, and each gone their separate ways. Liam walked home in the dead of night, his pockets heavy with gold. He tried to feel optimistic about his future with Cora. He was glad they now had enough money to run away together, but he couldn't stop thinking about the two injured footmen. If they even survived the trek out of the forest, their lives would never be the same. The Bricks had gone too far this time. It was only by God's grace that they missed their targets, and the men still lived. But even if their injuries weren't fatal, they could die later if they weren't able to work again. The rift between Liam and the Bricks was as vast as the ocean now, though Boyd was pretending like everything would go back to normal. It was just as good Liam was leaving. He never wanted to see any of their faces again.

Liam slid his hands into his pockets, rubbing one of the smooth coins between his fingers. With stone-cold clarity, he suddenly realized that he and Boyd were no longer as close as they'd once been. They'd been stealing ever since they were lads, and they'd stayed together out of necessity. The friendship was based on their shared struggle to survive, but when it came down to character, they weren't the same anymore. Maybe they never had been. Seeing Boyd flippantly dismiss the Bricks' actions tonight made Liam realize just how much they'd grown apart. Boyd had become harder and more bitter over the years. More mercenary. What would happen when the twins got better at shooting and they actually killed someone? Would Boyd be there to witness it, and would he care? The fact that Liam couldn't answer that weighed heavily on his mind.

When he reached the field near his brother's tiny cottage, he stopped at the low stone wall dividing the land. Kneeling in the dirt, Liam felt around for the loose stone he'd pried free years ago. Inside was a small hollow where he kept his secret stash. He placed the gold coins in the hole and replaced the stone, then sat with his back against the wall.

God, if Cora had any idea of all the sins he'd committed over the years, she'd never love him. But he could change, dammit. He *would* change. With a weary sigh, Liam stared up at the bleak night sky. A million stars shimmered above him like tiny beacons of hope, and he found himself saying a silent prayer for the future. Maybe somewhere up there, someone would have pity on him for Cora's sake. Because even though he knew he was just a common thief who didn't deserve her, it didn't stop him from wanting to be a man who *could*.

6

Providence Falls,
Present Day

"YOU GOTTA GIVE HER THE ILLUSION OF FREE-
dom, so she thinks she's in control," Magnus said from the passenger seat of the Mustang GTI on Sunday afternoon. "She'll
be feisty on those turns, and she'll want to skid out, so watch
your speed until you get to the straightaway. Then when you've
got her purring for you just right, take over and show her who's
boss." He patted the leather dashboard with a chuckle. "Cars
aren't any different than women, when it comes down to it.
You get me?"

Liam nodded, eyeing the racetrack with the enthusiasm of
a conquering warlord heading into battle. The car was a sleek,
magnificent beast with an intoxicating amount of horsepower.
He could feel the engine thrumming with unleashed fury, the
car champing at the bit to break free and fly down the track. It
was his second day at the Extreme Precision and Stunt Driving
School, and so far he'd mastered every challenge. Yesterday's
class had focused on proximity work, grid work, various brak-
ing methods and Liam's favorite—the ninety-and one hundred

eighty–degree turns. After only a few hours of practice, Liam had perfected each lesson as if he'd been doing it for years. While he suspected his skill had something to do with the ability the angels had bestowed upon him, he still felt a satisfying prickle of pride when Magnus had called him a "natural" at the end of the day.

"So we'll be doing high speed lane changes for the first six circuits over there," Magnus said, pointing to the course ahead of them. White lines on the tarmac ran parallel to each other down the mile-long track, with markers showing where to change lanes. "And on the final lap we're going straight into skid turns over there on the right. See that center wall? The car's going to fishtail out of the high-speed turn, and she's going to want to head straight for the wall, but you're not going to let her."

"Right," Liam said, adjusting the mirror. The center *wall* was just a visual barrier made up of empty plastic barrels, but the drivers knew to treat it like a solid block of concrete.

"She's all yours, man." Magnus relaxed into his seat like he was settling in to watch a TV show. "Take her out."

Liam stomped on the gas. The car shot off like a rocket, speeding down the course and eating up the track until the world outside streaked past in a blur. He loved the feel of the engine accelerating at his command. The squeal of the tires. The burning scent of rubber on the hot asphalt. Gripping the wheel, knuckles white with wild anticipation, he switched lanes at each designated mark. With every successful maneuver, his wicked smile grew until he felt as though he was one with the machine. No thoughts. No worries. Just the sensation of soaring across the earth with nothing weighing him down. It was pure freedom.

"I think you were born to fly," Magnus said with a chuckle on the fifth lap around. "Now, don't brake into that turn up ahead. When she loses traction—and she will—it's going to feel like we're heading straight into the wall, but remember what we talked about yesterday. Focus your energy on where you *want* to go, not where it looks like you're headed. If you focus on the wall, then all your immediate thoughts are given over to that wall, and what happens?"

Liam's fingers tightened on the wheel. "You crash into it."

"Exactly. So when you're spinning out at a hundred miles per hour, your gut's going to tell you to look at the looming danger ahead, but you're going to need to override that feeling. Don't focus on that wall."

"Got it," Liam said, keeping the speed steady as they neared the mark. Three...two...one. He jerked the wheel into the left turn. The car slid sideways, and the tires skipped across the asphalt, screaming in protest. Liam felt the sharp snap of the seat belt across his chest as they spun out. The car careened toward the wall of barrels.

"Focus," Magnus said sharply.

Liam tried, but the wall was coming at them fast. It rushed toward them like a bad omen, and he couldn't look away. All he could see was their inevitable collision. He gripped the wheel and spun it as hard as he could, but it was too late. With a jarring crash, they hit the barrels, skidded past the barricade and came to a screeching halt.

Adrenaline surged. Liam's heart thumped against his rib cage. He grimaced at the mess of orange barrels scattered around them. Disgusted with himself for failing so spectacularly, he slapped his hands against the steering wheel and swore like an angry sailor.

A choked sound drew his attention to Magnus, who was slouched in the passenger seat, his shoulders shaking with silent laughter. "Well, that's a relief."

Liam scowled. "What?"

"You're a mere mortal, after all," Magnus said with a smirk. "I think I was beginning to hate you a little. Ever since you got here yesterday, you've mastered each test with a skill that most people take months to hone. I've never seen anyone learn as quickly as you. But now that you've gone and crashed into the wall, my pride has been restored." Magnus waved a hand at the track. "Let's go again. Unless…you need a break?"

"No," Liam said with grim determination. "I'm not stopping until I get it right."

"Good man." Magnus thumped a fist against the dashboard as Liam backed onto the track. Two men in blue jumpsuits rushed to reassemble the wall of barrels.

Liam drove to the starting point when Magnus's phone rang.

Pulling it from his pocket, Magnus made a deep hum and answered in a voice like smooth malt whiskey. "Sheena. Of course I haven't forgotten. Yeah, baby, you know I'm easy like that. Whatever you want. Listen, I'm working right now, but I'll see you at seven and you can tell me all about it." He talked for a few moments longer, then hung up with a satisfied smile.

"Girlfriend?" Liam asked with forced nonchalance.

"Yeah, Sheena and I go way back," Magnus said. "She's a good woman."

A cool rush of relief swept over Liam. When Cora had made the comment about Magnus getting her phone number the other night, Liam had been deeply bothered at the idea of them dating. It wasn't only because she was supposed to be with Finn; it was because Magnus was… Well, he was *Magnus*. He was like a tiger on the prowl, and Liam would be damned if he'd let Cora fall prey. The man seemed to seize whatever he wanted out of life, no matter the cost. And that wasn't a bad thing, on the surface. Liam even admired him for it and felt a kinship with him, but when it came to Cora, Liam was fiercely protective. But he needn't waste his energy worrying over it. Magnus was in a relationship with another woman, and Cora had already made it clear she was too busy to date. Besides, Liam had more important, pressing matters to focus on. Like saving his immortal soul, for example. But first…

He gripped the gearshift and concentrated on the driving

course with the single-minded attention of a rooftop sniper. First, he was going to focus on mastering *this*.

"Ready, man?" Magnus asked, scrolling through his phone messages.

Liam nodded once.

Magnus set his phone in the center console. "Let's see what you've got."

Not a lot, apparently. To Liam's utter annoyance, he couldn't seem to master the high-speed turn. Again and again, he spun the wheel, skidded out and hit the wall. With every failed attempt to get it right, Liam's expression grew darker. On the final try he managed to just sideswipe the wall instead of crashing directly into it.

"Progress!" Magnus slapped Liam on the back as they walked off the course at the end of the day. "Don't beat yourself up, man. This is one of the hardest tricks to master. Everything else makes logical sense, but in this one, you have to override your instincts. Just practice, and you'll get there. You can pay to use the track by the hour during the weekdays, if you want. There aren't any classes going on, so feel free to schedule something."

Grumpy and hungry, Liam stopped at a drive-through for a double cheeseburger and an extra-large order of French fries on the way home. Even in his mood, he couldn't help but appreciate the glorious brilliance of fast food. It was one of his favorite things about the modern world—a person could have a hot meal at their fingertips within a matter of minutes. He could never have foreseen something so decadent. Cora called it "garbage food," which boggled the mind. Beef and cheese, as much as anyone could want? The only place he could fathom tossing something so mouthwateringly delicious was straight into his belly.

Savoring a mouthful of fries, he drove home mulling over the day's lessons and making plans to practice later in the week. He didn't like failing at anything, and he was determined to get it right. Maybe next weekend he'd take the add-on course to hone his newly acquired skills.

Something soft tickled his nose, and he absently brushed it away. A few seconds later another bit of white fluff floated near his face. Then another. He sneezed and rolled down the windows.

It wasn't until he shoved his hand into the fast food bag for more fries that he realized something was amiss. Instead of warm, perfectly salted potato wedges, he brought up a handful of…feathers? Frowning, Liam tossed them out the window, but it was no use. Soon, the interior of the car was swirling with downy fluff.

"Rogue," a cool voice said in his ear.

Liam yelped in surprise and slammed on the brakes. The car swerved dangerously. A driver behind him laid his hand on the horn, yelling obscenities as he passed, but Liam barely noticed. His gaze was locked on the sudden appearance of the two passengers visible in his rearview mirror.

The angels sat in the backseat as calmly as if they were carpooling to work. Samael, the blond, had his usual stoic expression completely at odds with his sweet, choirboy face. Agon, the tall, dark-haired angel, should have been imposing due to his immense size, but his kind smile helped soften the blow. Mist swirled around their neatly tucked wings, and their bodies were lined in a soft, glowing light. Against the backdrop of the shabby upholstery, they looked like they'd been plucked out of a dream. But it wasn't a good dream, as far as Liam was concerned. He'd always thought of angels as ethereal, divine beings of light who bestowed glad tidings and lit the way for wayward travelers, but not these two. Since day one, they'd been content to sit back and let Liam run headlong into all kinds of trouble, and they never even came when he called. Of all the heavenly guides, Liam cursed his infernal luck that he got stuck with them.

"By all that's sacred," Liam said through clenched teeth. "Can you not warn a man before you materialize like this?"

"We sent notice." Samael looked bored as he brushed a bit of fluff off his shoulder. "You should be grateful we're so accommodating."

"The feathers were my idea," Agon said cheerfully. "To announce our impending arrival and to symbolize hope. Was it adequate?"

"No," Liam grumbled. "I didn't have a chance to make the connection before you snuck up on me like a holy heart attack."

"I see," Samael said blandly. "You need something more obvious. A plague of locusts, perhaps?"

"Samael did suggest blaring celestial trumpets in your ears, but I thought it lacked subtlety," Agon said. "Don't worry. We will endeavor to do better next time."

Liam pulled the car to the side of the road, then twisted to face them. It had been an exhausting day, and his patience was wearing thin. "Look, if you've come to impart some of your doom-and-gloom wisdom, can we please get on with it? It's been a long week, and I've just finished an intensive driving class."

"Yes, two days wasted on selfish pursuits that have nothing to do with the task we've given you," Samael pointed out. "Time is not your friend, thief. You have precious little of it, and you'd do well to use it to your advantage. In this era meaningful social gatherings often happen on weekends, and now you've gone and squandered what could have been a valuable opportunity to get Cora and Finn together."

"I can't just force her to love him," Liam snapped. "I'm not bloody Cupid with a bow and arrow."

"Enough," Samael said. The temperature inside the car turned downright chilly. As annoyed as Liam was, he needed to remember they were powerful beings who held the fate of his soul in their hands. He ought to be respectful, but they didn't make it easy. Every time they appeared, he walked away feeling like a naughty schoolboy who'd been slapped on the hand with a ruler.

"You're supposed to find ways to bring them closer together, yet you seem utterly incapable of making the right choices when it matters." Samael's cherubic face was pinched with disapproval. "Last week you allowed Cora to skip the Fourth of July party. Instead, she spent it cozying up with you, watching fireworks on the roof. That party would've been an excellent opportunity for her to interact with Finn. They could've talked and perhaps made weekend plans, but now that avenue is lost to you."

"How was I to know the party was crucial?" Liam asked, throwing his hands up. "You're not exactly forthcoming with information. Cora and I were both exhausted from a grueling day on the job. A young woman was murdered—in case you haven't been following—a college girl who just last week was alive and well with her whole life ahead of her." The loss of Lindsey Albright had been a shock to everyone, and even in his own bleak circumstances, Liam couldn't help the wave of sadness he felt over the senseless death of such a youthful, vibrant soul. Cora had taken it especially hard. She'd been so quiet after viewing the body in the woods, and Liam knew she was still struggling with it.

"None of that is your concern," Samael said coolly.

"Like hell, it's not," Liam shot back. The temperature dropped further, and his breath misted, but he was too annoyed to care. "Everything that happens to the people in this town is my concern because it deeply affects Cora. She grew up here, and she loves this place and the people in it. She's made it her life's work to protect them and keep the peace. Now, with two unsolved murders, Cora's in a tailspin, trying to track down a possible serial killer, and I'm supposed to be helping her do it. It's not like I can just pull her aside and say, 'Oh, so sad about the poor lassie who got murdered, but, hey. Look! Doesn't Finn Walsh cut a fine figure in that penguin suit of his?' In case you're unfamiliar with females, let me assure you that dead bodies and unsolved murders do not typically inspire feelings of romance."

"Be that as it may, you must find a way to guide her toward Finn," Samael said.

"Have faith, ruffian." Agon was holding a French fry between two fingers. He turned it this way and that, studying it in the sunlight in fascination. Liam frowned, wondering how he'd missed the angel pilfering a piece of his dinner. "Even in the darkest times, there are opportunities to experience light. You just have to know how to recognize the moments when they arise."

Too tired to decipher the angel's cryptic words, Liam sighed heavily. "Fine. I'll try to stay alert for these opportunistic blasts of light. Any other bits of wisdom you'd like to impart? Anything, oh, I don't know...*useful*, for a change?"

The snowy-winged pains in the backside didn't bother answering. Of course. Instead, they began to fade like wisps of fog dissolving in sunlight. Apparently, the meeting was over, and they weren't going to dignify Liam with a response.

"His arrogance knows no bounds," Samael said to Agon as they shimmered away.

"All humans are riddled with imperfections," Agon commented. "But they can change for the better."

"Can he?" Samael's skeptical voice grew fainter until it was nothing but a soft echo in the distance. "I rather think he enjoys being difficult."

"Funny, I thought the same of you," Liam muttered. But they were long gone. Liam was alone in the car once again, with nothing but a bag of cold fast food for company.

7

CORA CREPT THROUGH THE OVERGROWN GRASS
with Liam close behind her. Taking care not to be seen, she approached the young man's hideout behind his mother's house with cautious steps. "Slice Biddlesworth," she said under her breath. "You are not the sharpest—"

"A *tool* shed?" Liam snorted in disbelief, taking in the rickety wooden structure against the fence. He didn't bother keeping his voice down because it wouldn't have mattered, anyway. "Is the man daft? This is no proper hideout."

Cora had to agree. For one thing, Slice's motorcycle was parked right outside the shed, and his Booze Dogs club jacket was draped over the seat. For another, empty beer bottles littered the grass outside the door, and loud music blared from within. Finally—and this was the real tipoff—the shed door was wide open, and Slice was slouched on an old futon couch, drunkenly hollering the lyrics to Radiohead's "Creep." He wouldn't have been easier to find if he'd placed a blinking neon arrow in the yard pointing the way.

It was late afternoon on Monday, and Cora and Liam had finally tracked down Slice's mother's house. They'd arrived with the intention of questioning Mrs. Biddlesworth on her son's whereabouts, but it hadn't been necessary.

Cora dodged an empty beer bottle as it came sailing through the shed door, then called out, "Mr. Biddlesworth?"

The young man swiveled his head toward the entrance, regarding her and Liam through bloodshot eyes. Deep lines of fatigue were etched into his boyishly handsome face, and his blond hair stuck up in all directions like a porcupine. He was wearing a pair of rumpled jeans, worn motorcycle boots and a beer-stained T-shirt. It looked like he hadn't slept in days. "Who are you?" he mumbled.

"Can you please turn that down?" Cora yelled as politely as she could. The music was so loud, every note was like sharp little jabs to her eardrums.

Slice fumbled for a remote in the futon cushion and finally shut off the music. Oh, blessed, blessed silence.

"Thanks," Cora said. "Mind if I come in?"

Slice rubbed his bleary eyes and shrugged. "Fine. What do you want? I told my mom not to say where I was."

"She didn't. We figured it out." Cora reached into her pocket, withdrawing her badge and introducing herself and Liam.

Slice's attitude changed so fast it was almost comical. He went from a morose drunk to a sloppy, nervous wreck in under five seconds. He lurched up from the futon and tried to steady himself on the wall, his gaze darting frantically between them. "I don't know anything!"

"All we want to do is ask you some questions about Lindsey Albright," Cora said calmly. "We need you to come with us to the station now."

"I heard what happened, and I didn't do it," Slice slurred, trying to lean against the wall, but miscalculating the distance and stumbling. How drunk was he? "I would never hurt Lindsey... Never *ever*. She was my girlfriend." He squeezed his eyes shut and sobbed. "I *loved* her."

"I'm sure you did," Cora soothed, approaching him slowly, like she would a frightened animal. The poor man was so distraught, she felt a sudden stab of pity for him. Guilty or not, his pain was etched all over his face, and being drunk only compounded it. "Come with us to the station, and you can tell us all about it." She gave him her most encouraging smile and softly patted him on the back. After a few kind words of understanding, she was leading Slice out the door and across the yard. Cora did her best to keep him engaged in conversation, and he seemed too drunk to realize where they were headed.

"Lindsey was the best," he said with a hiccup. "She was my best girl."

"Of course she was." Cora signaled Liam to quickly open the car door. Liam was letting her take the lead on this, probably sensing that Slice wouldn't respond well to his more aggressive style of persuasion. So far, so good.

But the moment Slice saw the open car door and Liam standing beside it, he balked. Cora couldn't blame him. With his granite expression and muscular build, Liam looked like one of those guys in mafia movies who were sent to "persuade" people.

"Not going anywhere." Slice took a jerky step back.

"It's only for a little while," Cora coaxed, but her control of the situation was quickly slipping.

Slice began to back away fast.

In swift strides Liam covered the distance between them until they were face-to-face. "Look, man, we can do this the easy way or the hard way. You come along without making a fuss, and you'll make that sweet thing happy. See?" He tipped his head toward Cora, keeping his gaze on Slice. "You want to make her happy, don't you?"

Cora pasted a huge smile on her face and nodded in encouragement. She felt ridiculous, like an adult trying to persuade a grumpy toddler to eat a spoonful of mashed vegetables. She also wasn't thrilled with Liam's comment, but hey. If it worked, she wasn't going to complain.

Slice blinked owlishly at her, and for a moment it seemed he was going to capitulate. But somewhere in the distance, a car horn blared, and that was all it took to yank him from his stupor. He was off like a startled deer, diving through the rosebushes and making a mad dash across the neighbor's yard.

Liam tipped his face to the sky. "Why do they always have to run?"

Cora pulled handcuffs from her pocket and dangled them in front of his nose. "Go get him. *Sweet thing.*"

For a drunk person, Slice was surprisingly fast. He also knew the neighborhood better than Liam, so he was five houses away by the time Liam tackled him to the ground. He put up a good struggle, but quickly lost steam once the handcuffs were on and Liam was reading him his rights. In a matter of minutes he was stumbling toward the car, so exhausted that Liam had to drag him the last few steps.

By the time they got to the police station, Slice was passed out cold in the backseat.

"What now?" Liam peered over his shoulder at the snoring man. "Should I give him a good wallop on the face to wake him up?"

Cora turned the engine off. "Absolutely not."

"Very well," he said decisively. "A bucket of icy water works better, anyway. I'll drag him onto the pavement while you fetch that bucket near the ice machine in the lunchroom."

"Don't you dare," Cora said, half laughing. She knew Liam well enough that he might just do it. He was unconventional, and she wouldn't put it past him. "We're going to put Mr. Biddlesworth in a holding cell and let him sleep it off, then we'll question him tomorrow when he's sober."

"That will take too long," Liam said matter-of-factly. "And

frigid water works quite well to wash away the cobwebs of in-ebriation. Believe me, I've firsthand experience."

"Why does this not surprise me?" Cora said, getting out of the car.

"It works like a charm," he assured her. "There was this horse trough back in my village near the tavern, and in the dead of winter, even the town drunk would emerge sober as a priest on Sunday after being doused in that frigid—"

"He's going in the holding cell," Cora said over the roof of the car.

"Fine," Liam said with a sigh. Then he gave her a cheeky grin before opening the back passenger door and hauling the young man out. "But an ice bucket would be much more fun."

By Tuesday afternoon Cora thought Slice might have bene-fited from that bucket of icy water, after all. The nervous young man sitting in the interrogation room across from them smelled like he'd been marinated in stale beer and sweat. With dark cir-cles under his bloodshot eyes and a scratch across his cheekbone from his dash through the rosebushes, Slice looked even worse than he did yesterday. He kept shifting in his seat, trying to get comfortable, but Cora knew from experience it wasn't going to happen. The interrogation room was a cramped, cinderblock-gray chamber with a spartan set of chairs and a steel table. It was cold and uninviting, which was by design. People tended to spill information quicker if they were out of their comfort zone.

Slice took a sip of water from his paper cup, glancing uneas-ily at them while Cora reviewed her notes.

Liam was silently regarding the young man with a cold, un-yielding expression. He'd slipped seamlessly into "bad cop" mode, leaving Cora to be the understanding good cop, which suited her just fine. Something about Slice brought out her pro-tective instincts. He reminded her of a lost puppy, with his sad, soulful eyes and scruffy hair. But she'd been in her profession long enough to know that looks could be deceiving. If Slice had anything to do with Lindsey Albright's death, she was determined to find out.

Cora flipped her notebook to a fresh page. "Let's start from the beginning, Mr. Biddlesworth."

"Slice," he said, nervously. "Just Slice."

Cora nodded. Maybe it was a Booze Dog thing, and they all had vaguely menacing nicknames. Bear's had certainly been appropriate. He'd growled like a grizzly and looked strong enough to crush a human head with his bare hands. Cora tried not to think of reasons why Slice got his nickname. She doubted it had anything to do with expert chopping skills as a culinary chef.

"It's my real name in case you're wondering," he added. "On my birth certificate and everything."

She looked up from her notes. "Does it mean anything?"

He scoffed. "Only that my mom's the queen of dumb decisions. She got a greeting card in the hospital when I was born that said, 'Congratulations on your little slice of heaven,' so she chose to name me Slice."

"It's very unique," Cora said with a smile.

"I'm okay with it." He relaxed back in his chair. It was a good sign. The more comfortable he felt with her, the more forthcoming he'd be with information. "I hate Biddlesworth, though. It was my stepdad's last name. I'm changing mine to something cooler and more legit someday, but I haven't decided yet. Dangerfield, maybe."

"Right." Because Slice Dangerfield sounded very respectable. Not at all like a cartoon villain. "Well, it's a big decision. Definitely take your time on that."

He nodded. "Yeah. I'm thinking—"

"Enough." Liam slapped a hand on the table in disgust.

Slice flinched.

"You're wasting our time, Mr. Biddlesworth," Liam said. "Let's start over, shall we?"

Slice seemed to curl in on himself. So much for breaking the ice. Any progress Cora had just made was gone. The poor man couldn't have looked more reluctant if Liam had been looming in the corner in a black hooded cloak, beckoning him with a scythe.

Liam fixed him with a steely glare. "Where were you on the night of Tuesday, July third between the hours of ten and midnight?"

Cora studied the young man's reaction. The specialists from Raleigh had been able to pinpoint the time of the murder. If Slice had been involved in Lindsey's death, the mentioned time frame might cause a flash of alarm in his eyes, or a sudden shift in his posture, or a nervous tick, but he didn't exhibit any behavior beyond sadness and exhaustion.

"I—I didn't do it," Slice stammered. There was a haunted look on his face when he whispered, "I didn't kill her."

Liam braced his elbows on the table. "Then why did you run when we tried to bring you in yesterday?"

"I don't know." Slice's gaze darted around the room like he was looking for answers, but the two-way mirror on the wall gave nothing away, and the security camera in the corner just glared with its blinking red eye. "I was drunk. I panicked."

"Why were you hiding out in your mother's tool shed?" Liam pressed.

"Because my buddy Bear called to say the cops were asking for me. He told me what you said—that my girl was…dead." Slice swallowed hard, his Adam's apple bobbing up and down. "That's not exactly feel-good news, you know? It messed me up bad. I needed a minute."

"The only reason a man runs from the cops is if he's guilty of something," Liam said coldly. "Tell us where you were between ten and twelve last Tuesday night."

"I wasn't with Lindsey."

"That's not what I asked."

Slice finished his water in one gulp, then fidgeted with the paper cup again. Cora studied him, taking in his clenched jaw and rapidly blinking eyes. He was stalling. "Can I get some more water?"

Liam sent the empty cup flying off the table with one swipe. "Answer the question, Mr. Biddlesworth. Or do you enjoy the idea of a life behind bars?"

"I told you I didn't do it!" Slice said in frustration. "I loved Lindsey, okay? You've got the wrong guy."

"I believe you," Cora said. And she did. Her gut instinct said he wasn't a murderer, but she had a strong feeling he was still hiding something. Maybe he had information about what happened to Lindsey, and he was afraid to rat someone out. There were worse things than getting thrown in jail.

"*She* believes you," Liam said with a scoff. "Me, not so much."

Cora nudged Liam's foot under the table, warning him to tone it down. She needed to get Slice to talk, and Liam's way wasn't working.

"Look, Slice," she said gently. "We both want the same thing here. If you can tell us about Lindsey, anything at all about the last time you saw her, or the night she died, it could help us track down her killer. That's what we both want, isn't it? Justice for Lindsey?"

Slice slumped in his chair with a heavy sigh. "I didn't go out with Lindsey last Tuesday night. She was with me at The Doghouse over the weekend, and we partied like we usually do. On Sunday she came back to my apartment and stayed for a couple of days. The last time I saw her was Tuesday afternoon."

"What time did she leave your place?" Cora asked, jotting down notes.

"I don't remember exactly. Maybe four."

"Did Lindsey mention where she was going?"

Slice shook his head, rubbing the scruff on his jaw. "Just that she had an important meeting later."

"Did she say where, or with whom?"

"No, but I figured it had to do with school. She was taking summer classes, and sometimes she had study groups in the evening, but it's not like I kept track of her schedule. We never talked about her college stuff."

"Why not?" Liam asked. "You were together, and college was a big part of her life."

Slice frowned. "I'm a mechanic, man. I never even finished high school. Got my GED when I turned eighteen, and now I work on cars. That's how we met. Lindsey brought her car into Zippy Lube a few months ago, and we hit it off. I knew she was out of my league, but she was cute, and she flirted with me and…" He trailed off, his eyes glittering with emotion. "At first, we just had fun together. I never expected it to go anywhere. A guy like me doesn't get to keep a girl like her."

"What do you mean?" Cora asked.

"Lindsey was too good for me," he said simply. "She was going places, and I knew it wasn't going to last. But she was always down to party, and the Booze Dogs throw the best ragers. So I started taking her with me to parties, and it became a regular thing. *We* became a regular thing. She was one of those good girls who'd been wound up a little too tight, and she just wanted to let loose. Her parents were crazy strict, and she'd always had to be perfect growing up. So I told her anytime she wanted to go wild, I was her guy. She liked that. I may not have known any of that fancy college crap, but she liked that I had no expectations, and I didn't judge her. I just wanted to be with her, that's all." He glanced down at his hands. "I never expected to fall for her, but you can't force your heart not to love someone, can you? You can't tell yourself how to feel." He searched their faces for a flicker of understanding.

"Aye, and that's the hell of it," Liam said in a soft, rough voice. His Irish accent became more pronounced. "The heart's a bull-headed mule when it comes to taking orders."

Cora wondered if he was thinking of his former lover Margaret again. Sometimes, in quiet moments when Cora caught him unawares, he got this achingly sad, faraway look on his face that made him appear so lonely. Cora felt as if she'd never be able to reach him, even if she tried for a hundred years.

"Anyway, that's why Lindsey and I didn't talk about her school life," Slice continued. "It wasn't a part of us. She was with me to get away from all that pressure, and I cared enough about her to give her that."

The room fell into silence while Cora wrote down a few more notes.

Liam straightened in his chair and finally said, "It's a lovely story, Mr. Biddlesworth. Very moving. But you still haven't answered the question. Where were you on the night of July third between the hours of ten and midnight?"

Slice sighed. "I was hanging out with friends."

"What friends?" Liam asked.

He gnawed the insides of his cheeks and glanced at the exit door. "Just a couple of guys from the club."

Liam slid the notebook and pen over to him. "Names."

Slice reluctantly picked up the pen and scribbled down names.

"Can you tell us what you were doing?" Cora asked.

"Nothing much." He fidgeted with the pen, unable to meet her eyes. "We just went for a drive. Kind of a lot's happened since then, so I don't really remember all the details."

"Well, now, that's a crying shame," Liam drawled. "Maybe a few more days in a holding cell will help jog your memory."

"That won't be necessary," a deep voice said from the doorway.

Cora's gaze flew to the broad-shouldered man standing at the threshold like a crusader in an Armani suit, and her mouth opened in surprise.

8

FINN WALSH SWEPT INTO THE ROOM WITH THE easy grace and confidence of a man in his element. He looked the same as he usually did, from his neatly styled hair to the crisp lines of his collared shirt and silk tie, but his cool, professional mask eclipsed any warmth Cora was used to seeing on his handsome face. He gave a perfunctory nod to her and Liam, then introduced himself as Slice's attorney.

Slice looked confused. "But I don't have a lawyer."

"You do now." Finn took a chair from the corner of the room and slid it to the table, seating himself beside Slice.

"I can't really afford—"

"Don't worry about that," Finn assured him, setting his briefcase on the table. "It's all taken care of."

"So, what? You're my court-appointed guy? Like on TV?" He took in Finn's bespoke pinstripe suit, his Italian leather briefcase and the Rolex Submariner on his wrist. "Dang. Business must be hopping."

Finn gave Slice a warm smile, and for a moment Cora saw a glimmer of the easygoing man she knew. "No, Mr. Biddlesworth. I'm an attorney with Johnston & Knight, but sometimes I do pro-bono work. Today's your lucky day."

Slice perked up a little. "Jackpot, me. How did you know I was here?"

"We have a mutual acquaintance, but that's not important right now. Let's focus on getting you out of here, shall we?" Finn turned to address Cora and Liam, his professional mask back in place.

Cora blinked at the sudden change. It was weird to see Finn in "power attorney" mode. This was the man who sometimes met her for drinks with her friends after work. The man who'd just taken her to the annual charity ball a few weeks ago and made her laugh. They'd danced. They'd shared stories. But now, for the first time since she'd known him, Finn Walsh was kind of... *ignoring* her. Cora felt an odd prickle of something. Whatever it was, she didn't care to examine it. Finn was a great attorney with a rock-solid reputation, and he took his work very seriously. Cora admired him for it. That was the important thing here.

"For the record, I'm submitting evidence in the form of video footage proving my client was not with Lindsey Albright at the time of her murder."

Slice sat bolt upright. "What evidence?"

Finn opened his leather briefcase and pulled out a laptop. Then he plugged in a USB stick, and after a few clicks to the keyboard, he showed them the screen.

Cora saw grainy footage of a gas station parking lot. Slice and two other guys pulled up on their motorcycles, parking at the pumps.

"How'd you even know I went out there?" Slice asked.

"Your mother was kind enough to show me her credit card statements," Finn said briskly. "She said you'd borrowed her card that night, and the transaction history indicated where you were. Most gas stations have cameras, so this was simple enough to obtain."

"Dang," Slice said under his breath. "My mom found out I—"

"Borrowed her credit card?" Finn interrupted. "Yes, and she was happy to help."

"Great," Slice whispered, scratching the side of his neck. From the look on the young man's face, it was clear he thought dealing with his mother was going to be even worse than this.

"Note the time stamp in the corner," Finn said, addressing Liam and Cora. "Nine fifty-seven p.m. on Tuesday, July third."

In the video Slice appeared to be doing exactly what he'd said—nothing much. He and his friends gassed up their bikes and bought drinks and cigarettes from the convenience store.

Cora and Liam continued watching as the gas station video footage played out, with Finn occasionally sliding the bar along the bottom of the screen to speed up the film. Slice and his friends spent more than a couple of hours outside loitering on the sidewalk, drinking and smoking and shooting the breeze. For a while they appeared to be watching sports on Slice's phone, their heads bent over the screen as they spoke animatedly. Occasionally, the team would score, and the guys would jump up, whooping and laughing and thumping each other on the back. By the time Slice and his buddies drove away, the time stamp showed that it was well past midnight.

When it was finished, Finn shut the laptop and handed over the USB stick. "The gas station in this video is located east of Providence Falls, about an hour away. As you can see from the footage, my client was at this location during the time of Lindsey Albright's murder on July third."

Liam frowned at Slice. "There's not much near the hills an hour east of here, save for a few acres of farmland and some state parks. What were you doing all the way out there in the middle of nowhere on a weeknight?"

"You don't have to answer that," Finn said as he snapped his briefcase shut.

Cora was wondering the same thing, but the evidence Finn had just provided was irrefutable. Slice did not kill Lindsey.

"Do you have any further questions for my client, or are we done here?" Finn asked.

"We're done," Cora said with a sigh. "Mr. Biddlesworth is free to go."

"Yes," Slice said, pumping his fist. For the first time since they'd arrested him, he broke into a smile. It transformed his face. The sadness and fatigue were still there, but the grin he gave Finn was nothing less than hero-worship. "Thanks, man. You really came through for me."

Finn nodded, thanked Cora and Liam for their time, then ushered his beaming client from the room. On his way out the door, Finn gave Cora a smile. For some reason that tiny acknowledgment lifted her spirits. Underneath the smooth, emotionless veneer of power attorney, the Finn she knew was alive and well. She liked that.

"Slice is hiding something," Liam said as they left the room. "If Finn hadn't showed up today like the bloody north wind to blow our chances to hell, I could've found out."

"Oh, come on. Finn was just doing his job."

"Aye, and now it will be that much harder for us to do ours."

Later, they sat in Captain Thompson's cluttered office, briefing him on the interrogation, then listening to him grouse about Slice walking free.

The captain paced behind his desk with his tie askew and his face lined with stress. He was only a few inches taller than Cora, but his commanding presence and solid build somehow made him seem bigger. The captain's close-set eyes darted between her and Liam, his mouth pressed in a grim line. Every once in a while he ran a hand through his hair, leaving the cropped, dark curls to stick up in all directions. Normally, he controlled it with some sort of pomade, but today it looked as though he'd forgotten to use it. The pressure from the higher-ups was clearly getting to him.

"Now we're SOL with that kid, and he was the best lead we had." Captain Thompson grabbed a bottle of Tums from his desk and popped a couple, chewing them like candy.

"There's something else, sir," Cora said. "Both Liam and I thought Slice was hiding something. The video proved he wasn't with Lindsey at the time of her murder, but he was acting sketchy during the interview. It could've just been nerves, but until Finn showed up, Slice was stalling. He didn't want to tell us anything about where he was, or what he'd been doing."

"So you think he's still involved somehow?" Captain Thompson asked.

Cora shook her head, unsure. "Maybe, maybe not. But I'd like to question the two men with him in that video."

"Yes. Good." Captain Thompson seemed appeased for the first time since they'd entered his office. "I still think that kid, or someone he knows, is connected to the murder. He isn't exactly a pillar of the community. He's a Booze Dog, for Christ's sake." He stopped pacing and sank heavily into his chair. "Young man from the wrong side of the tracks gets himself a girlfriend with a shiny future ahead of her. Maybe he falls harder than she does. Maybe he gets possessive. She tries to end it, and he doesn't want to let her go. If he can't have her, no one can, so he pays to have someone off her and dump her in the woods. In cases like these, it's almost always the boyfriend or husband who's responsible."

"With all due respect, sir," Cora said, "I don't believe Slice had an active hand in her murder. He might be keeping information from us, but he seemed to really love her."

Captain Thompson snorted. "Since when has love stopped a man from doing something stupid or irrational?" There was a bitter edge to his tone that gave Cora pause. She suddenly thought of the captain's wife, Alice, wondering if he was speaking from experience. Alice Thompson was a blonde bombshell with the zillion-dollar wardrobe and the high-maintenance personality to match. She'd worn sky-high stilettos to their annual company picnic and flirted outrageously, though not with her husband. The last time Alice came into the station, she'd gushed over Liam and made him uncomfortable. Cora had assumed the captain didn't notice, but maybe he'd brushed it off because he was used to it. Or maybe their relationship had lost its luster long ago, and he just didn't care.

"Very, very true," Liam mused, staring at the ceiling. He'd been quiet through most of their briefing, and was slouched so low, he looked ready to fall asleep.

Cora glanced at him. "What is?"

"Men doing irrational things," Liam said through a yawn. "For love."

"I'm sorry, O'Connor, are we keeping you from your nap?" Captain Thompson's face began to grow red. Not a good sign.

Cora shot Liam a warning look. For some reason Liam always seemed blasé when dealing with the captain. He wasn't exactly disrespectful, just...overly familiar. Maybe it was because they'd been boyhood friends together back in Ireland, but that was a long time ago, and things were different now. Liam needed to tread carefully.

"Sorry, Captain. I was just agreeing with you," Liam said smoothly, sitting up straighter. "I also agree with Cora that Slice wasn't involved in any aspect of Lindsey's murder. He doesn't have it in him."

"And you know this for certain, because...?"

Liam shrugged. "A man who kills the woman he loves is someone who's controlled by passionate rage or a darker ambition. Maybe there's something he wants to acquire that he believes is more valuable than her. Jealousy. Greed. Power. Any of those things could drive a violent man to kill. But Slice doesn't strike me as violent. He's a simple man. He's got a job. Friends.

Family. A community where he belongs. He told us Lindsey was too good for him, but there was no bitterness when he admitted it. He met a girl, fell in love and for however long it lasted, he was determined to enjoy it. Simple as that. Recent tragedy aside, I think Slice is a man who's truly content with his life, and he doesn't have that driving need to try to change it." Liam paused for a moment, then gave a self-deprecating smile. "If he could bottle that emotion and sell it, I'd be first in line to buy it."

Cora was too surprised to comment. She'd thought Liam was just phoning it in during this briefing with the captain. She also hadn't realized how deeply he'd connected with the young man they'd interrogated earlier.

"And I'd be right behind you," the captain said gruffly. "But seeing as how I don't have the time to wax philosophical when I've got murders to solve, I prefer to look at the *facts*. Slice is with the Booze Dogs, and they're not trustworthy. He was dating a girl who just showed up dead in the woods. There's too much of a connection to disregard him or his motorcycle club. Therefore, I'm not ruling him or any of them out, and neither should you. Now, go." He shooed them out with a wave of his hand. "Get me something we can actually use."

9

LIAM CHECKED HIS PHONE ON WEDNESDAY EVE-
ning, waiting for Magnus to confirm the racetrack was free for
practice. There'd been no new leads on the investigation ever
since Finn confirmed Slice's alibi, and the overall atmosphere at
the station had been heavy with frustration. Liam could think
of no better way to lift his spirts than getting back behind the
wheel of a powerful car. The sheer anticipation of it—the freedom of flying down the track at dizzying speeds—had him pacing the tiny living room like a caged tiger.

"Going somewhere?" Cora entered the room with a handful
of take-out menus and a steaming mug of cinnamon tea. They'd
been home for less than an hour, and already she'd tossed her
hair into a messy bun and changed into a pair of plaid pajama
pants and a tank top. He'd been living with her for several weeks,
but it still hit him like an arrow through the heart to see her
like this, relaxed and happy in her home. *Their* home. She was
so effortlessly beautiful it made his soul ache.

"If luck is on my side," Liam said, forcing his attention back
to his phone. "I'm waiting for Magnus to tell me if there's room
to practice at the racetrack tonight."

"That's impressive." Cora sank onto the couch.

Liam's chest puffed with pride. "I'm a bit of a natural, or so I've been told."

"Oh, I'm sure you are, but I meant Magnus." She dragged a fleece throw blanket over her lap. "The man's an attorney, yet he still finds the energy to teach stunt driving on weekdays. He must have the stamina of a demigod."

Liam's skin prickled with jealousy. "Magnus doesn't teach during the week. He only offered to check the schedule for me because I signed up at the last minute."

"That was nice of him," Cora said absently, browsing through the take-out menus.

Her cat Angel sauntered into the room, announcing the glory of his arrival with a lofty meow. He was a white fluffball of regal indignance, treating most people like human scratching posts, but to everyone's shock, he'd adored Liam the moment they'd met.

Cora took a bright red menu and slapped it on the coffee table. "Let's get Thai food. I want a double order of chicken satay this time. With extra peanut sauce. I didn't eat lunch today, and I'm starving."

Liam's phone chimed with a text from Magnus.

It's a go. You have the Mustang from 7 to 9.

"Can't stay. I'm off to the track." Liam texted a quick thanks to Magnus, grinning in sweet anticipation.

"Whatever you say, Speed Racer." Cora scooped her cat onto her lap, settling back against the overstuffed cushions. "Looks like it's just you and me tonight, Angel."

The cat gave a forlorn meow as Liam waved goodbye and was out the door. If, in the back of his mind, there was a nagging suspicion that he was wasting valuable time on a selfish pursuit, he tried not to examine it. It was only Wednesday evening, after all. What could he possibly do to play matchmaker for Cora and Finn right now? It wasn't like she was going to go falling in love between dinner and bedtime. The angels had accused Liam of squandering the precious weekend, so he'd just work on getting Cora and Finn together Saturday or Sunday. It wouldn't be hard, since Finn always jumped at the chance to see Cora. Along with being an uptight bore, he was painfully predictable. Liam could read the man like an open book, and it was clear he was head over heels for Cora and would do anything for her. Why the angels chose that man for her, Liam would never understand, but he'd dwell on it later. For now, all he wanted to do was get behind the wheel of that magnificent car and soar.

Liam left the driving track two hours later with a spring in his step and a satisfying sense of accomplishment. He'd gone through most of the maneuvers he'd learned the previous weekend, and he'd even managed the high-speed turn without hitting the wall. Twice. It was still a challenge to focus when the car skidded out of control, but he'd finally managed it. By the time he turned onto his street, all he could think about was telling—

Magnus?

Liam pulled his car up to his house with a growing sense of confusion. Magnus Blackwell was opening the passenger door of his shiny, gunmetal-gray convertible. What the hell was he doing there? With dawning dread, Liam watched a woman's slender, toned leg in a strappy sandal emerge from the car. He *knew* that leg. Cora emerged in a pretty floral sundress, smiling shyly at Magnus as he held the door.

No. Liam yanked his keys from the ignition. This was wrong. All kinds of bloody wrong. When Magnus whispered something in Cora's ear that made her laugh, it catapulted Liam into motion. He bolted from the car and approached them with ground-eating strides until he swooped in beside Cora.

"Oh!" Cora slapped a hand to her chest and laughed. "Liam, you startled me. I didn't see you drive up."

"Magnus, how interesting to see you. Here. At my house." He stared Magnus down, a muscle ticking in his jaw.

"Liam," Magnus said in greeting. He looked amused. "I was just telling Cora how lucky you were to have such a charming roommate."

Was she blushing? This was even worse than he'd thought. She tucked a lock of hair behind her ear and said, "How was the racetrack?"

"Good. Great. Very entertaining." Liam kept his gaze on Magnus. "I didn't realize you two had plans."

"It was spur of the moment," Cora explained. "Magnus called me out of the blue right after you left and invited me to dinner. I figured it would be more fun than having takeout with the cat."

"I'd like to think it was my sparkling personality that convinced you," Magnus told her with a teasing smile. "But now that I've met your cat, I can see why you chose to run away with me." He held up his hand, showing a red scratch along the underside of his wrist. "That thing is a demon on four legs. I think I may need holy water for this."

Cora stifled a laugh, reaching for Magnus's hand to examine it. Liam felt his blood begin to simmer. He curled his fists, straining to keep from shoving Magnus away from her. An old Irish curse rang in his head, and he struggled not to shout it aloud. *May the cat eat you, and may the devil eat the cat.*

"Please don't take it personally," Cora said to Magnus, letting his hand go. "My cat Angel hates almost everyone."

"Except me," Liam reminded her. He felt nothing but smug satisfaction knowing Angel had taken a swipe at Magnus. The feisty cat deserved extra treats for that. Angel was definitely on Liam's side. They were brothers-in-arms.

"He *does* like Liam. It's really weird," Cora said. "Even my dad was surprised the first time Angel jumped into Liam's lap."

"Must be the demonic energy," Magnus said with mock severity. "Like calls to like, you know."

"Oh, is that so?" Cora teased. "Must be why you and Liam get along so well, then."

Magnus locked eyes with Liam, and they had another one of those silent man-to-man conversations.

Are we cool, or are you going to challenge me?

Liam clenched his teeth. *She's far too good for the likes of you.*

Maybe. Probably. Hasn't stopped me before.

You'll never touch her.

Magnus smirked. *Care to put a wager on that?*

Liam was seconds away from slamming his fist into Magnus's arrogant face when Cora said, "I'm going to head in. It's getting late, and tomorrow's another long day at the salt mines. Thanks again for inviting me to dinner."

"It was my pleasure," Magnus said. "Next time we should check out the new sushi place downtown."

"Sounds good." She gave Magnus a bright smile.

A scalding bitterness coated Liam's insides, worse than the infernal coffee drink everyone seemed to love. That man didn't deserve Cora's smiles. He didn't deserve anything from her.

After Magnus drove away, Liam stormed into the house after Cora.

She was slipping off her shoes near the front door with a dreamy look on her face.

"Cora," Liam said, shutting the door behind him. "Please tell me you're not seriously thinking about dating Magnus."

Cora looked up in surprise. "Why not? I thought you liked him."

"Not for you," he said forcefully.

"What's that supposed to mean? You said Magnus was a guy who knew how to have fun and enjoy life, and I happen to agree with you. He was easy to talk to, and we had a great time at dinner."

"You can't trust a man like him," Liam blurted, following her into the kitchen. "Magnus is very slick with the ladies. I've seen it."

Cora let out a huff of laughter, reaching for a glass and filling it with water. "I appreciate you caring, but there's something you should know about me. First of all, I can take care of myself. I've told you that. I'm a pretty decent judge of character, and I'm not going to get into anything I can't get myself out of. Second, I've been dating long enough to recognize when someone's putting on a show. I know Magnus is a smooth talker and he's dialing up the charm right now, but you're the one who said there might be more to him on the inside."

Liam scowled. "I never said that."

"Yes, you did." Cora took a sip of water and leaned against the kitchen counter. "You said just because a man knows how to live life and have fun doesn't mean he's insincere or flippant with his feelings. No, let me finish." She held up her hand when Liam opened his mouth to interrupt. "Third, and most important, I don't need an overbearing father breathing down my neck, telling me who I should and shouldn't date. I grew up with one of those, and I'm so over it."

She marched out of the kitchen, and Liam followed her down the hall.

"Listen, I just think you should—"

"When I want your opinion, I'll ask for it," Cora said, opening the door to her room. She turned to face him, and Liam recognized the determined, stubborn tilt of her chin. There'd be no reasoning with her tonight. "Who I decide to date is really none of your business."

If only he could tell her how wrong she was. "You deserve much better than him. He's not the kind of man to take a relationship seriously."

"Okay. Let's say you're right," Cora said, crossing her arms. "Has it occurred to you that maybe I don't care? Maybe I'm not looking for anything serious, either. Maybe I just want to blow off some steam and have fun with no strings attached."

"Blow off steam?" Liam didn't like the sound of that at all. "What exactly do you mean by that?"

Cora rolled her eyes. "Think about it. Smart guy like you? I'm sure you'll figure it out. Good night, Liam." With that, she shut the door in his stunned face.

Liam's blood simmered to an angry boil as his mind filled with all sorts of wicked images involving Cora and Magnus blowing off steam. Hell would freeze over before he allowed that to happen. There'd be absolutely no blowing and no steam between the two of them, *ever*. Not if he could help it. Magnus was an arrogant libertine with too much confidence when it came to reeling women in, but Liam knew exactly how the man worked. He could knock him down a peg. All he had to do was find ways to hit Magnus where it counted—his pride. And Cora had to witness it.

Knowing he wouldn't be able to sleep, Liam went back outside to breathe in the warm, jasmine-scented air. He sat on the front porch step, trying to wrangle his disturbing feelings into something useful, like a plan. A week ago Liam had respected the hell out of Magnus and admired the way the man lived. But now that Magnus was sniffing around Cora like a hungry mongrel, everything changed. In the course of just one night, Magnus Blackwell had gone from being the most admirable person Liam knew in Providence Falls to the most manipulative, scheming reprobate in all the world. Magnus's style of reeling women in didn't bother Liam at all until he had Cora on his hook.

A soft meow came from the bushes as Angel sauntered out to greet him.

"Wandering the neighborhood again, I see." Liam scratched the purring cat under the chin. There was a small cat door in the back of the house that allowed him to come and go as he pleased. For the most part Angel was content to laze around in-

side, but sometimes he liked to wander at night when the neighborhood was asleep. "I saw what you did to that rat bastard's
hand earlier. Good job, you wee crafty thing."

Angel's purring grew louder as he stared adoringly at Liam
with big headlamp eyes. It was a comforting sort of purr. Very
soothing. But then the cat opened his mouth, and the most
alarming noise emerged.

A sound like the blast of a thousand golden trumpets rico-
cheted through Liam's eardrums, making his teeth vibrate and
his skull ache.

He slammed his hands to his ears, scrambling off the step and
backpedaling into the yard. "What was *that*?"

The cat twitched his nose, utterly unperturbed by the noise
he'd just made. Then he plopped onto the step, stuck a hind leg
in the air and began licking himself in a most ungentlemanly
manner.

"Did you not hear me, cat?" Liam sputtered. "That thing you
just did, with your…snout." He waved a hand in the direction
of the cat's nose and mouth.

Angel opened his mouth and "trumpet-meowed" again, only
this time the sound was even louder and longer and more bone
jarring.

"Stop!" Liam commanded, trying—and failing—to block
the terrible horn blasts from rattling his brain. The unearthly
melody roared through his head, pulsing deep into the marrow
of his bones until he lowered to his knees in the grass, shaking.

When it finally ended, Liam cautiously lifted his head from
the ground and risked another glance at the cat. What he saw
made him groan. "I should've known you two were behind
this."

Three angels now sat on the front step—a furry one who
couldn't be bothered to stop licking himself, and two heavenly
sentinels with wisps of mist clinging to the tips of their sparkling
wings. Even under the old porch lamp covered in cobwebs, Sa-

mael and Agon glowed with an otherworldly grace that defied the laws of nature.

Liam sank back on the grass, rubbing his chest. His arms. His scalp. The booming, soul-deep cacophony had stopped, but he could still feel the residual effects of it pulsing under his skin. The sound had affected him on a visceral level, snapping along every nerve ending with a heady, sharp energy that was too powerful to harness and too vast for a mere mortal to comprehend. Liam felt as if he'd just sipped lightning from the holy grail itself.

"Was that supposed to be fair warning before you appear?" he croaked.

"It was Samael's idea," Agon said with his usual cheer. "He thought since we'd already mentioned it earlier, our sudden appearance would be less startling if preceded by the glory of celestial trumpets."

Liam's emotions were so scrambled from the evening's events, he couldn't stop the nervous laugh that tumbled from his chest. "You sure you two work for the man upstairs, and not the other one?"

Samael looked unimpressed, but that was nothing new. "Your attempt at humor is unappreciated, ruffian."

"Oh, I wasn't joking," Liam said, rising from the grass and slapping dirt from his hands. "I've wondered about it often, but no matter. We've got a problem on our hands, lads. Cora went out to dinner with a man who's all wrong for her, and she enjoyed herself. He's a charmer, this one, a real wolf in sheep's clothing. Manipulative, self-absorbed and mercenary."

"Yes, it appears she has a type," Samael said coolly. "Why is it, Liam, that every time we warn you to stay focused on your task, you seem to bungle things up even worse?"

"There's been no bungling on my part," Liam said with feeling. "I haven't done a thing."

"Obviously. If you'd been doing what you were supposed to do, this wouldn't have happened."

"This is all Magnus Blackwell's fault," Liam said in frustration. "He swooped in on Cora tonight while I was away, and I have a very bad feeling he's going to become a problem. She—" He lowered his voice and whispered, "She wants to *blow off steam* with him." There. That would show them the severity of the situation.

Agon looked intrigued, but Samael just sighed and said, "Once again, you're in a bind, rogue. Cora's no closer to loving Finn, and now you've got a potentially disastrous problem to fix."

"Perhaps throwing Magnus into the mix was not the best plan," Agon said to Samael.

"You arranged to have Magnus and Cora meet?" Liam gaped at them. "What kind of angels are you? It's like you're working against me."

"We did not arrange for *them* to meet," Samael said. "But more to the point, we have our reasons, and you need not concern yourself with things you're not ready to understand."

"Oh, aye. I'm too much of an imbecile. Fine. Keep your angelic secrets," Liam said in annoyance. "I can fix this problem myself. I've got a plan. I just haven't figured out the details."

"Having a plan is a good start," Agon said with encouragement. "We have faith that you will succeed. Cora has a natural warmth and generosity of spirit. She can be persuaded back onto the right path."

Liam sighed. Even if Agon was right, it wasn't going to be easy. "Look, I know Cora's supposed to love Finn, and I'll do everything I can to try and make that happen, but let's be honest." He held the palms of his hands out, like they were a balancing scale. Then he lifted one. "On this side you've got a boring, forgettable man with the personality of a wet mop who probably irons his bedclothes before going to sleep." Liam lowered that palm and raised the other. "And on this side, you've got a thrill-seeking devil like Magnus Blackwell who wants to take Cora for a wild ride, and not just in his sports car. He'll do whatever it takes to get what he wants. Lie. Cheat. Manipulate."

"How can you be so sure?"

"Because I ran with a band of thieves, if you'll remember. I dealt with shady people all the time. I'm very familiar with the mind of a man who manipulates others into getting what he wants." Liam kicked at a clump of mud on the grass. "I've seen the way Magnus is with women, rotating through them like they're items on a menu. He can't be trusted to do right by Cora."

"Indeed." Samael gave him a piercing look that Liam couldn't decipher.

"Magnus is not good for her," Liam continued. "But Cora doesn't know that."

"Then I suppose it's up to you to show her." Samael rose from the step and floated into the air.

Agon gave the purring cat one last pat on his head, then followed Samael into the night sky.

Liam watched the angels leave with an odd mixture of determination and hopelessness. "Wait!"

They paused, shimmering against the backdrop of stars.

"I'll find a way to show Cora how wrong Magnus is," Liam said. "I'll think of something. But what about Finn? Is there anything you can do to make him more appealing? I'm not asking for a miracle, here." Lord knows it would take one. "Just... a bit of a boost."

"Finn doesn't need anything from us," Agon assured him. "He has very fine qualities already."

"*Fine* isn't enough," Liam said in exasperation. "The man has no *spark*. Nothing to pique her interest. Cora is a lively, passionate woman with a bright imagination and a deep capacity to love and care for people. She's got a feisty streak a mile wide, and she needs a man who can appreciate that side of her. The Finn I've seen would melt into a puddle at the first sign of trouble. Cora needs a man who's strong. In both character and body. Someone who loves fiercely and would protect her with his last breath. Someone who—"

"Patience, rogue," Samael said. "There's more to Finley Walsh than you know. She will soon see." With a flick of his hand, a pocket of mist opened up, and the angels disappeared.

10

"SO?" SUZETTE GRINNED WICKEDLY OVER THE rim of her cocktail as Cora placed her drink order with the bartender. "I've waited all day for the juicy details about your date with Magnus. Start talking."

"Shh," Cora whispered, tipping her head in the direction of Rob Hopper, Liam and some of the other officers at a nearby table. "I don't want them to hear."

It was after hours and Cora had agreed to meet her friend for Thursday night drink specials at Danté's bar. Over the years the place had become the preferred hangout for Cora and some of her colleagues. There were no pool tables or dartboards, and Danté's had never hosted live bands or karaoke, but the dark velvet booths, intimate mood lighting and relaxing music made it the perfect place for professionals to unwind after a long day.

"Who cares if they overhear us?" Suzette said, flicking a hand at the guys behind them. "It's not like anyone expects you to live like a nun. Women go on dates. Women like to have sex."

"Cheers to that," a man at the bar said, raising his glass to Suzette.

She smiled, tossed her red hair, then turned back to Cora. "Spill."

"It was only a first date," Cora emphasized, leaning against the bar. "I'm sorry to disappoint you, but sex didn't happen."

"And I had so much hope for you," Suzette said with a dramatic shake of her head. "Fine, tell me about it, anyway. What was he wearing? What did he say? Did he try anything? Please tell me he ran a hand up your leg under the table or tried to kiss you good-night. Give me something."

"He spoke Italian to the waiter," Cora offered. "That was kind of sexy. And he did try to ply me with a third glass of wine."

"He speaks Italian," Suzette said dreamily, sipping her drink. "Keep going."

"He showed up in a convertible Mercedes, then took me to this little hole-in-the-wall Italian place in Belletown Heights. I guess he's a regular there because the hostess knew him. He told me about places he's traveled, which was impressive. And he asked me a lot of questions about my job and growing up here."

"That's huge," Suzette said with a nod. "I've been on a ton of first dates, and in my experience, guys usually just want to go on and on talking about themselves. It's like my job is just to sit there and smile and nod and be impressed with whatever they say. And the only time my opinion matters is at the end of the date when they want to know if I'm down for a horizontal night cap. But I digress. Go on."

"That was really it," Cora said with a shrug. "And after dinner he drove me home."

"Finally, we're getting to the good part." Suzette's hazel eyes sparkled with anticipation. "How did you end the night? Did he give you one of those gentlemanly pecks on the cheek, or did he bypass all that and just go for it like the bad, bad boy I know he is?"

"Neither, because Liam rolled up right when we got home. The three of us ended up standing there talking for a bit." Cora glanced over her shoulder where Liam was in a discussion with one of the guys at the nearby table. He'd been so bothered that night, standing beside her on the sidewalk and glowering at Magnus like an angry boyfriend. That was what bugged Cora the most. She and Liam weren't together. He didn't even like her in that way, and he'd made it clear, so he had no right to comment on who she chose to date. It was none of his business.

"Mmm, so there you were. Sandwiched between two scorching-hot guys. Maybe there's hope for you yet. What happened next? Did the three of you go...inside?" Suzette wiggled her auburn brows.

Cora gave her friend a slow blink. "You're unbelievable, you know that?"

"Unbelievably awesome? Yes, I'm told often."

"So that's it. I said goodbye and went to bed." Cora sipped her drink, leaning her back against the bar to survey the crowd. "But Magnus did mention going out for sushi next time."

"And are you going to go?"

"I think so."

"What's there to think about? He's hot. You're single. Match made in heaven." Suzette said it like it was a foregone conclusion. Then her mouth opened in surprise as she caught sight of something across the room. "Oh, my gosh. Is that Finn? With a *woman*?"

Cora followed Suzette's gaze to one of the booths along the wall. A sconce with faux flames hung above it, casting a warm glow over Finn and a pretty young woman with blond hair.

"Wow, I can't believe he's actually with someone," Suzette said. "I could've sworn he only had eyes for you."

"We're just friends," Cora said as she watched Finn having an animated conversation with the young woman. "The only reason we were together at that charity gala was because Liam stood me up."

"For a hot minute I thought you and Finn would be good together," Suzette said. "But now that Magnus is in the picture... I mean, come on."

"What?" Cora watched Finn smile at the other woman. He seemed happy. She felt an odd twinge in her chest. Of happiness, of course. Finn was a nice guy, and he deserved it.

"Let's put it this way. Finn's the guy who'll help you paint your living room," Suzette explained. "He'll research the right kind of primer you need. He'll bring the drop cloth and all the tools and safety masks. He'll even tape off all the corners of the room for you, because everyone knows that's the crappiest part of the job. Magnus is the guy who will throw you up against that living room wall and screw your brains out until the two of you are rolling around on the floor naked, covered in nothing but wet paint and each other."

Cora turned her back on Finn and the room. "Sounds messy."

"Exactly," Suzette said. "Messy and wild and a little unpredictable. That's what you need right now. Escapism. When I look at Finn, I see a man who doesn't do anything without carefully thinking it through. But Magnus, now, there's your ticket to some pure, unadulterated *fun*."

"Work has been brutal lately," Cora said with a sigh. "We're at a standstill on the investigations, and morale is low. It's just been a cluster headache that keeps getting bigger. I think you're right, Suze. I just need to let loose and have some stupid fun."

"I'm on it," Suzette announced, slapping her hand on the bar. "Stupid fun is my specialty. I'm going to plan something for this weekend. You still owe me for bailing on the Fourth of July party, so you can't say no. You have to go."

"Go where?" Liam asked, sidling up between them. He signaled the bartender and ordered them all another round of drinks.

"It's a surprise," Suzette said. "We're going to have fun this weekend, and you can come, too, Liam. But only if you commit to the rules."

"Ach, rules," he said with exaggerated distaste. The grin he gave them next was steeped in mischief as he lowered his voice and said, "I much prefer breaking them."

Cora rolled her eyes. "Says the man who works in law enforcement."

"The rules are simple," Suzette said. "No dwelling on anything related to work. No talking about problems. No bringing up anything serious or important. We're seeking escapism in all its frivolous forms." Suzette nudged him with her shoulder. "Can you handle that?"

Liam gave a solemn nod. "I'll try to bear it as best I can. In fact, I know just where we can all go."

Cora's gaze wandered back to Finn and his mysterious woman. With a jolt, she realized he'd caught her attention and was waving her over to his table. The young blonde woman was smiling at her, too.

"I'll be right back," she told Liam and Suzette, who were now arguing about racing cars, of all things. She wove through the packed tables until she was standing before Finn and his date.

Finn seemed genuinely glad to see her. He stood and said, "Cora, I'd like you to meet my little sister, Genevieve. Gen, this is Cora McLeod."

Cora's brows shot up in surprise, but she beamed at the young woman as they greeted each other and shook hands. *Not a date, then.* She vaguely remembered Finn mentioning a sister, but he rarely talked about his personal life, and Cora never asked.

Genevieve appeared to be in her early to midtwenties, though the light sprinkling of freckles across her nose made her seem younger. Now that Cora had a better look at the woman, it was obvious she and Finn were related. Although Finn's hair had darker streaks of caramel and gold, and Genevieve's hair was lighter, they both shared the same deep brown eyes with thick black lashes. The biggest difference was their size. Where Finn was well over six feet tall with broad shoulders and an athletic build, his sister was a tiny little thing. She looked delicate and fragile compared to him.

"Sit with us." Genevieve slid over so Cora could sit beside her. "I'm so glad to finally meet you. Finn's told me about you. He said you're the best law-enforcement officer in Providence Falls, and the city is lucky to have you."

A hot blush seared across Cora's cheeks as she slid in beside Finn's sister. "I'm not sure that's true."

"It is. You'll just have to own it." Finn smiled as he lounged across from them, his long arm slung over the back of the booth. It struck Cora how much more relaxed he appeared now, compared to the last time she saw him when he showed up to the police station. It had been fascinating to watch Finn working as Slice's attorney, but Cora much preferred this side of him. Here was the easygoing man she'd grown used to over the years.

"I didn't realize your sister lived in Providence Falls," Cora said.

"Not for long," Genevieve sang out. "Soon, I'll be off to New York City. Just a few more weeks, and my brother will have his house all to himself again. You're sad to see me go, huh, Finn? You can admit it. It's okay to cry. It won't make you any less of a man."

"I'm sobbing right now on the inside," he deadpanned. "How will I live without my house gremlins to liven up the place?"

"House gremlins?" Cora asked, glancing between them.

"They're these invisible little creatures who steal my T-shirts," Finn explained. "They also leave trails of crumbs in the kitchen and hide the TV remote in the freezer."

Genevieve gasped. "That was *one* time. And I only did it because I'd been cramming for that exam all night, and I was in zombie mode." She tossed a balled-up cocktail napkin at him, which he deflected easily.

"My sister was recently offered an internship at a law firm in

Manhattan," Finn told Cora. "Providence Falls will be losing a rising star when she leaves us."

Now it was Genevieve's turn to blush. The tips of her ears turned pink. She looked down at her phone, then she sat bolt upright. "Oh, crap! I have to go. I'm celebrating a friend's birthday across town." She gave Cora an apologetic smile. "It was so good to meet you. Come over! Finn, let's have a going away barbecue before I leave. Cora, consider yourself invited."

"Do the house gremlins really need a going away party, though?" Finn asked with mock puzzlement. "Every day has been such a party with them around."

Genevieve rolled her eyes. "Call it a housewarming party, then. To celebrate getting your bachelor pad back to yourself again." Her phone chimed, and she swore under her breath. "Gotta run. See you guys later."

Cora watched Genevieve hustle out of the bar, dodging tables as fast as she could. She accidentally knocked a pile of napkins off a table as she passed.

"If we end up having a barbecue, I'll be sure to invite you," Finn said with a laugh. "Although consider this fair warning about those house gremlins."

"I had no idea your sister was living with you," Cora said. There was so much about him she didn't know. Odd that she'd never thought to ask.

"I invited her to move in a year ago so she could focus on finishing grad school without having to juggle a full-time job."

"That was nice of you."

He shrugged. "Family." He said it like that explained everything, and maybe it did. Cora had never had siblings. Her mother died when she was little, and her father raised her the best he could. Hugh McLeod was now retired and lived a few hours away, but he'd once been a police captain in Providence Falls, and he'd taught Cora about the legal system and loyalty and justice. The two of them made it work, but there was an emptiness in their home that was never filled after her mom died.

"I always wished I had an older brother growing up," Cora said. "I used to fantasize about how he'd fight off my bullies or help me kick the vending machines at school just right, so free candy would rain down. Or sometimes he'd forge my dad's signature on an absent slip so we could play hooky from school."

"This fantasy brother of yours sounds like a bad influence," Finn teased.

"No, he was perfect for me. My dad was so controlling and overbearing, I needed someone in my corner to help me go a little wild."

"I guess that makes sense," Finn said. "I know your father, and I don't think he'd ever advocate stealing candy or playing hooky."

"Definitely not," Cora agreed with a laugh. "Hence, my desire for the naughty older brother who was my partner in crime. Did you ever do stuff like that for your sister? Like save the day and get in fights for her and all that?"

An odd expression ghosted across Finn's face. He took another drink, then set the glass back on the table. "Something like that."

"Well, I think it's wonderful that she's going to be a lawyer," Cora said. "You must've been a good influence if you inspired her to follow in your footsteps."

Finn's expression shuttered. "I think it was our similar upbringing, more than anything else."

Cora wanted to ask what he meant, but she didn't want to pry because he looked slightly uncomfortable. She quickly changed the subject. "I was surprised to see you at the police station on Monday. I didn't realize you did pro-bono work."

"It was part of my agreement when I signed on with Johnston & Knight. I keep a certain percentage of my time reserved for those cases."

Cora lifted her brows in surprise. That was commendable

of him. The more she learned about Finn, the more convinced she was that he was a genuinely good man. Suzette had once said Finn reminded her of Clark Kent, a superhero in disguise. A smile tugged at the corners of Cora's mouth.

"What?" Finn asked.

"Nothing. It's just really good of you to do that. What made you decide to take on pro-bono work?"

He stared down at the table for a few moments, like he was trying to gather his thoughts. Or maybe he was deciding whether or not to divulge personal information. Either way, Cora was intrigued.

"When I was eighteen, my father was wrongfully convicted of a crime," Finn said quietly. "He got involved with some bad people and ended up becoming their scapegoat. He was innocent and needed a good lawyer, but my mother was a preschool teacher and my father worked in construction. We didn't have the money to afford good representation. My dad got a court-appointed lawyer who meant well, but he was new to the job and already swamped with more cases than he could handle. It didn't work out in my dad's favor, and he was sent to prison for a crime he didn't commit."

Cora stared at Finn in shock. "That's terrible. What happened afterward?"

"Nothing good." Finn was wearing the cool, emotionless expression he reserved for the courtroom. There was a stark contrast between this mask and the warm, kindhearted person Cora knew him to be. "He died in prison. In his case, justice was never served."

"Oh, my God. Finn, I'm so sorry."

"It happens more often than we think," he said in an offhand manner that didn't fool Cora for one second. She could see that he felt deeply about the injustice, and she suspected it was the foundation for his chosen profession. "I decided after that I was going to study law and someday advocate for people who couldn't afford to help themselves."

"That's amazing," Cora said. "Truly. I can't think of a better or more noble cause. Not everyone could experience a tragedy like that and still find a way to embrace the system and help others."

Finn's cheeks flushed, and he took a quick drink. "Well, it was either study law or become a masked vigilante on a quest for vengeance." He gave her a self-deprecating smile. "I couldn't afford rent on a decent bat cave, so it wasn't a hard decision."

Deep admiration bloomed inside her as she studied the man across the table. He was quiet and unassuming, and she was suddenly overcome with the realization that she'd known him for years and never bothered to find out what made him tick. But now the more she learned, the more she admired. There was no subterfuge with a man like Finn—at least not from what she could tell. He was as he appeared. Honest, with nothing to hide. And he was moral and steadfast in his quest for justice. No wonder her father liked him. Suzette had said Finn wasn't the type of guy to sweep a girl off her feet. Maybe she was right, but deep down Cora had a feeling that someday, Finley Walsh was going to meet his perfect girl, and they were going to be very, very happy.

11

AT NOON ON SATURDAY LIAM LEANED AGAINST a faux barrel of ale outside a colorful tent with the words YE OLDE COSTUME RENTALS. He watched Cora and Suzette disappear into the shop, pointing to the brightly colored skirts and scarves dangling from hooks along the ceiling. Coming to the Annual Summer Renaissance Faire had been Suzette's crackpot idea of letting loose and having fun, and Cora had embraced the idea with enthusiasm.

Liam was still on the fence about the whole thing. While he appreciated the overall frivolity of the fairgoers and the exaggerated gaiety of the place, the anachronistic portrayal of centuries past made him feel like a hapless actor on a stage. It mirrored his actual situation a little too closely for comfort.

He scratched his head, turning in a circle as he took in the merchant stalls and costumed revelers. It was like standing in the middle of a Technicolored dream in which fantasy and modern entertainment were tossed into a bubbling cauldron of wildly inaccurate interpretations of the past. Here was a medieval princess in sunglasses clinging to a man in a wizard cape and blue jeans. There was a knight crusader wearing a baseball cap and eating a hot dog. A wood nymph in a fluorescent green bikini with tennis shoes wove through the crowd, trailing plastic vines and flowers in her wake. It was going to take Liam some time to ignore the glaring reminder that, like these actors and costumed revelers, he was just a player in this life, stumbling around on a stage not meant for him.

"Come, come, good sir!" A rotund man at the mouth of the costume tent boomed, beckoning to Liam. He wore poufy pantaloons over a striped doublet, a baggy velvet hat with a feather in it and a digital sport watch on his thick wrist. "Clothe thyself in our fine garb and catch a fair maiden's eye!"

Liam shot him a dubious look. The outfits were eye-catching, to be sure. The Day-Glo colors and gaudy, spangled ensembles were enough to stab anyone in the eye. Whether or not the costumes were appealing to the finer sex remained to be seen.

"Liam," Suzette called. "Get in here. We found something perfect for you."

Cora waved a white pirate blouse with billowy sleeves, laughing at Liam's expression. "Don't be a spoilsport. You promised to embrace the spirit of fun, remember?"

Frowning, he ducked under the hanging scarves and approached his doom. This day was not turning out as he'd expected. When Suzette said they were going to go wild and enjoy a day free of worry, he'd pictured trips to the beach or nightclubs or roller coaster theme parks. What he hadn't expected was to be immersed in a farcical reminder that he didn't belong in this century. Worse still, his attempt to include Finn had failed in the most spectacular way. Finn had declined Cora's invitation because he was flying to New York City with his sister for the weekend. Something about viewing potential apartment listings. When Cora announced he wasn't able to make it, Suzette chimed up with even worse news. She'd invited Magnus Blackwell. Liam grimaced. The day was set up for disaster, but he was determined to find a way to knock Magnus down a peg or two. He just had to make sure Cora witnessed it.

"Liam, we're typecasting you," Suzette announced, shoving a pirate costume at him.

He reflexively caught the wide-cuffed overcoat as Cora placed a leather hat with dreadlocks on his head. "You look like Captain Jack Sparrow."

"It's only fitting," Suzette explained as she ushered him toward the striped curtain concealing a small dressing room. "It was either this, or that Henry the Eighth-looking thing, and I just can't see you in tights and a codpiece." Neither could he, thank God for small mercies.

"What about something simpler?" He pointed to a pair of gray breeches and a coarse linen shirt. Though cleaner and softer, they weren't much different from the clothes he used to wear in his old life in Ireland. All they lacked was a fine layer of dirt, a handful of patched spots and several mended seams.

Cora looked up from a stretch velvet medieval dress she was considering. She tilted her head to the side and regarded him thoughtfully. "You know what's weird? It actually suits you. I feel like I've seen you wearing that costume before. Are you sure you weren't an extra on *Game of Thrones*, or something?"

He knew she was teasing, but Liam searched her face, wondering if some part of her soul remembered him. The angels had said Cora would never recall the life they'd once shared, but sometimes in moments like this, when she gave him that perplexed frown, the veil between this world and the other seemed to thin, and Liam allowed himself to hope. If Cora ever did remember—*truly* remember him and the love they'd shared—then that would change everything. The angels would have to accept she belonged to him, wouldn't they? A horned demon chose that moment to enter the tent with a plastic pitchfork, his nefarious laughter curling through the shop. Liam's shoulders slumped, and he turned his back on the devil. Or perhaps it wouldn't matter, and he'd be tossed into the fiery pits of hell, anyway.

"A peasant?" Suzette scoffed, wrinkling her nose. "You can't wear that. It would be a waste of your swashbuckling good looks. Now, go, Liam. Shoo. Embrace your destiny." She gave him a gentle push into the dressing room.

Ten minutes later Liam emerged from the tent in what the shop clerk called "Deluxe Caribbean Pirate" gear. He'd not gone four steps when a group of women in diaphanous fairy costumes eyed him coyly, whispering to themselves and giggling as they passed. One of them blew him a kiss before flitting into the crowd.

"Ahoy, there, Captain," a serving girl shouted from the ale tent across the way. "We've got plenty of booty over here for you to plunder!"

A bawdy laugh erupted from the tent, and Liam tipped his hat, giving them an elaborate bow.

"Suzette was right," Cora said, emerging from the costume shop. "Seems you're destined for a life of piracy."

Liam took one look at Cora and felt the air whoosh from his lungs. She was wearing a black corseted serving wench costume that showcased her feminine charms to tantalizing perfection. The blue-and-green skirts were hiked high enough to reveal glimpses of her toned legs, and the white blouse under her corset draped low, leaving her shoulders bare. She looked a far sight better than any barmaid he'd ever seen. Part of him wanted to haul her over his shoulder and carry her off someplace where they could be alone, and the other part wanted to rip his coat off and cover her, so no man with wandering eyes could ogle her.

Cora spun in a circle and held out her arms, grinning. "I'm a naughty bar wench. What do you think?"

Before Liam could find his tongue, Suzette breezed up with a loud, "Holy hotness, Cora. You look *smoking* in that getup." Suzette fingered the pink crushed velvet skirt of her medieval lady costume. Faux colorful jewels were sewn into the neckline, and she had a matching gold crown on her head. "Crap. Now I kind of feel like a Pinterest fail."

"You look beautiful and regal," Cora assured her, linking her arm through Suzette's. "Jimmy's going to be very impressed when he sees you."

"He'd better be," Suzette said, adjusting the neckline and tugging it lower. "He's been working at this fair all summer, and this is the first time I've had a chance to come and surprise him. Honestly, I don't know why I agreed to date him again. He's canceled on me twice already. I'm so over the excuses."

"Now, remember the rules, ladies," Liam said with mock severity. "We're to have fun today and not dwell on problems."

"Oh, right." Suzette gave him a sassy salute. "Aye aye, Captain."

"Come on," Cora said. "Let's go to the ale tent and get this party started. Magnus said he'd meet us there."

Liam grumbled at the mention of Magnus but followed them to the ale tent to order drinks. Within a few minutes they were standing in a roped-off area, people-watching and sipping beer from plastic cups.

"There he is!" Suzette said, bouncing on her toes. "He's not wearing a costume, but who cares?" She whispered something in Cora's ear that made Cora blush.

Liam watched as Magnus emerged from the crowd like a hawk descending on prey. He wore a black T-shirt, dark jeans and leather motorcycle boots, and he gave Cora a smoldering once-over as he approached. Liam gritted his teeth, even more determined to nip this—whatever this was—in the bud before Cora went off the rails with this man. He was a bad influence, and Liam would do everything in his power to prove it to her.

"Ladies, you look ravishing," Magnus said with a rakish grin. Then he took in Liam's costume and said, "What a remarkable outfit. I believe I had something similar when I was a kid. Good for you, man." It was a veiled insult, but only Liam caught it.

He gulped the rest of his beer while Magnus exchanged pleasantries with the women. For the next few minutes Liam had to listen to Magnus engage them in a detailed story of how he'd found parking, somehow managing to make it sound like a fascinating adventure. Cora and Suzette were obviously enraptured, which made Liam's blood begin to simmer and his skin begin to itch. He had to get out of the beer garden. He needed to *move*. Suddenly, at the far end of the merchant row, he saw the perfect diversion.

"Shall we walk?" he asked, interrupting Magnus. "There's a game stall over there that looks too fun to miss."

Forcing himself to adopt a meandering stroll through the crowd like the rest of them, Liam somehow managed to keep his excitement in check until they reached the booth he wanted. A man dressed in faux chain mail stood under a sign that read battle axes of valor. On a low table were several rustic hatchets with rope-wrapped handles. A wall of painted wooden targets lined the back of the booth twenty feet away.

Liam plunked down several bills, enough for all of them, then said, "Who wants to go first? Magnus?"

"Me, me, me," Suzette said with enthusiasm, elbowing her way to the front. She adjusted her crown, then lifted the ax with both hands. "How do we throw it?"

Liam showed Suzette how to place her hands on the handle, explaining where to aim and when to let go. To his annoyance, Cora had taken the spot beside Suzette, and Magnus was now giving her instructions. He was speaking to Cora in a low, intimate voice as he wrapped both arms around hers to show her how to stand and where to hold the ax. Liam scowled. Who made Magnus an expert on ax throwing? Surely, this wasn't a twenty-first century skill. He probably didn't have the faintest idea what he was doing and was just taking advantage of the situation so he could paw at Cora.

"I think the ladies can take it from here," Liam said through gritted teeth.

Magnus glanced at Liam in amusement, then stepped back with a final encouraging word to Cora.

Suzette went first. She hauled the ax over her head with both hands, her long princess sleeves fluttering in the breeze. With a warrior-like yelp, Suzette let the ax go. It flew in a high arc, but there wasn't enough power behind it. The ax landed in the dirt a few feet in front of the wooden target.

"No," Suzette said, stomping her foot. With a regal lift of her chin, she turned to the man in chain mail and held out her hand. "I want to try again."

He placed another ax in front of Suzette, explaining they each had five chances to throw.

Cora braced herself, drew back her hands and tossed her ax. It flew end over end through the air and smacked the wooden target, then fell to the ground.

"Oh, that was so close," Suzette said in encouragement.

Liam stood back with Magnus as the women practiced aiming and throwing. Every time, their axes smacked the wall and fell to the ground.

"It's like there's a secret way you have to spin it," Suzette said with frustration. "Mine keeps hitting the wall in the wrong spot, and it doesn't want to stick."

"Suze, I'm afraid ax throwing isn't for us," Cora said, laughing. "If we had to defend ourselves in battle like this, we'd be the first to die."

"It's all just a matter of timing," Magnus said. "I'm sure you'd be great at it with a little more practice."

"Take it, Liam." Suzette's shoulders slumped in defeat, and she handed him her ax. "You defend us. I'll just embrace my role as the medieval lady and hang in my castle with the minstrels and the mead."

"And I will be your serving wench at the castle," Cora said, stepping away from the table. "Serving myself all the mead."

Liam took the ax and stepped up to the table. He measured the heft of it in his hand, spinning it twice in the air, then catching the handle to test the balance.

"Oh, my God," Suzette exclaimed. "Cora, you missed it! Liam just spun his ax and caught it all *Braveheart*-style. Do it again, Liam."

"No spinning the axes," the man in chain mail boomed. He pointed to a sign on the booth where the rules were laid out in old English font. "Aim only for the targets, or forfeit your right to battle, milord."

"Bummer," Suzette said, shaking her head. "That was impressive."

Liam faced the target, lifted the ax easily over his head with one arm and lobbed it through the air. It was child's play. The ax flew end over end and the blade lodged into the center target with a satisfying *thunk*.

Suzette and Cora gasped, clapping their hands.

"How did you do that so easily?" Cora beamed at him, her blue eyes sparkling with admiration.

"I had a lot of practice growing up," Liam said, lifting another ax and sending it flying straight into the target. As a child he'd chopped enough wood for ten lifetimes, and had mastered the use of an ax, as well as hunting weapons to catch small game in the woods. It was amazing how fast one could learn to use a blade when the alternative was starving or freezing to death. For his final throw, Liam tossed the ax underhand from hip level with an expert flick of his wrist, sending it spinning to land in the direct center of the target once again. Cora and Suzette whooped and clapped, thoroughly impressed.

Liam barely had a chance to bask in their praise before Magnus stepped up to the table. He drew an ax over his head and let it fly. To Liam's annoyance, he hit the wooden target, too.

Both Cora and Suzette began commenting on Magnus's skill. It irked Liam no end when Magnus hit the target again. And again. By the time they walked away, Liam was downright fuming.

"How were you both so good at that?" Suzette asked a few minutes later. "Did you practice ax throwing when you were a kid, too, Magnus?"

"No, not at all," he said with a laugh. "I've only tried that once before, but it's fairly simple once you figure it out. Should we go watch the jousting?" He gestured to the crowded bleachers in the distance, then held his arm out to Cora, who—blast it all to hell—linked her arm with his, grinning up at him like he'd just slayed a dragon for her.

Grumbling under his breath, Liam followed them all to watch the knights in shining armor perform. He was so consumed with finding ways to knock Magnus off his pedestal, he barely noticed the show.

For the next couple of hours Liam repeatedly challenged Magnus to participate in activities of skill. He'd wanted Cora to watch Magnus fail, but time and again Magnus surprised Liam with his damned competence. The man was as good at crossbow targets as he'd been at ax throwing. At the strongman tower Liam swung the mallet hard enough to make the puck rise to the top and ring the bell, which was quite satisfying, until Magnus did it, too. It seemed that every time Liam tried to beat Magnus at a game of skill, Magnus proved to be just as competent.

Even worse, Magnus was playing the chivalrous knight to perfection. When Cora said she was thirsty, Magnus marched to the nearest beverage tent and brought back a round of ice-cold drinks for everyone. When the ladies oohed and aahed at the merchant cart selling painted silk fans, Magnus bought each of them one. As the day wore on, Liam's mood grew stormier.

Magnus acted noble and charming through it all, but he wasn't fooling Liam for one second. The bastard was playing the role he needed to play in order to win Cora over, and it seemed to be working.

Sometime after noon Liam purchased a giant turkey leg and leaned against a tree, brooding as Magnus and Cora rode the wooden carousel. He grimaced, tearing off chunks of smoked turkey leg and chewing forcefully as he watched the smiling couple. If only he had a jousting lance, he'd knock Magnus off that stupid painted horse. He could do it, too. He had good aim. Maybe he could just chuck this turkey leg at him when he circled back around.

"Why are you waving your food around like that?" Suzette asked from a nearby cart full of parasols. He ignored her and bit another chunk off his turkey leg.

"You're going to choke if you keep taking such huge bites, you know. I once saw a guy at a steak house who—" She gasped. "Oh, *hell* no."

Liam looked at Suzette's thunderstruck face and rigid posture. He followed her gaze to a sparkly tent with a sign that read Witch Hazel's Potions and Spells. The tent was filled with colorful bottles of perfume and body oils. Tied bundles of lavender spilled from baskets, and trays of scented bath soap were arranged on velvet tablecloths.

Inside the tent a tall, lanky man in breeches and a billowy shirt was locked in a heated embrace with a woman who appeared to be Hazel. She was wearing bohemian skirts, a plethora of gold bracelets and her long, dark hair was spangled with colorful ribbons. The powerful scent of patchouli incense wafted out of the tent. The man said something to Hazel, and she let out a throaty chuckle.

"Jimmy," Suzette spat under her breath. "He is so dead."

She bolted forward, but Liam reached out and caught her elbow. "Suzette, wait."

"I'm going to kill him," she said, barely restraining herself. "Then I'm going to let that witch bring him back to life with her magic spells, so I can kill him again." She shook her head in disgust. "This just proves what I already knew. Jimmy's a lying, cheating slimeball. I can't believe I gave him another chance. Why are men such pigs, Liam, hmm?" She pierced him with a glare, daring him to answer. Bright pink blotches stood out against her pale, freckled cheeks.

Liam hesitated. With her flashing eyes and flaming hair, Suzette looked like an angry tigress. He needed to tread carefully. He glanced toward Cora for help, but it looked like she and Magnus would be engaged at the carousel for a while. There was no way around this. He was on his own. Drawing himself up to his full height, he gave Suzette one of his most disarming smiles. "Come, now. Not *all* men are swine. Surely, you must admit some are quite decent."

Suzette scoffed. "Not that one." She jerked a thumb at Jimmy, who was now facedown in Hazel's magical cleavage. "He's a grade-A moron. See, this is my problem. I never learn. Maybe I'm destined to be alone. Oh, my God, that's it, isn't it? That's my fate. I'm going to grow old and be found dead in my apartment, eaten by my cats. I should just quit while I'm ahead and join a convent!"

"There, there." Liam gave Suzette's shoulder an awkward pat. Her face was growing alarmingly red. "Don't strap yourself to the wheel of pain just yet. Why don't you take some deep breaths, and we'll—"

"I can't take deep breaths. I'm running on fumes. Angry, noxious, patchouli-scented fumes!" She was on a roll, and it was clear she wasn't going to back down. "I need to go over there and confront him."

"All right," Liam said in resignation. If Suzette was determined to have it out with the man, then Liam would back her up. "Let's go talk to this halfwit, but first I have a question."

She was angry and insulted, yes, but something important was missing. Liam knew what love and heartbreak looked like, he knew what it felt like and he saw neither emotion on Suzette's face. That was a good thing. "You don't love him, do you?"

She wrinkled her nose. "No. I'm just angry at myself for believing he was being faithful, and I don't like being played. But I'm not head over heels for him or anything. It was never like that."

"Good," Liam said, tossing his turkey leg in the nearest garbage bin. "Then this is going to be easy."

He followed Suzette as she whirled and marched over to the tent, her pink velour gown trailing behind her. At the entrance she stopped and jammed her hands on her hips. "Jimmy. What a surprise."

The skinny man pulled himself from Hazel's embrace very slowly, as if he was waking from a dream. When he saw them standing at the entrance, he jerked, scrambling off the velvet floor cushions. "Suzette?" All the color drained from his face. "What are you doing here?" He yanked his flowy shirt over the front of his breeches, but it was quite clear where his feelings stood.

"Oh, no. You don't get to ask the questions." Suzette whipped her head back and forth between him and the witch. "Looks like you've been keeping *very* busy at the fair, Jimmy. At least you weren't lying about that."

Hazel appeared confused. She smoothed her bohemian skirts and went on autopilot, gesturing to a table of multicolored glass bottles. "May I interest you in a potion, milady?"

"Sure. Do you have any rat poison?" Suzette drawled. "I have a very large rat I need to exterminate from my life."

Jimmy stepped closer and lowered his voice so Hazel couldn't hear him. "Suzette, I can explain. Hazel's just a friend. She's been going through a lot, so I've been trying to cheer her up this week to make her feel better, that's all. You're still it for me. This doesn't mean anything."

Liam stepped up beside Suzette and, to his surprise, she snaked an arm around his waist and snuggled closer. Liam played along, drawing her tight against his side.

"Who are you?" Jimmy had the audacity to look affronted.

Ignoring him, Liam deliberately bent down and whispered in Suzette's ear, "You're doing grand, woman. He looks flustered enough to topple over in a thin breeze, but I'll still clock him in the face for you, if you like. Just say the word. It'll be fun."

"Maybe later." Suzette gave him a secret smile that probably looked downright flirty to the gaping man watching them.

"You did promise me a day of frivolous fun," Liam reminded her.

"Suzette, who is this guy?" Jimmy sputtered, crossing his scrawny arms and glaring at Liam.

"Oh, he's just a friend." Suzette fluttered her lashes and gave Liam an extra-tight squeeze for emphasis.

"Yes, and I'm going through a lot, myself," Liam deadpanned. "Suzette's been making me feel…*much* better."

"Come on, babe," she said breezily. "Let's get out of here. I'm done with rats. Have a nice life, Jimmy."

"Wait! What about us?" Jimmy started toward her, but Hazel seemed to have finally caught on.

"Jimmy, what the hell?" Hazel said. "You told me you were single."

"He is now," Suzette sang out, tugging on Liam's arm to leave.

Hazel backed Jimmy into a corner, spewing such colorful swear words, Liam had half a mind to stay behind just to listen. Maybe there'd be a few he could add to his ever-growing list. But Suzette was ready to go, and his role was to play her adoring paramour so he couldn't linger.

By the time they reached Cora and Magnus, who were exiting the carousel, Suzette was in a much better mood. "Did you see the look on his face?" she asked, rolling her eyes.

"I don't envy the dumb beast," Liam said. "From the looks of it, Jimmy's going to be drowning in Hazel's curses and hexes before the day is through."

"What happened?" Cora asked.

"I caught Jimmy cheating on me with that witch over there." Suzette tilted her head to the tent. "So I went to confront him, and Liam came to back me up."

Cora looked shocked. She stood on tiptoe to see the tent through the crowd. "Suze, that's terrible. I can't believe Jimmy would do that."

Suzette let out a derisive snort. "I can. Honestly, I shouldn't have been surprised he was cheating. Jimmy changes his mind about jobs and friends as often as I change my nail polish. He's never been steadfast about anything."

Cora laid her hand gently on Suzette's shoulder. "Are you okay?"

"Believe it or not, I am," Suzette said in surprise.

Cora searched her friend's face with concern. "Should we leave? We can get out of here right now if you—"

"No way." Suzette gave Cora a quick hug. "I promise, I'm okay. It's actually nice to be free of him. I feel pretty dang good about it. Liam pretended to be my boyfriend and made Jimmy jealous, which was awesome. Thanks for that." She smiled at Liam.

He gave a theatrical bow. "Happy to be of service."

"And then Jimmy's witchy girlfriend started yelling at him," Suzette continued. "As far as breakups go, it was extremely satisfying."

"It seems we missed all the excitement." Magnus casually wrapped his arm around Cora's shoulders. Cora did nothing to dissuade him. In fact, she seemed to like it. Liam felt as if a dark cloud suddenly covered the sun.

As they strolled away, a cold desolation overcame him. Any sliver of fun he'd experienced while helping Suzette was now gone, and in its place was the bleak realization that Cora liked the wily, conniving womanizer walking beside her. She didn't seem to notice the way Magnus's gaze lingered on her breasts, nor did she witness the hungry, wolf-like glint in the man's eyes when she bent over to adjust her skirts. Somehow, Liam's plan to make Magnus look bad had backfired, and Cora seemed to like him more than ever now.

By the end of the day Liam walked stiffly toward the parking lot with Suzette chatting gaily beside him. Ahead of them, Magnus and Cora were *holding hands*. Liam wanted to dash back to the fair, snatch one of those battle-axes of valor and send it flying straight at Magnus's back. That would solve the problem once and for all, though it sure wouldn't win him any points with Agon and Samael. Or Cora, for that matter. He sighed with frustration.

"Hey," Cora called, turning back to wave at them. "Magnus and I are going for a drive. I'll see you guys later."

"Sounds good," Suzette said, waving back.

Like hell it did. Liam started forward. "Cora, wait—"

"Shh!" Suzette elbowed him in the ribs. "This was the plan all along. Cora needs to have some fun and she likes him, so just go with it."

"She doesn't need a man like him," Liam grumbled, rubbing his ribs. "He spent the entire day ogling her charms like the lecher that he is."

"Ogling her charms?" Suzette snorted. "You've really embraced the Renaissance lingo."

"He was," Liam insisted. "I witnessed it myself."

"Liam, did you see the costumes in that place? It's a Renaissance Fair. Corsets and cleavage are practically mandatory. And anyway, Magnus was the pinnacle of chivalry compared to some of those guys I saw in that beer garden back there. Trust me."

"You're supposed to be Cora's friend," Liam said. "The last thing you should want is for a man like that to sink his hooks into her."

"I am her friend. The oldest and dearest. And that means I know her better than anyone else. She spends a lot of her life with her head down at work, and it's been a long time since she's let loose and had a good time with someone. All I want is for her to be happy."

"As do I, but a man like Magnus Blackwell is not going to make her happy," Liam said. "I know the type of person he is, and I've seen the way he flirts with other women. He only wants one thing from Cora, and she deserves more than that."

"Oh, yeah?" Suzette gave him a quizzical look. "Like what?"

"She deserves a man who's going to treat her with respect and genuine affection. Someone who will appreciate her brilliant mind, her kind heart, her loyal spirit. She's beautiful, of course, but Magnus only sees what's on the surface. He has no idea that her true beauty lies within, and he'll never know because all he wants is a quick tumble in the hay."

"Oh, my God." Suzette gaped at him. "You like her."

"Of course I do." Liam spotted the car in the distance and began walking briskly toward it. "We work together and live together. I care very much about her well-being."

"That's not what I meant, and you know it." Suzette grabbed his arm, so he had to stop walking. "You *like* her."

Liam shook his head.

"She thinks you're not attracted to her, you know. She told me."

"I'm...not." The lie scraped like thorns across his tongue, but he managed to get the words out, anyway. "I'm not interested in her in that way, but I am aware of her good qualities. I want to see her with a man who can appreciate all that she has to offer. A man whose personality is compatible with hers.

Someone who can enhance her life in all the best ways. She deserves nothing less."

"I agree," Suzette said. "But it sounds like you're talking about The One. A soul mate or something. People can spend a lifetime looking for that person and never find them. Frankly, I think soul mates are like unicorns. I'm not convinced they exist."

"They do," Liam shot back, wishing he'd never met those blasted angels who had confirmed it.

"Fine, I'm happy to be wrong," Suzette said, holding up her hands in surrender. "I'll be thrilled when Cora finds a great guy to settle down with, but in the meantime, let a girl have some fun. Ease off the pedal, okay? Just be her friend and quit with the growly big-brother act." She started to walk and added, "Oh, and for the record? I know it's exactly that—an *act*. Because no matter what you say, I'm pretty sure you have a thing for Cora."

Liam opened his mouth to deny it, but Suzette didn't give him a chance.

"Hey, keep it to yourself if that's what gets you through the day." She slapped him on the shoulder and changed the subject to the different fast-food restaurants they could hit on the way home. It was a subject quite near and dear to his heart, but he was too bothered to think about food.

It was just past twelve when Liam heard Cora arrive home that night. He was lying in his room with the cat, Angel, beside him, wondering how the hell he was going to untangle Cora's growing affections for Magnus and transfer them to Finn. Another week gone, and he was no closer to completing his task and saving his immortal soul. Time was running out, but with Finn off to New York City for the weekend, there wasn't much more Liam could do until next week.

As if sensing Liam's distress, Angel rose from the bed and repositioned himself, curling around Liam's head. Soon, all Liam could hear was the loud rumble of the cat's purr.

"Get off my pillow, you mangy thing." Liam pretended to

act annoyed, but there was something very comforting about having a cat for earmuffs. He'd never had the luxury of a pet in his old life, so he hadn't understood the lure. In his village most animals were kept for sustenance, and with crops beginning to fail, even farm animals were becoming scarce. So it came as a bit of a surprise that he was growing attached to Cora's feisty feline. In truth, it was no small thing when such a lofty, regal creature as a cat chose to love you.

"Purr all you want, but it's not going to help," he grumbled as he smoothed a hand down Angel's back. "I'm on borrowed time, cat. Unless you want to give me one of your nine lives, you're useless to me."

Angel ignored Liam's complaints because he was a cat, and therefore above such trivial things. Instead, he continued to purr and settled more firmly around Liam's head.

Grumbling one last time for good measure, Liam closed his eyes and tried to think of ways to drag Cora from Magnus's clutches, but it all seemed futile. Not even the cat listened to him. What hope did he have that Cora would?

12

THE ZIPPY LUBE AUTO SHOP WAS EMPTY ON MON-
day morning, save for an old station wagon in one of the stalls. It
was located at the edge of a strip mall near a McDonald's, where
cars were already lined up for the drive-through window. Liam
had half a mind to skip the auto shop and get in line for one of
those lovely melted cheese-and-egg sandwiches, but he stayed
the course because he was a responsible police officer on an important mission. That, and he'd just had breakfast.

Pulling his car up to the first garage bay at Zippy Lube, Liam
rolled down his window. He'd left Cora at the police station
to get caught up on paperwork, and since he would rather do
anything than tackle the pile on his own desk, he'd decided to
pay Slice Biddlesworth a follow-up visit. It was a long shot that
Slice would have any new information to divulge, but it was a
good excuse to get out of the office.

The young man emerged from a side door wearing a black
mechanic jumpsuit with an oil-stained rag hanging from one
pocket. Though his clothes were soiled from work, the dark cir-
cles were gone from his eyes, and he looked much more rested
than the last time.

"You." Slice slowed to a stop before reaching the window. Liam could tell from his expression he wasn't thrilled to see him.

"Morning." Liam tried to look cheerful and unassuming. "I've come to get my car one of those tune-up things."

Slice took in the state of Liam's ancient sedan, unimpressed. "When's the last time you had the oil changed?"

"A few years." It seemed like a better answer than the truth, which was *never*. How often did a car even need its oil changed, anyway? Liam handed Slice the keys and hopped out of the vehicle.

Slice looked at Liam like his brain needed a tune-up. "I'll get you signed in and have Arnie take a look." He gave the keys to a squat man with sunburned cheeks and a shaved head, then led Liam into the cramped office. Other than a counter along one wall and three plastic chairs in a tiny waiting area, the place was mostly bare. It smelled of stale cigarette smoke and motor oil, and the only thing hanging on the wood-paneled wall was a poster of a woman on the hood of a convertible wearing a swimsuit.

Slice typed some information into a computer, then grabbed a Zippy Lube invoice off the printer and slid it over to Liam. "This is the basic package price, but I'd recommend upgrading to synthetic oil to extend the life of your vehicle." He ticked off boxes with a pen. "Air filter change, coolant flush, fuel injector cleaning. Your car looks super old, so you may also want wiper blade replacements and—"

"Just do it all," Liam interrupted. He had no idea what the man was going on about, and he had more important things to be concerned with. "Whatever the car needs, I'll leave it to your expert opinion. Charge me for everything. The works."

Slice began ticking off more boxes on the invoice, launching into all the upgrades Liam would be receiving with the premium package. Liam nodded at all the appropriate times, hoping to speed the process along. Once the invoice was filled out, Arnie was notified and the transaction was complete, Slice leaned his back against the counter, twisting an oil rag in his hands. "Any news on Lindsey's case?"

"I can't discuss it." Liam took a seat in one of the plastic chairs. "How are you?"

Slice crossed his arms. "Not sure I want to discuss it."

Fair enough. The young man had been through a lot, and he didn't owe Liam anything. "I'm sorry about your girlfriend and that whole business at the station," Liam said solemnly. "Truly. It's a terrible thing to lose someone."

Slice searched Liam's face. "Have you?"

"Aye, and it's hell." Liam looked him straight in the eyes. "I know."

Slice glanced away. "I've got my buddies at the club around. Makes it easier to deal."

"I imagine it does," Liam said, then added casually, "How's everything with the Booze Dogs?"

Slice's expression soured. "Is this another interrogation, or are you just asking to kill time?"

"A little of both, I suppose," Liam admitted. "Just because I'm not here in an official capacity doesn't mean I've stopped trying to find out what happened to Lindsey. She didn't deserve what happened to her. If you've heard anything that could be useful in the case, it would help to tell me."

Slice was quiet for a long time. Then he gave a heavy sigh and rubbed the back of his neck. "There's something, but I don't think it has anything to do with her."

Liam waited.

"There was a big dustup at The Doghouse this past week," Slice finally said. "A lot of money went missing from the club. Like, a ton of money. Prez went ballistic when they discovered it was gone, and there was a bunch of infighting. Nobody knows what happened yet, but they're determined to find out who did it. Things could get ugly."

"When was it stolen?" Liam asked.

"They don't know for sure. Could've been days, maybe even weeks. Only Prez and a couple of other guys even know where they keep the club's cash."

Liam wondered if Lindsey's death had anything to do with the stolen money, but he didn't want to upset Slice by mentioning it. "If anything else comes up and you think it might be useful, let me know."

Slice studied him for a moment, then shook his head. "I want to help you guys, but I'm not going to do anything to jeopardize my brothers at the club. We're a family, you understand?"

"I do," Liam said. "And I don't envy your position. But if you really want to get justice for Lindsey, I hope you remember that we're on the same side."

After paying what seemed to be an exorbitant amount of money for his auto tune-up, Liam got back on the road and called Cora, filling her in on what he'd learned.

"The Booze Dogs haven't reported any stolen money," Cora said over the phone.

"Aye, but they wouldn't. From the way Slice talked, they're keeping it in the family and doing their own investigation."

"That's disturbing. Those guys don't play by the book, and I don't even want to think about their interrogation methods, or the depths they'd sink to in order to get information. I need to talk to the club president. I'll see if I can arrange it."

"How?" Liam asked, remembering the last time they'd gone to The Doghouse. "That place is locked down, and that giant bear of a man wouldn't even let us step one foot inside. It's going to be nigh impossible to get an audience with their leader if he's not in the mood to talk."

"I have an idea, but it's a total crapshoot," Cora said. "I'll fill you in later when you get back."

Cora got off the phone with Liam and headed out of the building. She'd spent the better part of the morning responding to calls and dealing with paperwork, and after one look at Captain Thompson yelling on the phone in his office, she'd decided it was a good time to talk to the Booze Dog president. Anything to get out of the station. If her hunch was correct— and it was a big *if*—maybe she'd even find the man and gather something useful from the meeting.

She pulled her phone from her pocket, leaned against her car and selected a number she'd never dialed before.

Finley Walsh answered on the third ring. "Walsh."

"Hey, it's me," she said, then quickly added, "Cora. I'm sorry to bother you at work."

"Cora." She could hear the surprise in Finn's voice. "It's no problem at all. How are you?"

"I have a favor to ask." She bit her lip. "But I don't want to make you nervous or uncomfortable."

"When you start with something like that, I'm already halfway there," he said with a chuckle.

"It's nothing bad. It's just kind of personal. But first I want you to know that if you don't want to talk about it, or you can't, it's totally okay. I'll find another way that doesn't involve you. I don't want you to get in trouble or anything."

"Cora," Finn said kindly. "Talk to me."

She took a deep breath. "Okay, you know how you came in to represent Slice Biddlesworth as his attorney last week?"

"Yes."

"Well, I heard you tell him you had a mutual acquaintance, so I figured someone contacted you to help get him out of hot water. And all I need to know is if that person was in any way connected with the Booze Dogs."

There was a long pause. "Why do you want to know?"

"I need to speak to the club president," she said. "I think there might be a connection between a robbery that just took place at the compound and a case I'm working on."

"You think Lindsey stole something from the Booze Dogs and got killed for it?"

Dang, he was sharp. Cora hadn't wanted to reveal anything about the investigation, but he'd gone and jumped to the right conclusion, anyway.

"I can't really discuss it. Look, I know this is a shot in the dark, but is there any chance you could introduce me to the club president? I just want to ask him some quick questions."

"Eli Shelton is not the kind of guy who'd take kindly to questions," Finn said. "Especially not from law enforcement."

"So you do know him." Maybe she'd get lucky, after all.

"I've represented a few of his club members in the past."

"Can you at least tell me if you know where he is? Is he at The Doghouse?" Cora asked. "Last time Liam and I went there looking for Slice, this man named Bear wouldn't let us past the gate. But I'm flying solo today. Maybe he'll be easier to talk to if he sees me without Liam."

"Bear?" Finn sounded incredulous. "You'd have a better chance trying to reason with an actual grizzly."

"If you can't tell me anything, it's okay. I get it. I don't want to put a strain on any business relationship you might have with them."

"Cora, please don't go to The Doghouse alone," Finn said urgently. "It's not a good scene. They won't let you past the gate unless you're a club member or there on official club business. There's only one other exception that would gain you entrance, and you're certainly not it."

"What's the exception?"

Finn paused. "Women who are there for a party or pleasure."

"Oh," Cora said, deflated. "Yeah, I guess that's not me."

He gave a resounding, "No."

She sighed. "I have to talk to him. Maybe if I go as one of those women and sneak in during a party—"

"Cora," Finn said in alarm. "Good God, tell me you're joking."

"Shh, let me think about this for a sec." If she found a way to buddy up with a group of women before they arrived at The Doghouse, and if she could get past the front gate—

"Listen, I know where Eli Shelton is," Finn said. "He owns Choppers, a bike shop on Fifty-Fourth. It's where he hangs out during the week."

Relief washed over her. "Good. That's much easier than waiting until the weekend to try and infiltrate The Doghouse as a party girl. It's exactly what I needed to know. Thanks, Finn. I owe you one."

"What are you planning to do?" He sounded worried.

"I'm just going to pop over there," she said, mentally calculating the time it would take to get there and back with traffic. "I need to ask Eli a few questions about the robbery, that's all. Thanks for telling me where to find him. I won't reveal your name or anything. I promise."

"I don't care about that," Finn said quickly. "Just... Hold on." Cora heard a few muffled words between him and someone who must've been his administrative assistant. Finn told the person to cancel an appointment and reschedule. Then he got back on the phone and said, "Are you at the police station?"

"Sort of. I'm in the parking lot, but I'm about to head out."

"Just wait for me, okay? I'll meet you there and go with you."

Cora leaned against her car, surprised. She hadn't expected him to go that far to help her. "Finn, you don't have to do that. I know you're busy, and I can take care of it myself. I appreciate you letting me know where to find him. It saved me a lot of hassle trying to track him down."

"Cora, we're talking about Eli Shelton," he said as if the name packed a punch. Maybe it did to other people, but to Cora it didn't mean much.

"I know."

"Eli doesn't trust anyone, especially not cops. He'll take one look at your badge, and he'll shut down and lock up like a bank vault. You won't get anything out of him. The Booze Dogs keep to themselves in all business matters, especially when it comes to club secrets. They have a strict code of honor. It'll be an exercise in futility if you go all the way out there by yourself. Eli doesn't know you from Adam. But there's a small—and I mean very slight—chance he'll talk to you if I vouch for you."

She sucked in a surprised breath. He really was willing to go out on a limb for her. "You'd do that?"

"Yes."

Cora felt a sudden wave of gratitude for Finn. The fact that he was even willing to try meant a lot to her. "Do you think it will work?"

"I think it's the best chance you've got," Finn said.

13

FINN DROVE CORA ACROSS TOWN, PULLING HIS car into a gravel lot just off Fifty-Fourth Street. Eli Shelton's motorcycle shop was a single-story building at the end of a one-way road running parallel to the north highway. The sign above the shop had the word CHOPPERS painted between a set of wicked-looking canine teeth, complete with salivating fangs.

Across the street was a gas station no longer in business, its boarded-up windows and weathered paint adding to the overall aura of neglect. Aside from a nearby vacuum repair store and a grungy diner on the corner, the rest of the area seemed abandoned. Nothing about the place was warm or inviting, which made it perfect for the president of the Booze Dogs.

Cora stepped from Finn's shiny Porsche, feeling as out of place as his car looked in such a seedy environment. There were three open garage bays with motorcycles in various states of repair, and at least ten burly biker men hanging around inside. A few were working on bikes, but most were sitting on fold-out chairs, talking and drinking beer. Several Harley-Davidson motorcycles were parked in front of the main shop entrance, and Def Leppard's "Pour Some Sugar on Me" boomed from one of the open bays. Cora felt like they were about to step into an old MTV music video.

"Ready?" Finn asked over the hood of his car. He gave her an encouraging smile. His hair was as neatly combed as ever, and today he was wearing a charcoal designer suit with a blue silk tie. He was tan and clean-cut, like he should be at a country club or in a high-rise office—anywhere but this place. Once again, Cora felt overcome with gratitude that he'd gone out of his way to accompany her. He didn't belong there, and neither did she. In her soft red blouse, dark jeans and low wedge boots, she felt overdressed for a visit with the Booze Dogs.

"Come on." Finn led the way like a man completely at ease with who he was and where he was going. It was impressive, considering the dark looks they were getting from some of the men in the garage.

One of them made Cora quicken her pace. The man was bald and big as a mountain, with huge arms and corded muscles along his neck, but it wasn't his size that made her nervous. It was the look in his flat black eyes. She'd seen an episode during shark week on TV once, where a great white attacked a seal. The shark's eyes were dead and expressionless, void of all emotion. Just like this man. He was even bigger than Bear, which she wouldn't have thought possible until now.

One of the guys caught sight of her and Finn. He smirked and called, "Jaaack," drawing the name out into a low rumble. Another man joined in, then hollered something at them Cora didn't catch. She hurried toward Finn and entered the shop.

The inside of Choppers was so unexpected, Cora's mouth dropped open in surprise. It was a sparkling showroom. Rows of gleaming bikes were parked on raised platforms across the shining tiled floor. The walls were painted a slate gray, with black-and-white framed photographs of motorcycles speeding down the open road. A few of the framed images were more abstract, and upon further inspection, appeared to be close-ups of gears, handlebars, or other engine details. There was a wait-ing area near an office with black velvet chairs, a soda machine and low tables filled with magazines. Beyond the office door was a short hallway leading to another garage.

"Wow," Cora said, stepping into the showroom. The overall atmosphere was understated, sophisticated and elegant.

"Eli doesn't kid around when it comes to his business," Finn said. "The outside is deceptive on purpose." He walked past a counter near the wall and rapped on the office door. When no one answered, he tried again. Muffled swearing and the sound of clanking tools could be heard from down the hall.

"Eli," Finn called.

There was a scraping sound followed by a hacking cough and another metallic clang. Then a raspy voice barked, "Out back."

Finn motioned to Cora, then led the way toward the garage.

A grizzled old man with a scruffy white beard was hunched down, working on a bike. He was tall and wide with a beer gut to rival Santa Claus's bowlful of jelly, but there was nothing soft or cheerful about his appearance. Deep lines were etched on his face from a lifetime of too much sun and tobacco, and his arms and shoulders were thick in the way of a retired weightlifter. If Santa quit his job and took to the streets, picking fights, swigging beer and chain-smoking cigarettes, he'd look like Eli Shelton.

"Eli," Finn said.

When the old man saw him, his weathered face splintered into a grin. "Well, well. Look who decided to step off his high horse to come visit."

"It's been a while." Finn leaned his broad shoulder against the doorway.

Eli snorted. "Too long, but that ain't on me. You're the one who likes the view better from the moral high ground."

"It serves its purpose," Finn said with a shrug. "And yours, on occasion."

"Ain't that the truth. It's the only reason you still got that pretty face, Jack." Eli let out a hacking cough that ended on a chuckle. "You may have changed venues, but you still don't lose, do you?"

Finn's shoulders stiffened. Cora only noticed because she was half-hidden behind him in the doorway. He seemed suddenly uncomfortable, but his voice was smooth when he asked, "How's the family?"

"Mabel hasn't stopped singing your praises ever since you took her mama's case and got the charges dropped. She thinks you walk on water."

"How about the kids?"

"Both married now," Eli said. "Got two grandkids driving me batshit crazy."

Cora had a hard time imagining Eli as a grandfather. He didn't seem like the kind who would teach you baseball and read bedtime stories when you were afraid of the monster under the bed. He looked more like someone who'd take your baseball bat, drag out the monster under your bed and bludgeon it to death.

As if he could hear her thoughts, the old man finally noticed Cora in the hall. He rose from his crouch near the bike and asked Finn, "That your woman?"

"She's a friend." Finn shifted to let Cora into the room. He seemed reluctant to do so, which made her wonder just how bad this Eli Shelton really was.

"Hi." Cora's smile felt like plastic, but she forced it, anyway. She stepped through the door, grateful for Finn's warm presence at her back. He wasn't joking when he said Eli Shelton did not take kindly to strangers. The old man gave her a shrewd once-over, assessing all her parts as if she were a bike he might want to purchase. Or dismantle. It was hard to tell.

He smirked at Finn. "A fine young filly."

Cora bristled. Was this guy for real? "Not a filly. My name is Cora McLeod."

His bushy white eyebrows shot up. "Sassy, too. You better lock that down, Jack."

Cora sucked in an annoyed breath, but before she could respond, Finn took over. "Eli, I brought Cora here to meet you because she'd like to ask you a few questions."

All humor vanished from Eli's face. Now he looked deeply suspicious. "McLeod. I heard that name before."

Cora braced herself and dove in. "I'm with the Providence Falls Police Department, and—"

"McLeod," Eli interrupted. "You Hugh McLeod's brat?"

"No, I'm his daughter." She didn't want to get on Eli's bad side, but he made it so tempting. "My father was the police captain years ago. He's retired now."

"I remember him. Better than most, but still a pig." Eli turned his head and spat. "Now he's got his kid holding down the fort. What are you doing in my house, girl?"

This was her moment, so she had to make it count. "I'm investigating the murder of a young woman that took place on the night of July third."

"And why should I care?"

"There's a chance it may be connected to the recent robbery that happened at your compound."

Eli's face darkened like a thundercloud. "Who told you about that?"

Cora swallowed. "I'm not at liberty to say."

Eli made a sound of disgust. Then he dismissed her, turning on Finn. "You bring this noise into my house, Jack? A cop. Poking around in club business. Of all the bull—"

"Eli, she's here to help you," Finn interrupted.

"I don't need any help from the cops," Eli boomed. "You should know that better than anyone. When's the last time the local law enforcement went out of their way to help the Booze Dogs? I'll tell you. Never. That's how long it's been."

"Mr. Shelton," Cora began.

He jerked his head. "Get out."

"Someone robbed you of a lot of money," Cora said. "Don't you want to find who did it? One of your club members was dating a girl who showed up dead in the woods. Lindsey Albright."

"The boy's in the clear," Eli growled. "He had nothing to do with it."

"Yes, but what if Lindsey was somehow involved in that robbery? If there's a slight chance her death and the theft are connected, we might be able to help each other by sharing information."

Eli's lip curled into a sneer. "Get her out of here, Jack. Now, or I'll get one of the boys to haul her out."

"Eli, you should talk to her," Finn reasoned. "You might be able to help each other. Cora's straight. When have I ever steered you wrong?"

Eli gave a stubborn shake of his head and turned his back on them.

"Come on, Prez," Finn tried again. "What's it going to take to give her just ten minutes of your time?"

Eli's back straightened. He turned slowly to look at Finn, his expression calculating. It was a scary look coming from a man like him. "You want me to help your little girlfriend?"

Finn blew out a breath. "I just think you could both benefit from a conversation. That's all I'm asking."

"All right," Eli said easily. Too easily. "She can meet me at The Rolling Log bar on Friday night around nine. I'll have a little chat with her then."

"But that's days from now," Cora blurted. "Why Friday?"

Eli's eyes glittered with anticipation. "Because your man needs to do me a little favor first."

The hair on the back of Cora's neck rose. Whatever Eli wanted, it couldn't be good.

"I've got a lot of casework this week." Finn sighed, rubbing the back of his neck. "But if one of your guys is in trouble, I might be able to—"

"I ain't talking about legal counsel." Eli stared Finn down. "You know what I'm talking about... *Jack.*"

Finn froze, then swore under his breath. He looked as if Eli had just punched him in the gut. Eli crossed his arms in challenge, waiting for Finn's answer. What the hell was going on? Cora's flight instinct was kicking in hard. She needed to shut this down fast.

"Come on, Finn. Let's just go," she said, heading toward the door.

Finn didn't move. A muscle ticked in his jaw, but he was staring at the old man with a look of pained resignation, which Cora found even more alarming. Whatever Eli wanted, Finn looked like he was going to agree to it.

"Run along to the waiting room, little girl," Eli told her. "The men need to talk."

A nice roundhouse kick to the face was what Eli really needed, but she refrained. "Finn, come on. I'll think of something else. I'm done here." She gave him a gentle push in the direction of the door, but it was like pushing against a brick wall. He didn't budge. Instead, he looked down at her with a cool, unreadable expression she remembered from the interrogation room.

"Cora, I need a moment to speak with Mr. Shelton alone," Finn said in that clipped, professional tone she was beginning to resent. The sudden formality was like an ice cube down her back. "If you could be so kind as to wait in the showroom, this won't take long."

Cora clenched her teeth. She'd be so kind as to kick his butt into high gear so they could get the hell out of this place. "Don't you lawyer-speak to me in that tone of voice," she mumbled under her breath. "I don't know what that deranged, misogynistic, North Pole reject is asking you to do, but I'm not on board with it. Do you hear me?"

Finn's lips twitched, and for a moment his mask slipped. "I promise I'll make it quick, Cora. Please?"

She wanted to argue further, but he looked just as determined to talk to Eli alone as Cora was to go, so she firmed her features. "Sure thing. I'll be in the waiting room when you're ready."

Stomping down the hall, Cora made sure to cough a couple of times, so they heard her leaving. After a few seconds she spun on her heel and tiptoed back, stopping right before she reached the doorway. She could just make out their conversation over the muffled sound of the radio in the garage.

"Who's up?" Finn's voice was low and cold. "Give me something."

"Goes by the name Meat."

Finn made a noise of disgust. "Are you trying to get me killed, Eli? I'm not even in the scene, and I've heard of that guy."

"Just do your thing. Get in and get out. Keep it simple."

"Easy for you to say, old man."

"You've kept up." It sounded like Eli slapped Finn on the back. "I can tell. We can make it worth your while, too. Just like the old days."

"No. I don't want anything."

Eli let out a raspy laugh. "Look at him now, ladies and gentlemen. A fine, upstanding law man."

"Just tell me when and where."

"Wednesday night, ten o'clock." Eli rattled off an address, and Cora quickly entered it into her phone. When the map pinpointed the location, her mouth fell open in shock. It was the gas station from the video footage where Slice and his friends had been hanging out on the night of Lindsey's murder. Something wasn't adding up here. This didn't make any sense. Why would Finn need to go to a rundown gas station in the middle of nowhere on a Wednesday night? Was Eli running drugs with some guy named Meat? No, Finn would never get involved in that kind of thing. It had to be something else.

"Why me?" Finn asked him. "Surely, you have someone better suited for it."

"No one like you. Makes things interesting."

"What are the odds?" Finn's tone was grim.

Eli cackled. "Either way, I come out ahead."

There was a long pause. "Fine. Just keep your end of the deal for Cora, and I'll do my part."

"She must be something special to get you jumping like this," Eli said.

There was a shuffling sound near the door, so Cora bolted.

She ran down the hall to the waiting room and sank into one of the velvet chairs. Utterly confused, she stared at the tiled floor, replaying what she'd just heard. What the ever-loving hell was going on? Eli and Finn had a history; that part was clear. Cora never would've guessed it. She knew Finn had represented some of the club members in court, but this conversation was different. It sounded downright *shady*. Maybe even dangerous. If it were anyone else, Cora wouldn't be that surprised, but Finn? The idea of someone as clean-cut as him willingly doing something bad for her sake made her feel sick.

Until recently, Finn had always been on the periphery of her life, just someone she knew through her father, but things had changed in the past few weeks. She'd gotten to know him more, and she genuinely liked him. He always did kind, thoughtful things for others. He cared about his sister and supported her. He donated his time and expertise to help the less fortunate. Everything about Finn screamed "good guy." So whatever just went down in that garage felt wrong on too many levels to count. Cora was used to dealing with the underbelly of the city; it was her job. But Finn's battles took place in courtrooms, on phones and behind mahogany desks surrounded by books. She hated the idea that Eli could be putting him in harm's way. *Are you trying to get me killed, Eli?* Finn's words echoed in her mind as a dark sense of foreboding curled in her belly. This was bad.

Whatever was about to happen, it sounded like Finn was going alone and without backup. She couldn't let that happen.

"Ready to go?" Finn strode calmly from the hall with his back straight and head high, but she could tell by the firm set of his jaw that he was on edge. She hurried to keep up as they crossed the parking lot.

Once they were on the road, Finn was back to acting like his normal, easygoing self. He didn't mention anything about the private conversation he'd had with Eli. Instead, he talked about the weather, the meeting he had back at the office and his sister's tiny apartment they'd found in New York City. Cora tried to follow along, but she was too preoccupied. When they were ten minutes from the police station, she couldn't hold it in any longer.

"Finn."

He gave her a questioning glance.

"Whatever favor Eli asked of you, please don't do it. Tell him you changed your mind. I don't trust that guy."

"You have nothing to worry about. It's not a big deal."

"Then tell me what it is."

Finn didn't answer right away. She waited a full two minutes until she realized he might not answer at all.

"Look, I have a really big imagination," she warned. "Huge. If you don't tell me, I'm just going to imagine you doing all sorts of nefarious deeds in the worst possible scenarios. And then my brain will start spinning up all the ways you could get into trouble, and I'll be forced to endure crushing guilt because it'll be my fault."

"Nefarious deeds," he said in amusement. "Like what?"

Cora lifted her hand, ticking her fingers one at a time. "Drug smuggling mule. Scapegoat for a mafia hitman. Driver of a get-away car for lazy bank robbers."

His lips twitched. "Why lazy?"

"Because they'll dawdle, and they won't run fast and they'll still be shoving money into their duffel bags when the police arrive."

"But I'm driving their getaway car, yes? I could just take off and save myself."

"No, because they were too lazy to fill the gas tank."

"Ah, that would be a problem." His expression was serious, but his voice was thick with concealed laughter. "I can safely promise I won't be doing any of those things. I'm not going to be in danger, Cora."

"How can you be so sure?"

"Trust me, I'll be fine. More important, Eli Shelton agreed to talk to you and answer your questions. That was the goal today, wasn't it?"

She nodded because he was right, but she wasn't happy about it.

"Good. Mission accomplished."

Cora squeezed her eyes shut, torn between gratitude and guilt. "I know I should thank you for helping me today. Please know that I'm deeply grateful, even though I'm worried. Thank you, Finn."

"Any time."

"But also know that I have this crazy urge to lock you up at the station for the rest of the week so Eli can't cash in on this favor."

"You couldn't hold me," he teased. "I'd *lawyer-speak* my way out." His warm brown eyes sparkled with mischief, and the slow curve of his smile did strange, swirly things to her insides.

She turned away in confusion, focusing on the brilliant blue sky and the dappled sunlight through the trees lining the street. It was a beautiful summer day. If only she could roll her window down and let the languid breeze carry her worries away, but they were far too heavy for that. Two nights from now Finn was going to do something outside his comfort zone, all because of her. With steely resolve, Cora began to make a plan. Even if he was right, and it wasn't dangerous, she wasn't going to take the chance.

14

ON WEDNESDAY NIGHT CORA REVIEWED HER plan as she pulled on a pair of black jeans, a black T-shirt and her black knee-high boots. Then she wrapped a long black scarf around her neck, winding it high until it covered her chin. A loud clap of thunder sounded outside, and she yanked her bedroom curtain back to see a flash of lightning illuminate the street. Of all the nights for a summer storm, why did it have to be the night she needed to be an undercover superstalker?

Angel was curled on a chair in the corner, watching her rush around the bedroom. He didn't seem the least bit concerned that she was dressed like a cat burglar, about to race headlong into a storm and possible danger. That was the wonderful thing about cats; they never interfered when you were busy making mistakes.

"Is this a bad idea?" she asked Angel, pausing to scratch him between the ears.

He meowed, which Cora preferred to interpret as a resounding *no*.

"Good, because I have no idea what I'm heading into. Wish me luck."

She tossed her hair into a bun, grabbed a dark hooded jacket from her closet and hurried before Liam could grill her on where she was going. She'd thought about inviting him to tag along, then decided she had to keep this adventure a secret. Finn was not the type of person to do anything shady, but Eli Shelton definitely was. If Finn got caught up in something that could jeopardize his reputation and career tonight, Cora didn't want anyone else to witness it. She felt protective of Finn. He was genuine and kind, and he cared deeply about other people. Cora trusted Liam to back her up, but she knew he wasn't crazy about Finn. If something went wrong tonight, Liam would blame him. She didn't want that. Therefore, tonight was a solo mission.

It was eight-thirty when Cora rushed down the hall and made a beeline for the front door.

"Where are you off to, then?" Liam asked.

She startled, whirling to see Liam on the sofa. "Oh, I didn't see you over there."

He blinked sleepily at her. "Where else would I be? *Appalachian Housewives* is on soon, and they're about to make a right mess of things with the cider still."

Cora smiled as she zipped on her jacket. She wondered if Liam realized his Irish accent grew more pronounced when he was on the verge of sleep.

"Are you to market?" he asked. "We're out of those wee black biscuits with the sugar paste filling." He was sprawled on the sofa with a fuzzy throw blanket and a bag of chips balanced on his perfectly flat stomach. It wasn't fair that he ate like a starving man and never gained an ounce. He must've done something pretty stellar in a past life to be gifted with such a high metabolism in this one. If only she were that lucky.

"They're called Oreos," Cora said, grabbing her keys from a hook by the door. Sometimes he sounded like he was raised in an underground bunker. That village where he grew up in Ireland must've been more rural than most. Or maybe his memory was like his accent—it slipped when he was tired.

"Aye, lovely Oreos," he said dreamily. "Straight from heaven, those."

"Well, you'll have to make a trip to the pearly gates on your own. I'm heading out to meet a friend, so I'll be back late."

"What friend?" He sat up, beginning to look suspicious. This was her cue to leave. "It's already late."

"Have fun with the cider still!" She gave a cheery wave and was out the door before he could grill her further. This whole interrogation routine with him was getting old. It seemed every time Cora went somewhere alone at night or—heaven forbid—she had a date, he practically waterboarded her with questions afterward. And no matter how many times she reminded him it was none of his business, he still acted like a cross between a broody, jealous lover and an overprotective older brother. It was so weird. He wasn't interested in her romantically, so why did he care? Maybe Suzette was right, and it was a cultural thing. Suzette said Irish guys were territorial about two things: their whiskey and their women. But Cora wasn't Liam's woman. At some point he was going to have to understand that.

Her phone alarm chimed, reminding her it was time to get on the road. She quickly entered the address Eli had given Finn at his motorcycle shop and was soon heading north out of Providence Falls.

Half an hour into her drive the sky opened up, and Cora found herself in the middle of a torrential downpour. Heavy sheets of rain beat down on the windshield, making it almost impossible to see. She slowed her car to a crawl, checking the clock every few minutes in agitation. Why didn't she think to check the weather? Summer storms weren't uncommon in this part of the state. It was one of the things tourists remarked on whenever they visited. The day could dawn bright and cheery, only to turn into a summer squall by nightfall, complete with thunder and lightning. If she hadn't been so preoccupied with worry, she would've planned better.

When the rain finally cleared, she was way behind schedule. By the time she rolled into the gas station, it was twenty minutes past ten.

Gritting her teeth in frustration, she pulled to the side of the road just before reaching the gas station parking lot. The place looked deserted, the same as it had in the video footage of Slice and his friends. There was no sign of Finn or his car.

She was too late. Cora smacked her steering wheel, mentally kicking herself for not leaving her house sooner.

Suddenly, two men emerged from inside the store, carrying plastic bags and drinks. One was heavyset, with carrot-red hair, and the other was skinny with neck tattoos. Cora had never seen them before, but she did recognize the Booze Dog jackets they were wearing. Like Slice and his friends, the men settled against the wall. She could just make out their two motorcycles parked on the side of the building.

"What are you guys up to?" she whispered. When ten minutes passed, and they did nothing but talk and puff on cigarettes, Cora blew out a frustrated breath. *Do something!* She couldn't just sit there for the next few hours, and she hated the idea of driving home a failure. It was just past ten-thirty. Finn was long gone by now. If she wanted to find out what Eli Shelton and the Booze Dogs were up to, then she was going to have to use her own skills as a shrewd, cunning police detective.

She checked her reflection in the visor mirror. With her hair in a tight bun, her pinched expression and the black hooded jacket and scarf, she looked like a cross between a Disney villain and a ninja assassin. Not going to work. If she wanted to charm a couple of biker guys and strike up a conversation, she'd have to look more approachable than this.

After shucking off her jacket, she unwound her scarf and tossed them both in the backseat. Then she pulled her hair free to hang loose around her shoulders, dug around in the center console and applied some lipstick. The result wasn't great, but it was a little better. At least now she looked like an unassuming person out for a pleasurable, late-night cruise through a thunderstorm in the middle of nowhere. Not suspicious at all. She found a random music station, turned up the volume, rolled down her window and drove into the gas station parking lot.

The red-haired man gave her a cursory glance when she parked in front of the store, then turned his attention back to his phone. But the man with the neck tattoos blew out a plume of cigarette smoke and eyed her like she was a prize side of beef.

Cora gave him a doe-eyed smile, wondering what the hell she was going to say. She checked her phone to stall for time.

"You shouldn't be here, sugar," Neck Tatts said.

"Um…" *Tell me something I don't already know.* Cora looked at her phone again, then feigned confusion. "I'm so sorry. I think I took a wrong turn somewhere."

"Barn's that way." The man pointed to a dirt road about twenty yards away. It was partially hidden by a copse of trees. "Came in on the wrong side. This is the lookout. You're supposed to enter from the south."

"Ohh." Cora nodded, like that made all kinds of sense. She did the Bambi-eyed thing again, with the blinks and the vacuous smile. Not her proudest moment of cunning detective work, but hey. Whatever got results.

"S'all right, baby. Just head down that road about a half mile. The noise'll hit you before the crowd does." He chuckled and took another drag on his cigarette.

"Okay, thank you so much." Cora threw her car in Reverse before they had time to ask her questions. And, also, before she had time to chicken out. Adrenaline pumped in her veins as she took the hidden back road leading to the mysterious barn. It was pitch-black out there, but she could see taillights from a car in the distance headed in the same direction. She focused on the lights and kept going.

She had no idea what she was heading into, but it sounded

big. Neck Tatts had said *noise* and *crowd*. If that gas station was the lookout point, and Eli was up to something illegal, then those guys were there to watch for cops. No wonder Slice had been so reluctant to tell them what he'd been doing. With a jolt of alarm, she thought of Finn. What if he was there now? She picked up speed, bouncing over the dirt road until she turned a corner and slowed to a stop.

A sea of cars, trucks and motorcycles was parked haphazardly in an open field. In the far distance bright lights spilled from a huge wooden barn. Every once in a while the roar of a crowd could be heard from inside, the shouts and hollers interspersed with sharp commentary from someone on a microphone.

Cora found an open spot between two pickup trucks and parked. Then she stepped into the sticky summer heat, adjusting her custom sports bra with the concealed gun holster. Tonight she carried her Glock 42 tucked just under her arm. Its compact size was perfect for undercover work like this. The slight weight of it was negligible, and it didn't show through her T-shirt. Though it gave her a sense of confidence to have it, she dearly hoped she wouldn't need it.

She picked her way carefully through the wet, overgrown field, using her phone's flashlight until the ambient light from the barn made it unnecessary.

The noise from inside rose and fell like a living, breathing thing. At the entrance people were so jam-packed, Cora had to scoot sideways to slip through. It was sweltering hot inside. The sheer amount of testosterone and the scent of mud, sweaty bodies and beer hit her in the face like a wet gym towel.

All she could see was a wall of backs. Bikers in Booze Dog leather jackets and men who looked like gang members shouted over each other, jostling for space. The few random women looked like they'd done hard time on a booze cruise, with harsh makeup, teased hair out to there and skintight clothes. Ear-splitting shrieks, drunken bellows and the cracking sound of fists hitting flesh made Cora feel like she was caught in a mosh pit at a death metal concert.

Inching along the wall, she ducked past a greasy-haired man waving a fistful of cash in his drunk buddy's face. "Ten-to-one odds, you idiot! The window's about to close, so place your bet now."

Then Cora saw the cage. She sucked in a breath as everything snapped into place. The Booze Dogs were running an underground fighting ring.

A chain-link cage was erected on a raised platform in the middle of the barn. Inside it two shirtless fighters were locked in what appeared to be the tail end of a brutal battle. Cora understood martial arts, but this was something different. This wasn't even boxing; it was more like the MMA fights she'd seen on TV, but without any rules. Kicks to the groin, elbows to the face and low-blow kidney punches appeared to be fair game here.

She winced as one of the men grabbed his opponent's arm and bit down. The poor excuse for a referee broke it up, but he only gave the biter a warning. This was no Wild West brawl; this was more like a post-apocalyptic death match.

Dragging her gaze from the fight, Cora frantically began searching for Finn. When she'd eavesdropped on the conversation at Choppers, Eli had talked about the *odds* and *winning*. It dawned on her that he must've wanted Finn to be the bookie tonight. Finn was brilliant and trustworthy, so it only made sense he'd be asked to put his skills to good use. He was probably somewhere in this madness taking bets and keeping track of the house money. Guilt lay heavily on Cora's shoulders when she thought of him enduring all this chaos just to do her a favor. She had to find him and make sure he was okay.

Spying a wooden crate near the wall, Cora moved in that direction, turned it over and climbed up to peer over the sea of people. Once she tracked Finn down, she would keep an eye on him until the last bet closed. If all went well, he'd never even know she was there.

An air horn screamed, signaling the end of the match. Music swelled from speakers attached near the rafters, and the winner did a victory lap as the other man hobbled out of the cage.

Cora exhaled in relief. She'd witnessed her share of fights, but this savage style of combat was hard to swallow.

"And now for tonight's grand finale," a man on a microphone boomed. "I'm not going to drag this out because you all know why you came tonight."

Techno music, heavy on the bass, began thumping over the noise. Everyone grew louder, more frenzied, jostling this way and that like a herd of restless cattle.

Cora teetered on the rustic crate, bracing a hand against the wall to keep from slipping. Her makeshift stool was rickety, but it gave her a good vantage point to see over the much taller crowd.

"I'm talking about the bone crusher," the man on the mic said theatrically. "The annihilator. Your reigning champion. Ladies and gentlemen, give it up for... Meat!" The microphone echoed on his name.

Cora whipped her head to the doorway. *Meat?*

A giant mountain of a man burst through a double set of doors on the far side, surrounded by an entourage of guys holding back the crowd. She recognized him instantly. He was the biker with the dead shark eyes from the garage outside Eli's shop. He was even more intimidating tonight, with his pale, steroid-pumped body in blood-red shorts and gloves. Yoked with huge slabs of muscle around his shoulders, chest and back, he had to be around six and a half feet tall, and with his Neanderthal brow and bald head, he looked like an orc heading into battle.

A tiny fissure of dread crackled down her spine.

"And here to challenge our champion tonight," the man on the microphone shouted, "is a special guest many of you may remember. The legend, himself. A blast from the past. Still undefeated. Ladies and gentlemen, give it up for… The Jackrabbit!"

Music boomed, the crowd roared and people began chanting, *"Jack. Jack. Jack."*

Cora's heart lurched, then kicked into a gallop. Eli Shelton's words came flooding back like a tidal wave. *You know what I want.* Jack.

The double doors swung open.

The crowd went berserk.

Cora took one look at The Jackrabbit, and her mind went blank.

15

Kinsley, Ireland
1844

THIS WAS MADNESS. LIAM CROUCHED BEHIND the rosebushes outside Squire McLeod's house. It was broad daylight, and he knew he shouldn't be risking his neck like this, but he had to see Cora. He missed her dreadfully. It had been over a week since they'd last met, and he needed to hold her in his arms and reassure himself that all was well.

For the past several days Liam had been working tirelessly to prepare for their plan to run away together. He'd gone to the next town over to arrange for passage to the coastal town of Cork. He'd slowly gathered supplies they'd need between here and there, squirreling everything away in random hiding spots. Cora had assured him she'd have the two horses in her father's stable ready to go. In three more days they'd be leaving Kinsley, Ireland, for good, traveling to the coast. There, he'd pay the clergyman the steep price to perform a last-minute marriage ceremony, and then he and Cora would be off to America. Just the thought of it sent a thrill of excitement through him because Cora would finally be his, and he'd be a new man heading to a better life.

Part of him felt guilty for what he planned, knowing that he was never going to see his brother again. His brother's wife and kids had grown to rely on him, as well, but if Liam didn't take this chance, he knew he'd never get another. He only wished they could come with him. Last week over a supper of cold porridge, Liam had asked his brother if he'd ever consider taking his family to America. His brother had just laughed and called him gone in the head. He'd said Ireland was in his blood, and he'd be dead in the ground before he ever left.

Now, as Liam ducked under Cora's drawing room window, he thought perhaps he *was* gone in the head. No man in his right mind would risk lurking about Squire McLeod's house like this in the middle of the day, but he couldn't go another moment without seeing her.

Crouching under the window ledge, he lifted his head to peer into the room where soft piano music played. The walls were painted bird's-egg blue, with delicate floral patterns in muted greens. A silk-covered settee and dainty chairs were gathered in front of a massive marble fireplace, and in the center of the seating arrangement was an intricately carved low table. Though the carpet was faded, and the furniture worn, the overall impression was still beautiful, in the way of a watercolor painting that had begun to fade with age.

The sight of Cora sitting at the piano made his heart soar. Today she wore a rather pretty dress of pale blue silk. It appeared to be new, and it accentuated her figure quite nicely, unlike the dull gray and brown dresses her nanny usually made her wear. Her blond hair was swept into curls on the crown of her head, with a blue silk ribbon woven through the coils. Liam was struck by how beautiful she looked and, once again, overcome with awe that she'd chosen him. Someone up in heaven must've been distracted the day he'd stumbled into her life, but he wasn't going to wait around for them to realize their mistake. No, he was going to hold on tight to Cora and run as far and as fast as he could. A thief knew a true gem when he came across one, and she was a treasure more precious than anything he'd ever encountered.

He tapped lightly on the window.

Cora looked up from the piano, her big blue eyes flying open in surprise. Her smile was bright as the sun as she ran to the window and threw it open. "Liam, what are you doing here?" she asked in a voice tinged with laughter. She glanced behind her at the closed drawing room door. "Someone will see you."

Liam hooked a leg over the edge of the sill and climbed into the room. "Let's make it worth it, then." He swept her into a hug and kissed her soundly.

"I missed you," Cora said breathlessly. "Did you get everything we need?"

He nodded, sliding his fingers through the hair at the nape of her neck. "We're all set, love. I just couldn't wait to see you again, and I wanted to make sure you hadn't changed your mind about me."

Her eyes grew glossy and soft. "Never, thief. I want to be with you forever."

Liam drew her closer and nudged her nose with his. "Three more days, and the adventure begins." He was just lowering his head to kiss her again when a loud knock came at the door.

"Miss?" one of the maids called.

Cora's eyes flew wide. "Hide!" She pushed him behind the heavy velvet curtains.

She spun around and adjusted her hair. Liam reached out to tickle her, and she batted his arm away. "Come in."

Through an opening in the dark drapery, Liam saw a maid enter the room. She wore a white cap and apron, and she appeared flustered. "Your betrothed is here to take tea with you, miss."

Cora's spine went rigid. "Right now?"

"Yes, miss. He's only just arrived to town."

"Well…" Cora looked around the room helplessly, as if the faded furnishings and dainty floral arrangements could provide her an escape. "Did you tell him my father isn't home, at present?"

"He knows, miss. It was your father's invitation that brought him to see you."

"I hope you don't mind." A man's voice came from the hall behind the maid.

Cora lifted her chin and nervously patted her hair, then walked away from Liam's hiding place behind the curtain. "Of course not. Do come in, Mr. Walsh."

"Finn," he said, entering the room behind the maid. "Please call me Finn."

Cora smiled politely, and Liam felt an angry stab of jealousy. Finley Walsh was not old and decrepit like he'd imagined. On the contrary, the man who entered the room was tall, broad shouldered and lean. He looked to be in his early thirties, with not a gray hair in sight. On top of all that, he appeared rather fit in his tailored suit and shined shoes. No signs of gout at all, the bastard.

"We'll take tea now, Mary," Cora said to the maid, who was just leaving.

The maid closed the door behind her, leaving Cora in the room alone with Finn.

Liam gripped a fold of the velvet curtain with his fist. If the man tried to touch one hair on her head, he'd jump out and box his ears, hiding place be damned.

"Won't you have a seat, Mr. Walsh?" Cora asked, sitting opposite a small tea table. It gave Liam a smug sense of satisfaction to hear her calling him by his formal name.

Finley arranged his coat and sat stiffly on the faded silk settee. He appeared nervous. "Thank you."

An awkward silence befell them, and Liam lapped it up like a contented cat. Every time Finley tugged on the collar of his shirt, Liam's smile grew wider. The man had no idea how to talk to her. "H-how have you been?"

Cora folded her hands primly in her lap. "Quite well, thank you. And you?"

"Good. Very well." Another awkward silence. This was bloody marvelous.

The maid came into the drawing room with a tea tray. She set it down and left, leaving Cora to pour steaming tea into dainty china cups. "Would you like sugar, Mr. Walsh?"

He shook his head. "No, thank you."

Liam grinned. Of course he didn't want sugar. No amount of sweetener could fix his bland personality.

"I see you received the dress I sent," Finley said, his gaze flickering over Cora's blue gown.

"Oh, I hadn't—" Cora stopped and blushed to the roots of her hair, smoothing the silk folds of her skirt. "I'm so sorry. It only came this morning, and I thought… I thought my father sent it." She stared at her lap. "Thank you." Her voice was so faint, Liam could barely hear the last part. She looked beyond uncomfortable at the idea she was wearing a gift from Finn. It made Liam want to beat his chest with satisfaction.

Finley searched the room frantically, as if trying to come up with a less uncomfortable topic. "Your father tells me you collect seashells."

Cora looked up in surprise. "Yes. I dearly love them."

Finley smiled. "Now that I know, I'll bring you some when I next visit the coast."

Liam scowled. He'd do no such thing.

Cora blushed again, only this time she seemed intrigued by Finn's offer. Liam didn't like it one bit. "I didn't realize you traveled that far away." Liam wanted to take the teapot and bash it over Finley Walsh's perfectly combed head. The only thing stopping him was the knowledge that Finley could make whatever promises he wanted, but he'd never get the chance to follow through on them. Cora would be long gone by the time Finley came back with his blasted shells.

"I travel quite a bit, actually," Finley said, sipping his tea with the precision of a man born into a genteel life. He had perfect manners. Yet another reason for Liam to dislike him. "I'm often to the coast and, on occasion, London."

"Really?" Cora tilted her head in interest. "How lovely to travel and see the world. I've always wondered what that must be like."

Finley seemed pleased with her reply. He cleared his throat. "You know, after we are married, I expect to travel often."

Cora's smile faltered. "Of course." She lowered her head and took a sip of tea.

"Would you like that?" he asked nervously.

Cora raised a delicate brow. "I would like you to carry on with your business as always, Mr. Walsh. I can assure you that I'd never expect you to stay home on my account."

Finley looked startled, then he rushed to say, "N-no. That's not what I meant at all. I was hoping we could—"

"Ah, Mary," Cora said, standing when the maid entered with a plate of spice cakes. "That looks lovely, but I fear I've a headache coming on. Mr. Walsh, would you please excuse me?"

Finley stood so fast, it was almost comical. "I'm sorry you're unwell. Is there anything I can do to help?"

"No, no." Cora waved a hand. "I must apologize. Perhaps we can take tea another time. Thank you for visiting."

Finley bowed and wished her a good day. The maid had barely closed the door before Liam swept into the room from behind the curtain.

"Good God, Cora. If that was Finley Walsh, it's no wonder you want to run away. Truth be told, I've been quite flattered you'd chosen to flee with me, but now I realize you just needed to jump at the first opportunity, and I happened to be it." He wrapped his arms around her and spun her in a circle.

Cora gave him a reproving look that ended on a giggle. "I was so nervous with you in the room. I could barely speak."

"You were a blasted chatterbox compared to that man's stilted conversation."

"I don't think he can help it," Cora said. "He's always been that way, which is strange, don't you think? For a solicitor, one would think he'd be more verbose." She walked over to the tea tray and handed him the spice cakes with a glowing smile. Liam had a fairly good idea why Finley was so tongue-tied around Cora. She was like an angel.

"He said he'd bring me seashells," Cora mused, lifting her teacup.

Liam frowned. No one would bring her seashells but him. "Did you hear what he said about after you were married? How he'd continue to travel and leave you home alone all the time?"

"He did say that, didn't he?" Cora sipped her tea, looking more subdued. "That would be terribly lonely. I'd very much hate to sit around embroidering cushions while my husband was off seeing the world without me."

"Well, speak no more of it," Liam said firmly. "In three days you and I will be on the adventure of our lives, together. And I can safely promise you I'll never expect you to sit home embroidering cushions."

Cora beamed at him. "I am very glad to hear it."

"But if you want to bake me these lovely spice cakes once in a while, I won't say no to that."

"I almost feel sorry for Finn," Cora said with a sigh, placing a cake on her plate. "I do believe he means well, but even if he did grow to love me someday, he could never understand my desire to go on adventures. Can you imagine him doing anything like that?"

"And risk creasing those immaculate suits?" Liam asked.

"Never. It's plain to see Finley Walsh is not the adventurous type. He'd never do anything wild in the name of love."

Cora nodded in agreement and kissed him sweetly. She tasted like cinnamon and nutmeg and the promise of a better future. Once again, all was right with the world.

16

West of Providence Falls,
Present Day

SOMEONE HAD HIJACKED FINN'S BODY.

It was a full-on mutiny; that was the only explanation. Because the clean-cut man Cora knew—the man with the warm eyes and the friendly smile and the neatly combed hair—wasn't steering *this* ship tonight.

Cora gasped. Her brain short-circuited as she tried to make sense of what she was seeing.

He walked in alone. No entourage. Just a shirtless, chiseled powerhouse of a man, slowly easing his way through the screaming throng of people with smooth, masculine grace.

The crowd flocked toward him, pressing in on all sides until some of the bikers had to intervene and push everyone back.

"Finn," Cora whispered hoarsely.

But everyone kept chanting, "Jack."

She watched in stunned shock as he made his way toward the cage.

Finn was The Jackrabbit? Finley Walsh, the guy who blushed when she gave him compliments, was an underground, cage-fighting legend? It was impossible. Cora felt like Alice down the rabbit hole, as if she'd slipped into some weird, alternate reality. It was unsettling to see him like this. Gone was the custom-tailored suit, the pressed, collared shirt and the designer silk tie. Now all he wore was simple black fight gear: shorts and a pair of open-fingered gloves. This was a boss-level version of the man she knew. A lean, honed, muscular version with six-pack abs and—

Hold on, was that a *tattoo*?

At the cage door Finn twisted his torso and Cora caught sight of his back. A Latin phrase in wicked black font scrolled across his broad shoulders. She couldn't decipher it; the looping words were as foreign as this fevered dream she'd stumbled into.

The reality of what was about to happen suddenly hit her like a freight train. Overcome with panic and fear for Finn's safety, Cora began cataloging all the possible ways she could break him out of there before he got himself killed. The exits were blocked. There were too many people between her and Finn. If Meat started beating him to death, she wouldn't even be able to draw her gun to defend him because there were too many civilians in the way, not to mention the chain-link barrier.

For the first time in all the years she could remember, Cora was furious at Finn.

How could he willingly be so stupid to put himself in this situation? And for what, just to buy her some time to talk to a cranky, sexist jerk like Eli Shelton? Cora wanted to grab Finn and shake him until his teeth rattled, she was so mad. She really ought to be angry with Eli. He was the one who thought it would be entertaining to toss Finn into a cage with the bone crusher. But Cora wasn't going to waste her energy on someone as stupid as Eli Shelton. Finn, on the other hand, should've known better. He should *never* have agreed to this. He may have been some legendary fighting champion from the past, but that didn't mean he could hold his own tonight. Just looking at the freak show Finn was up against made her sick to her stomach.

Meat was pacing inside the cage, seething with pent-up fury. Even from where Cora was standing, she could see his ego was taking a hit because the crowd kept cheering for Finn. Meat was probably used to getting all the glory, and he didn't look like the type of person who embraced the spirit of sharing. It should've been a relief to see an actual expression on the man's face, but it wasn't. Cora much preferred his dead, lifeless eyes to *this*. Right now he was tracking Finn's movements like a great white shark, circling a wounded seal. Pale shoulders rippling, fists clenched, Meat emanated so much hungry, pent-up aggression, she wondered how Finn had the courage to jump into the ring. Didn't he know the sharks were supposed to be on the outside of the cage?

But Finn didn't seem concerned. He lithely pulled himself onto the platform and entered the cage like it was just another day at the office. Like he wasn't chum in the water for the predator now circling him. Finn's face was cold and unreadable, and Cora suddenly realized it was the same mask he used when he was in power-attorney mode. She'd thought he honed it in the courtroom over the years, but now she realized he must've perfected it for this.

It worked, because no one could guess what Finn was thinking. He circled the cage, as calm and cool as the eye of a storm, rolling his shoulders and stretching his neck and arm muscles to warm up. Bouncing on his feet, he breathed deeply and stared Meat down with a look so devoid of feeling, Cora barely recognized him.

Meat began jeering and throwing insults at Finn, though it was impossible to hear over the noise. But Finn remained unfazed. If anything, he seemed bored.

Cora let out a harsh breath. Did he not realize he was about to get slaughtered? Granted, Finn was in spectacular shape. She'd never have guessed that underneath all the pristine suits and stiff, collared shirts, he was hiding the ripped figure of an Olympic swimmer. Suzette had once said Finn reminded her of an undercover superhero. Even then, Cora hadn't given it much thought, but her friend hadn't been wrong. Whatever Finn did in his spare time, it really worked for him.

Still. Meat was a ham-fisted giant puffed up on steroids, and he had at least seventy pounds on Finn. One swipe of his arm, and a regular man would go flying. The only way Finn could survive this fight was if he had a skeletal frame of adamantine and the retractable claws to match.

"Are…we…ready…to…rumble?" the announcer bellowed, drawing out the words with dramatic flair.

The crowd shouted its approval as a referee stepped in to talk to each of the fighters. Finn nodded. Meat spat an insult. Both men moved to their corners. Cora squeezed her eyes shut. A nightmare was about to play out in front of her, and there was nothing she could do.

A bell clanged.

Cora jerked and lost her footing. She stumbled off the stool. The crowd let out a battle cry of bloodthirsty glee. Dread churned in her stomach as she scrambled back on her perch. The fight was on.

Choking with anxiety, Cora watched the two men circling each other in the cage. "If Meat doesn't kill you by the time this is over, Finley Walsh," she vowed under her breath, "I will."

Meat attacked first. He shot toward Finn and launched a massive right haymaker with enough power to end his life.

But the punch never landed.

As soon as Meat attacked, Finn jumped forward, *into* the punch, without even appearing to wind up for it. He leaped toward Meat, clearing at least six feet. In one swift motion he'd moved from Meat's center line to behind his right shoulder, somehow dodging the blow.

Cora's mouth fell open. It was an impressive jump. No wonder they called him The Jackrabbit.

Landing lightly on his feet, Finn was already coiled for a right reverse punch. Grounded with a firm forward stance, his hips, torso and shoulders moved in perfect harmony to accelerate his fist toward Meat's head. It all happened so fast. Meat's arm was still fully extended toward his target that was no longer there. He had just enough time to turn his head to witness the blow that connected with his temple.

Meat collapsed to the floor, motionless.

For the first time since she'd arrived, the barn fell quiet.

In another powerful leap, Finn cleared himself to the other side of the ring. He bounced on his feet, fists clenched at his sides, waiting for whatever came next.

The referee was visibly stunned. He gaped down at the mountain of a man who had, until this night, been the undefeated champion.

Meat's hands twitched, and he tried pushing to his feet in a feeble attempt to stand, but he couldn't do it. The fight was over.

The referee snapped back to his senses and called it.

The crowd exploded, and the man on the microphone announced The Jackrabbit was the victor.

He won. Still perched on the crate, Cora slumped against the wall in relief. Her limbs felt weak and jittery, the way they did after a long session of rock climbing at the gym. She dropped her face into her shaking hands. Victory music blared from the rafters, and she peeked through her fingers at Finn.

He was leaning against the cage, facing the crowd with hands propped high. To Cora's annoyance, he appeared much calmer than she felt.

People swarmed the cage, jumping to the beat of the victory music and screaming like banshees.

For one split second Finn's mask slipped, and the corner of his mouth curved in a crooked smile.

And that was all it took. Cora's anger spiked hot all over again. He had the audacity to smile at *them*. The screaming mass of bloodthirsty animals who would've just as easily cheered for Meat, had Finn been beaten to a bloody pulp. These people didn't care about the real Finn. They didn't even know who he was. All they saw right now were dollar signs and the cage fighter who'd given them an evening's entertainment.

Suddenly, a drunk biker in front of Cora careened into the wall, missing her by inches but taking another man out on his way down. She flung her hands back to steady herself, teetering on the crate. Within seconds the men were throwing punches and shoving into other people.

Like a domino effect, more people were drawn into the fighting, and the energy in the room shifted from drunken revelry to dangerous aggression.

She pressed her back against the wall, knowing she had mere seconds before she lost her footing and went down. What now? She searched the rafters, wishing she could haul herself above the brawling crowd.

"Cora!"

She whipped her head toward the cage.

Finn was staring at her in shocked disbelief.

Cora felt as if time slowed. A tangle of emotions flashed across Finn's handsome face. She could count them in heartbeats.

Ba-boom. Confusion.

Ba-boom. Fear.

Ba-boom. Determination.

Time snapped back, and Cora swallowed hard.

The Jackrabbit was coming straight for her, his flinty gaze locked on hers. The muscles on his arms and chest bunched and flexed as he forcefully shoved his way through the brawling crowd. "Don't move!" he yelled.

But it was too late. Someone slammed into her, the crate underneath her tipped and down she went.

The floor was a forest of stampeding boots and legs and kicking feet. Cora tried to protect her head and push herself up, but she couldn't gain purchase.

Suddenly, she was hauled up and flung over a broad, muscular shoulder. She knew it was Finn because she caught a glimpse of his tattoo. He gripped her legs with one arm, fighting through the crowd with a speed and efficiency that would've surprised her before tonight. He didn't stop when they cleared the barn door, and she felt the cooler night breeze on her heated face.

"Let me go," she demanded. Hanging upside down was not only humiliating, it was disconcerting to be in close contact with his bare skin.

He ignored her, swiftly walking from the barn in long, ground-eating strides and making his way toward a lineup of cars. Low whistles and male laughter followed them.

"Give her a good one for me, Jack," someone cackled. Cora cringed when she caught sight of the leering old man with a face like a dried apple. He was leaning against the barn with a near-empty bottle of whiskey.

"Finn," Cora warned. The heat emanating from his rock-solid back was nothing compared to the anger simmering inside her. "Put me down *right now.*"

He stopped, and she heard a metal jerk and a squeal, then he set her gently on the open tailgate of a truck. Deep brown eyes searched her face. His chest rose and fell, either from the exertion of carrying her out, or a strong emotion he was battling. "Are you hurt?"

"No." Cora angrily slapped dirt off her jeans, reluctant to meet his eyes. Instead, she took in the rusted truck with pale blue chipped paint. "Whose truck is this?"

"Mine. You sure you're not hurt?" He studied her face, shoulders and limbs as if he didn't believe her.

"I'm *fine.*" She bristled, shoving the mass of curls away from her face. She wasn't hurt; she was embarrassed. She'd come there to be his backup, and she'd ended up being the one who needed rescuing.

Finn's gaze skimmed the people milling around outside the barn. "Did you come alone?"

"Yes." Thank God. Liam would've been impossible to live with if he witnessed her in that cage-fighting scene. At least she could be grateful she'd had the foresight to leave him at home.

Finn swore under his breath and spun away, running both hands through his hair in frustration. When he faced her again, his expression was grim. "You shouldn't have come here, Cora. This scene is dangerous."

She gave him a sardonic look. "Says the man who just climbed out of a fight cage."

"It wasn't a big deal," he said in dismissal. "I was doing Eli a favor."

"No, a favor is feeding someone's cat for them while they're on vacation. Or picking up someone's dry cleaning on the way home. Favors don't involve jumping into a cage fight with a guy known as the *bone crusher*." Her voice rose in accusation, but she couldn't help it. She wouldn't let him brush it off like it was nothing. She'd actually been scared for Finn's life in there, and she hated being afraid. He'd made her feel that way. This was all his fault.

"How did you find out about all this?" he asked suddenly.

Cora shifted uncomfortably on the cold metal tailgate. As mad as she was at this stunt he'd pulled tonight, there was no denying the underhanded method she'd used to get here. For years she'd thought of Finn as a stuffy guy who spent his evenings playing chess in a library, sipping cognac and discussing stock market fluctuations. Though he'd been nothing but kind, his impeccable manners and unshakeable composure always made her feel just a little bit unsophisticated. Old habits must die hard, because right now she felt like a kid about to be reprimanded, and it just ticked her off even more.

"You listened in on my conversation with Eli," he said. It wasn't a question. It was one of those statements he made with no tone inflection, like he was analyzing the situation and searching for facts to build a case.

Her simmering anger finally boiled over. Screw this. Why should she care if Finn knew she'd eavesdropped? He was an active participant in tonight's shady operation, and he'd just blown the old stereotype she'd given him to smithereens. She'd never look at him the same again. From now on, when she imagined him sitting in a tufted leather chair in a library sipping cognac, he'd be shirtless and tattooed, with washboard abs and mussed-up hair. It wasn't fair!

"Okay, yes. I did eavesdrop on you guys," she said, lifting her chin. "But obviously, you're no stranger to breaking the rules, so don't stand there with that holier-than-thou look on your face."

He blinked in surprise. "I'm sorry… I'm just trying to piece together how you knew. Look, this was a one-and-done thing for me. Eli knows I'm not in the scene and have no wish to be. He just has a devious streak, and he likes to stir up trouble for fun. If he can somehow profit from it, even better. He knew I'd win, which is why he asked me."

People were now pouring out of the barn, heading into the field for their cars. Some gave them curious looks as they passed, but Cora was too tired to care.

She crossed her arms. "Yeah, about that. How did Eli know you'd win? Pretty sure they don't teach cage fighting in law school. You strolled in there like you were heading to a Sunday picnic, and knocked that guy out in under a minute. Where did you learn to do that?"

Finn's expression shuttered so fast, she would've missed it if she hadn't been staring right at him. How did he go from being the warm, open man she knew to the cool, unreadable stranger in just the blink of an eye? "It doesn't matter. That's all in my past."

"Yet, here you are," she pointed out. "And you could've gotten *killed*."

"Cora." He tilted his face to the sky. "You're being a little melodramatic."

Oh, ho ho. Cora sucked in a breath of outrage and hopped off the tailgate to put some distance between them. "That's just rich coming from—" she made air quotes with her fingers ""—the undefeated, legendary Jackrabbit.'" She started to walk away, then spun back and stomped over until they were face-to-face. "I can't believe you said you wouldn't be in danger tonight. You lied to me. You're just a big, fat liar." Except he wasn't fat. Not even a little. She glanced at his torso then tore her gaze away. He was cut like Swarovski crystal, but that was neither here nor there.

"Cora, I never lied to you," Finn said in frustration. He reached for her, then seemed to think better of it and let his arms drop to his sides. "I wasn't in danger because I know how to fight. I knew I could take him."

She threw her hands up. "Of all the arrogant, asinine— You know, you surprise me, Finn. I didn't take you for one of those bragging men who lets their ego overrule their common sense."

"It ain't braggin' if he can back it up, lady," someone slurred.

She whirled, pointing a finger at the drunk old man leaning against the barn. "You stay out of this. We're having a private conversation here."

"Sounds more like foreplay to me," someone else snickered.

She hadn't noticed the small audience they'd attracted. A few of the people from the barn had stopped to watch. Some of the men looked amused, and a couple of the women were eyeing Finn like he was a hot fudge sundae with all the toppings.

Cora lowered her voice and told Finn, "I came out here in case you needed backup. I was worried you were going to be caught up in something illegal or dangerous, and I was right. Technically, I could arrest you right now."

He dropped his head. "I know, and I'm sorry. None of this should've touched you. I never wanted to put you in this situation, Cora."

"You didn't. *I* put myself here, but I'm walking away now. And even though it doesn't sit right with me, I'm not going to tell anyone what happened tonight. Out of respect for the relationship you had with my father, and the work you do to help others, I'll keep your secret. But I won't forget it." She leaned close enough to feel the heat emanating off his naked skin. It was distracting, which just added to her frustration. "I'm putting an end to this mess Eli's got going on. Not right away, because I have cases to work, and I need answers from him. But I promise you, I *will* make it happen."

"I know you will," he said softly. "You have an unwavering desire to see that justice is served, and I admire that. Not everyone's built that way. It's a rare and beautiful thing."

Cora felt an odd fluttering in her stomach at his compliment, but she shut it down fast. This night had been weird enough, and her emotions had been through the wringer. "Don't try to be nice to me right now, Finley Walsh. I'm still mad at you."

His expression turned wistful. "Just stating facts."

"Here's a fact," she said, backing away. "If I ever catch you doing something like this again, I'll throw you in that holding cell at the station. And no amount of lawyer-speak will get you out of it."

She left him standing by the truck and set off across the field. It was time to climb the hell out of this rabbit hole.

17

PRETENDING TO LOOK BUSY WAS THE WORST.
Liam hated it. He did all the required things other officers appeared to do at the station. He tapped away on his keyboard, rearranged the neglected stack of papers on his desk and reviewed the latest updates on the cases. He chatted with Mavis at the reception desk, and even walked back and forth to the kitchen in false pursuit of what everyone in this world seemed to think was nectar of the gods—coffee. He grimaced. How any of them could stomach the stuff was a mystery bigger than any he'd encountered since arriving in Providence Falls. But as much as he tried to blend in with the normal ebb and flow at the station, today was especially hard.

Something was wrong with Cora. She'd gone out last night to "meet a friend," and he didn't hear her come home until well after midnight. This wasn't her usual routine for a Wednesday. She was so quiet and introspective today that he was convinced something disturbing must've happened.

He stole another glance at her across the pen. She was on her computer, but she kept checking her phone. She seemed restless and preoccupied, continually worrying her bottom lip with her teeth the way she did when working on a difficult problem.

"I made the last of the Hawaiian Kona blend," Otto said cheerfully as he ambled over to his desk. He eased into his chair, setting two pastries and his mug on a paper towel. "Better hurry, Cora, before they finish it off. There's only the instant kind left after this."

"Hmm?"

Otto held up his mug. "The good stuff."

"Oh, thanks," she said absently. "I've got some."

Liam narrowed his eyes. No, she didn't. She hadn't had a single cup all morning. This was surefire proof that something was askew with her. Enough of this.

He lurched from his chair and walked over as casually as he could. Knowing Cora, it wouldn't do to attack her with questions straightaway. She had a stubborn streak that always rose to a challenge. Better to ease into it. He propped his hip on the edge of her desk.

Cora didn't even bother looking up. "Can I help you with something?"

"What the devil is going on with you?" he demanded. Okay, he'd just made a grand mess of that. It was hard to act casual when he was worried about her.

She gave him a curious frown.

"What I meant to say was, let's go to lunch. I'm starving." It was a bad save, but it appeared luck was on his side.

Cora's lips curled in amusement. "You're always starving."

"It's half past noon. I'm nigh faint from hunger. Also, you look like you could use some fresh air."

"Actually, I do need to get out," Cora said, pushing back from her desk and stretching her arms. "And I skipped breakfast, so I'll go if I get to choose the spot."

"Deal."

She chose the restaurant, but he drove, so they arrived in record time. He was getting better at driving assertively without inspiring others to honk and shout curses at him. Even though his own car was the equivalent of a swaybacked mare put out to pasture, he still managed to practice some of the things he'd learned in the class. Still, he deeply regretted bringing Magnus Blackwell into Cora's life. If her mood today had anything to do with that ass, he was going to make the man pay.

Cora chose The Rusty Spoon, a hipster breakfast and lunch bistro in the university district. It was situated near a small man-made lake with a paved walking trail, and it was a popular spot among the college crowd and local business people. From the moment Liam stepped inside the quirky restaurant, he was intrigued. There were rustic tables paired with plush, cushioned chairs, and odd chandeliers hanging at intervals along the ceiling. One was made up entirely of spoons; another was a birdcage wrapped with winding iron vines and flowers. There was even a wall of clocks in all shapes and sizes, with plaques marking the time in various countries across the world. Overall, Liam felt as though he'd stepped into an enchanted tavern, complete with the mouthwatering scents of grilled steak, seasoned poultry and sweet, crisp apple cobbler.

He salivated as one of the servers rushed by with a platter of fried chicken and frosty drinks. "You may need to find a new roommate because I think I want to live here."

Cora grinned as the hostess led them through the dining room and onto the back terrace. "Wait until you try the food. It's incredible."

A short while later they were enjoying lunch on the patio under a rainbow umbrella overlooking the lake. Lulled by the warm sunshine, lively atmosphere and delicious food, Cora finally seemed to relax.

Liam took a bite of his honey barbecue burger with onion straws, savoring the smoky, tangy flavors with nothing short of bliss. Jesus, this was amazing. He'd spent so much of his time in his past life trying to stave off hunger, it seemed he could never fill the void now. There were precious little upsides to this god-forsaken task the angels had given him, but the food was definitely one of them.

"Slow down," Cora said, laughing. "You're going to choke."

"I can't help it," he said between bites. "This is the most delicious thing I've ever had."

"You say that about every dish you eat."

"Perhaps, but this one is truly divine." He took a drink of his iced tea and stretched back in his chair, crossing his hands behind his head. "Tell me what's going on."

She blew out a breath. "There's nothing new, yet. We've got that appointment tomorrow night to talk to Eli Shelton about the robbery, but—"

"I don't mean the case. I mean you. Ever since last night you've been acting distant and preoccupied. Did something happen with Magnus?" Because if it did, he'd happily wring the bugger's neck.

"No," she said, looking out at the lake. "It's nothing."

"Cora, I know you well enough by now to see that something's been bothering you. Did Magnus do something to—"

"Of course not," she said with feeling. "Magnus has been great. We've had a lot of fun, and we're getting along fine. I've got no problems with him." She gave Liam a pointed look. "And neither should you."

"He's nothing but a wolf in sheep's clothing," Liam said in disgust.

Cora rolled her eyes. "Not too long ago, you were singing his praises. I don't know why you're so against him, Liam. You used to like him, and you even took his driving class. The two of you are like carbon copies of each other."

"I'm nothing like him," Liam said indignantly. She may have a point, but he'd be damned if he'd own up to it.

"I'm serious. Magnus reminds me a lot of you. He's funny and charming and maybe…a little racy." She ended on a breathless note. Was she blushing? He'd kill the man. *Racy* could mean a great many things, he knew from experience, and he didn't want to imagine Cora and Magnus doing any of them.

Liam suddenly wanted to smash something. He let go of his iced tea glass before it shattered, fighting to appear unfazed. Even though he knew Cora was destined for Finn, he'd never felt threatened by him. Maybe because in the back of his mind, Liam still refused to accept that he could lose Cora to someone so boring. But Magnus was a different story. If she went down this road with Magnus, they were all screwed, and hell might as well swallow him up right now. The angels had told him, time and again, that Cora's life always ended in tragedy. And until she embraced her destiny with Finn, she could never find true happiness. While Liam had big problems with this, one thing rose in importance above all others—Cora's well-being. As Magnus was all wrong for her, that could only mean one thing. Magnus was going to lead to Cora's tragic demise.

Not on my watch. Liam gripped the edge of the bistro table with grim determination. He was going to find a way to get Magnus out of her life for good, even if it killed him.

"And if you can get past this big brother act you keep insisting on," Cora continued, oblivious to his turbulent emotions, "I think the two of you could be good friends. It would be a lot easier on me if you'd at least try. I plan to see him again, you know. And there's nothing you can do about it." She lifted her chin, daring him to say something.

We'll see about that. Liam took an angry bite of his burger. They needed to stop discussing Magnus before he said something he'd regret. "What happened last night? You've been in a strange mood since you got home."

She shook her head and stabbed at the salad on her plate. "I don't want to talk about it."

He wanted to press her for details, but he was getting good at reading her moods. She wasn't going to change her mind. He'd have to let it go and try later. "Is there anything I can do to help fix it, at least? Any bodies you need help burying?"

"Not right now, but I'll let you know."

A shadow fell across their table. "Hello."

Margaret Brady, the widow of the recently deceased John Brady, stood over them. Liam was surprised to see her, because the last time they were together she'd made it very clear she wanted nothing to do with him. He couldn't even blame her. She believed they were lovers and he'd recently jilted her. On the night her husband was mysteriously murdered, Liam had taken her on a date to a shoddy restaurant, then made sure she drank enough to pass out. He hadn't known exactly how her husband was going to die, but the angels had told him there would be a tragedy at her house. After making sure Cora was safe, he'd rushed over to the house to get Margaret out of there, too. He used every trick in the book to lure her away for the night, because even though he didn't love her, he still wanted to protect her from harm. She'd thought he was trying to win her back, and she'd been very upset to realize later that he'd never intended to renew their relationship. Worse, still, was the morning after their "date" when they discovered her husband had been murdered in her home. Margaret had been devastated, and angry at both herself and Liam.

She looked much better now than the last time Liam had seen her. Tall and lovely, with dark hair pulled into a sleek twist, she was wearing a beige shift dress that was both casual and elegant. Now she looked more like herself, but her wide gray eyes were weary and sad.

"Margaret." He stood abruptly, searching her face. "How are you?" She hadn't returned his calls when he'd tried to check up on her.

"I've been better." She didn't appear to be angry at him any longer, which was a godsend. It seemed her heartbreak over her husband's death trumped any of the issues she'd had with Liam.

"Please, sit with us." Cora pulled out a bistro chair at their table.

"No, I can't stay." Margaret gestured to a blond man who was browsing a menu several tables away. "I'm here with a colleague, but I saw you both, and I wanted to ask if you've learned anything new about my husband's case."

"Nothing yet," Cora said. "But we're working very hard, and we'll make sure to keep you in the loop."

For a moment Margaret's face fell, but she quickly regained her composure. "I heard about Lindsey Albright. I read about it in the paper, and it's been a topic among the faculty."

Liam and Cora exchanged a look. Margaret taught botany at the university. There was a chance Lindsey's death was connected to the murder of Margaret's husband, but they didn't want to burden the grieving widow with that information until they were sure. She'd been through enough already.

"Did you know Lindsey?" Cora asked. "We reviewed her class schedule, but your name wasn't on the instructor list."

"I didn't know her personally. She wasn't in any of my classes. But I saw her at my gym sometimes when I went to Pilates," Margaret said. "I know that's not very helpful."

"What gym do you go to?" Cora asked.

"Kick Start Fitness." Margaret found a sudden interest in her wedding ring, which Liam noticed she was still wearing. He imagined it would be a long time before she decided to take it off. "I just keep thinking about that poor girl's parents. To lose someone you love in such a senseless way, and to not have answers. I know what it feels like." Her eyes welled with tears and she shook her head, clearing her throat. "Anyway, please let me know if you hear anything else."

"Come on," Cora said after Margaret left. "Let's get out of here and go investigate the gym."

On the way out, Liam caught sight of Margaret with her lunch date, wondering if they were more than just colleagues. For all he knew, Margaret had many lovers. The rules of society were different here than they were almost two hundred years ago. When he'd interrogated Margaret last month, he'd become irrationally jealous every time she talked about how much she adored her perfect husband. But now he only felt sadness for her. What if Margaret could never be happy in any century? Were they all just pawns on a chessboard, destined to make the same mistakes over and over again?

The angels seemed to think Liam could do the right thing and change the course of Cora's destiny. But since the moment he saw Cora, he'd wanted to keep her for himself. Just like he had in his past life. Was his failure here inevitable, or could he actually change? The disturbing thought had him brooding all the way to the gym.

18

"WELCOME TO KICK START FITNESS," A RECEP-
tionist with a high ponytail and a bright smile said to Liam and
Cora. She was standing behind the front desk, wearing a purple
polo shirt with the gym logo, and she was busy folding a stack
of towels. "You can just swipe your cards and go on in."

"We don't have cards," Liam said, taking in the sleek, indus-
trial decor. The gym was airy and upscale with chrome trim
on the floor-to-ceiling windows. In the background he could
hear the whirring and clanking sounds of exercise equipment
mixed with ambient, upbeat music. "We're here because of one
of your members. We want to ask some questions."

"Hey, that's awesome, man. Perfect, perfect." A young man
came strutting up to him and Cora, grinning and nodding as if
they were already in a conversation. He had closely cut blond
hair, a deep suntan and he wore a purple gym polo with Brad,
Lead Personal Trainer embroidered on the breast pocket. Giving
them each a sturdy handshake, he tilted his head toward a small
room off the entry. "Let's step into the office. Our manager's on
his lunch break, but I'll be happy to answer all your questions."

They followed him into a pale green room with dim lighting

and motivational gym posters. Brad took a seat and pulled out several colored pamphlets. "If you guys want to do the couples membership, you came at the right time. Half off the first three months, plus four free protein shakes at the Beverage Bar."

"I'm afraid you've got the wrong idea." Cora pulled out her badge. "My partner and I are with the Providence Falls Police Department. We're looking for some information on Lindsey Albright, and we understand she was a member here at your gym."

Brad's blond eyebrows shot toward his hairline. "Wow, that's not what I expected you to say. What'd she do?"

"She died," Liam said bluntly.

Brad's mouth formed a shocked O, and he stared at them for several seconds before recovering. "Oh, man, that sucks so bad. How'd she die? No, never mind. My girlfriend's big into crime shows, and we've seen a lot of them, so I know you can't give me details. But still. This is pretty much the worst thing I've heard all month. No, like all year. Let me just switch gears." He pushed the pamphlets to the side of the desk. "What's her name again?"

Liam repeated it, and Brad typed it into his computer.

"Were you acquainted with her?" Liam asked.

"No, but we've got over five hundred members here. Let me just see..." Brad scrolled through the screen and made a few clicks. "Okay, here we go. Lindsey Albright. Yeah, I recognize her photo. She joined back in March. Last time she checked in was June thirtieth." He sat back, shaking his head. "Man, I can't believe she died. Like, she was *just here*."

"Yes, it's difficult to accept," Cora said. "Anything else?"

He scanned her membership profile. "Just that she has two protein shakes left on her punch card. If you want to talk to the rest of the staff— Oh, hold up. She was a Booty Buster."

Liam peeked at the screen but saw only a grid of names. "What's that?"

"It's our summer fitness challenge. Says here she swam the

most laps in her category last month. Way to hustle, girl," Brad said in admiration. Then he seemed to remember why they were there. "You could try checking her locker."

Cora sat forward. "Lindsey had a locker here?"

"Yeah. They're normally just day lockers, but the Booty Busters get to have one for the duration of the challenge. It's one of the perks if they sign up." He checked the screen and wrote Lindsey's locker number on a sticky note, then handed it to Liam. "Number 433 downstairs on the women's side. I'll get someone to block the doors while you check it out. Let me know if you need anything else."

"Thanks," Liam said, already heading for the door.

"Hey, you sure you don't want to join?" Brad leaned back in his chair and linked his hands behind his head. "Looks like you work out, man. What do you bench, two, two twenty-five? I can hook you up with some training sessions at a discount if you sign up today."

Liam looked at Brad like he was cracked in the head. "You want me to give you money. So you can force me to exercise?"

"No pain, no gain, shut up and train," Brad said, grinning.

Liam opened his mouth to tell Brad exactly what he could do with his training, but Cora laid a hand on his arm and said, "I'm sure my partner would love to stay and hear all about your membership options, but perhaps another time when we don't have a murder to investigate."

"Right, yeah. No worries." Brad thumped his fist on the table. "I'll just give you my card when you guys are done."

"Don't feel like joining the gym?" Cora teased Liam as they crossed the gym floor. A few men were on various exercise machines that looked and even sounded like torture devices from the way the men heaved and grunted. One was squatting in front of a mirror with a bar and metal plates attached to the ends. He looked uncomfortable, and his face was bright red. Another man was lying on a bench, pushing a bar attached to heavy weights while a man stood over him, shouting encouragement. In all the things Liam had seen so far since arriving in this life, this was one of the most perplexing.

"I don't understand why they'd do this," he said as they passed two people whipping giant ropes between them. "It's as if they plan to go into battle, or they're preparing for an event, which would require them to build a home or fight for their lives. But from what I've seen, most people here live quite comfortably and have an abundance of everything at their fingertips."

"Exactly," Cora said with a laugh. "Our jobs don't require us to hunt and gather like the cavemen. Now most of us sit behind desks and have food prepared at the push of a button. Hence, the obsession with exercise. It balances out the laziness."

"I suppose, but this indoor nonsense is bollocks," he said as they took a hallway with a sign labeled pool. "I'd rather eat dried squirrel meat than stay in a tomb like this, surrounded by other people who look just as miserable as I'd feel. If I'm ever restless and have an excess of energy, you won't find me here. I'll be outside with the wind in my hair and the sun on my face. This is unnatural."

"Okay, a couple of things," Cora said in amusement. "One, have you actually eaten dried squirrel meat? No, wait. I don't want to know. Two, you act like you've never seen people working out in a gym before."

"Of course I haven't."

She gave him an incredulous look. "One of these days, Liam, that inhuman metabolism of yours is going to catch up with you, and you may just find yourself joining the rest of us poor mortals."

"In this purgatory on earth? Never."

Cora laughed. "Let's see where you are in ten years, and you can tell me that again."

It wouldn't be purgatory, that was for sure. Within the next few weeks he'd be headed someplace much more permanent. If he wasn't careful, it could be a lot worse than this.

They found the women's locker room at the end of a long hall. It smelled like bleached towels, damp concrete and chlorine. Lindsey's locker was in the right corner on the last aisle. It was locked, so it took another fifteen minutes for someone to come down with the master key.

Finally, Cora donned a pair of rubber gloves from her pocket and pulled the door open.

A mesh shower bag containing toiletries hung from one of the hooks. At the bottom of the locker was a striped beach towel and a swimsuit.

She pulled the towel out, and something tumbled onto the floor. *Stacks* of somethings. Fat bundles of cash were tossed into the bottom of the locker, each stack wrapped in narrow paper sleeves with a clawed paw print stamped on top.

"Oh, Lindsey," Cora breathed. "What have you done?"

"The stamp," Liam said, crouching down to look more closely at the money. He knew not to touch anything for fingerprints. "Booze Dogs. This could be the stolen money Slice was talking about."

"There's got to be thousands of dollars in here," Cora said, pulling her phone from her pocket to dial the station.

Liam stared down at the small fortune in cash. "Seems our young Ms. Albright was up to more than just partying at The Doghouse."

19

ON FRIDAY EVENING CORA DUG AROUND IN HER freezer for some prime quality jet fuel. She'd been saving the vacuum-sealed bag of Jamaican Blue Mountain coffee for a rainy day when she needed a good pick-me-up, and today was turning out to be that day. As far as she was concerned, it was time to bring out the big guns.

She prepared it, inhaling the deep, earthy scent of freshly ground beans, then waited for the pot to brew. It was a little after eight o'clock, and soon she and Liam would be heading to The Rolling Log to meet with Eli Shelton. The thought of talking to that man again was another reason she needed this liquid pick-me-up. He was a chauvinistic creep, whom she'd disliked within minutes of meeting him. And now that she knew about the "favor" he'd asked of Finn, she liked him even less.

Finn. She still couldn't believe he'd told her not to worry about him, and that he wouldn't be in any danger. Cora gritted her teeth and pulled a leopard-print mug from the cupboard. So many of the men in her life, including Liam, seemed to think she needed to be protected and coddled. It grated on her nerves, but she'd never thought Finn was one of them. He'd always seemed so open and honest and easygoing.

"Let's have a barbecue this weekend," Liam said, striding into the kitchen with Angel at his heels. He pulled open the fridge door and took out a covered dish of tuna, setting it on the floor for the ecstatic cat. Watching him spoil Angel was almost enough to make her smile. She wondered if he realized how often he did it.

"I want to make a honey barbecue burger with the crispy bits, like I had at The Rusty Spoon. I dreamed about it last night. We can invite Suzette." He paused, then went to the sink to wash his hands. "And I suppose we should invite Finn. We can make s'mores and—"

"No." Cora crossed her arms and watched the coffee brew, willing it to hurry up. She wasn't ready to see Finn at all, let alone have him over for a visit.

"Fine, no s'mores," Liam said. "How about—"

"No *Finn*." She pulled cream from the fridge and mumbled, "I'm not in the mood for liars."

"Fine, no lawyers," Liam said under his breath.

She didn't bother correcting him.

"Look, I know Finn seems as exciting as a long drink of pond water, but he can't be all bad. You never know. He could surprise you."

Cora scoffed. Been there, done that. But right now Liam was the one surprising her. "I thought you didn't care for Finn."

"I...like him just fine." If he thought to convince her, he was doing a poor job of it.

She opened her mouth to argue, but the doorbell rang. Liam went to answer it as she prepared her cup of Jamaican Blue Mountain. Cream, two sugars, one glorious sip, and life was good again.

"Bad news." Liam poked his head into the kitchen with his

handsome face in a deep scowl. "There's a shmucktacular dill-hole at the door for you. Should I tell him to go away?"

Cora's eyes flew wide. Crap! She'd forgotten about her date with Magnus. "No, I'll talk to him." Last Saturday after the Renaissance Fair, she'd agreed to have dinner with him. But after the crazy week she'd had, it had slipped her mind. As much as she wanted to go to dinner with Magnus, he'd have to take a raincheck. This could be the only time she'd ever get Eli Shelton to talk to her, and Finn had already paid the price for it.

Sighing, she went to give Magnus the bad news.

Liam and Magnus were facing each other in the doorway. Liam had his arms crossed and was guarding the door like a suspicious bouncer at a nightclub. Magnus appeared nonplussed. His face lit up when he saw Cora.

"Hi, Magnus," she said with an apologetic smile. She hip-bumped Liam, shoving him out of the doorway. "Please come in."

Magnus entered the small living room, sending Angel streaking under the couch to hide. Liam followed Magnus, and seeing them both standing together, it struck Cora that they could've almost been brothers. Magnus wasn't as broad in the shoulders as Liam, but they were close in height. With their dark good looks, cocky confidence and easy charm, the similarities were uncanny.

"I have some bad news." Cora lowered herself onto the couch, and Magnus sat beside her. "Something big came up at work, and I can't go to dinner tonight. I'm so sorry to do this to you at the last minute."

Magnus looked disappointed. "I'm sorry to hear that. What's going on?"

Liam dropped into the armchair. "We aren't at liberty to discuss important police business with you."

"We discovered evidence yesterday," Cora explained, ignoring Liam's testy attitude. "And I need to go speak with some-one about it."

"Anyone I'd know?" Magnus asked.

Liam scoffed. "Not likely, unless you're friends with the president of the Booze Dogs."

"Liam—" Cora began. For someone who didn't want to discuss police business, he was doing a poor job of it.

"No kidding?" Magnus said, impressed. "I've heard they're a rough and tumble lot."

"They are, which is why I'll be escorting Cora to The Rolling Log tonight," Liam said with arrogant satisfaction.

"Glad to hear it," Magnus said. "I know the place, and it's not for the faint of heart. In fact, Cora, I'd be happy to drive you, if you still want to go to dinner afterward. I can have a drink while you conduct your interview."

Cora's first thought was to decline his invitation, but why shouldn't she agree? Dealing with Eli was going to be the rotten cherry on top of the crazy week she'd had. It would be nice to end it doing something relaxing and fun with Magnus, a person whose superpower seemed to be showing her a good time with no stress.

Liam, who'd been looking rather smug up until now, snapped to attention. "She's not going anywhere with you. This is official police business, and anyway, Cora's not in the mood for lawyers."

"Liam, I don't need you to speak for me," she said in annoy-ance. His cocksure attitude just cemented her decision. "In fact, Magnus, that would be fine. Dinner afterward would be great, too. As long as you don't mind waiting for me in the bar while I talk to Eli."

"Cora, I'm going with you," Liam insisted. "We already talked about this, and I won't be left behind to worry about you. I'm part of this investigation, too."

"Eli will only talk to me," Cora pointed out. "There's really no need for you to come."

"Better me than him," Liam said, tilting his head in Magnus's direction.

"Hey, I don't want to cause problems," Magnus said easily. "Liam should come, too. Safety in numbers, right? Afterward, we can drop him home and then head to dinner."

Cora's phone alarm sounded, signaling it was time to leave. She wasn't in the mood to argue with Liam, so she made her decision quickly. "All right, let's get out of here. I'm sorry again about our plans tonight. Believe me, I'd rather talk to a fire-breathing dragon than Eli Shelton. The Rolling Log is the last place I want to go on a Friday night."

"It'll be fun," Magnus said with a roguish smile. "Sometimes the best memories are made when plans go awry."

Liam folded his arms and stared, unseeing, out the window of Magnus's Mercedes. He felt like the petulant child who'd been relegated to the backseat. This had been a poor turn of events, to be sure. If he'd known Magnus was going to show up to shoehorn his way into their evening, he'd have insisted they leave sooner.

The Rolling Log was in a run-down area on the north side of the city. It was just minutes from the freeway exit, which probably worked out well for the Booze Dogs. The place was close enough to be easily accessible, or close enough to make a quick getaway, depending on the situation. Most of the businesses on the same street looked as old as dirt, with chipped, faded signs and barred windows. They were all closed down for the night, save for one coin-operated laundromat with a few tired patrons visible through the windows.

"Here we are," Magnus said, turning into a grungy parking lot filled with motorcycles. He whistled low under his breath at the sight of the bar.

Liam didn't think it was anything to whistle about. A one-story redbrick building was planted on the asphalt as if it fell there. No architectural details, no front stairs or even a porch. There was only a sun-bleached red awning over the front door. Neon beer ads hung in the small front windows, and a metal pole beside the building held a swinging sign that read The Rolling Log. Several of the letters were burned out, and one was hanging by a wire.

"Look at this place," Magnus said. "I have a Harley and I enjoy it, but I've never felt the need to join a club or hang out in places like this." He pulled into a parking spot in the corner and turned to Cora. "Are you ready to slum it?"

He and Cora shared a smile, and Liam wanted to punch through the window. Instead, he clamped his mouth shut and got out of the car the moment Magnus parked.

When Cora stepped out, Liam leaned close and said, "Magnus should wait in the car. We'll win no points with these men if that swindling peacock follows us in."

"He's coming," Cora said. "It's a public bar, and it's a free country. Now, check your attitude because you look like you're ready to throw down, and if you don't knock that broody scowl off your face, I'll make *you* wait in the car."

She tossed her hair and walked straight in, not bothering to see if he followed. Swindling peacocks aside, Liam couldn't help admiring her. Cora McLeod could be a firebrand, and seeing her like this never failed to stir his blood.

The moment Liam stepped inside, he felt like he'd been dipped in a vat of aggression and desperation. The scent of hardcore partying seemed ingrained in the wood-paneled walls, soaked into the floorboards and diffused into the air. Alcohol-splashed tables, body odor and sweaty leather. Engine grease, heavy perfume, bile and cigarettes. All of it made an impression, and not a good one.

He stood beside Cora as Magnus stayed behind them. Like a hive mind, the bikers in the bar all noticed them at once. Conversations stopped, pool games paused and laughter ceased. The only thing still going was a song about a last dance with some girl named Mary Jane.

The bartender, a lanky man in a black leather vest called across the bar, "You folks lost?"

"I'm looking for Eli Shelton," Cora said, approaching the bar.

"And what would you be wanting with my husband?" A woman in the corner rose from her chair. She was shorter than Cora and older by about two decades. There was a tautness to her mouth and around her eyes, with faint lines and tired skin, but she had the appearance of a woman who'd once been beautiful before life stepped in and gave her a good thrashing. In jeans, motorcycle boots and a denim jacket, she looked like all the rest of the bikers—weathered, worn and gritty.

"He told me to meet him here at nine," Cora said.

"Is that so?" The woman bristled and started coming toward Cora. If she'd have been a cat, she'd have laid her ears back. "You think you can just waltz your skanky ass in here like—"

"Mabel," a gravelly voice said from a narrow hall. "Let her be. She's telling the truth."

Mabel eased off the pedal, but she was still idling, ready to charge.

An old, barrel-stout man with a white beard approached Cora. He was wearing dirty jeans and a weathered leather jacket. "Didn't think you were going to come, little filly."

Liam felt her stiffen beside him. "It's Cora McLeod. *Officer* McLeod," she said.

The atmosphere in the room shifted. Mabel wasn't the only one laying her ears back now.

"McLeod," Eli said, amused at Cora's correction. "I don't recall saying you could bring the pigs."

"This is Liam O'Connor, my partner," she said stiffly. "And Magnus is a just a friend. They'll wait at the bar while we talk."

Eli squinted at Liam and Magnus with obvious suspicion. To

Cora, he said, "I'll give you ten minutes, but your phone stays with them. Nothing gets recorded, you got me?"

Cora nodded and handed her phone to Liam. He slid it into his back pocket.

"I'll be quick," she whispered.

Eli jerked his head to a door in the back. "Let's go. And talk fast, McLeod. I don't got all night to do charity work."

"Wait." Liam grabbed her sleeve. "I don't like you going into that back room with him alone. Tell him to talk to you somewhere I can see you."

"Just try not to get into trouble out here, and I'll be back in a few minutes." She tugged her wrist free and walked away.

20

"YOUR MAN DID A MIGHTY FINE FAVOR FOR ME this week," Eli said as he shut the door behind Cora. They were standing in what appeared to be a makeshift office, but the room was small enough to be a broom or supply closet. She eyed Eli as he gave her a lascivious once-over, and barely refrained from rolling her eyes. For some reason, Eli hadn't gotten the memo that he was a foul, misogynistic creep who was old enough to be her father. Or maybe even her grandfather. What was it about some men that made them believe they were a prize stallion, even when they'd been put out to pasture long ago and looked destined for the glue factory? She would never understand it, but that kind of confidence—as ill placed as it was—never ceased to amaze her.

He eased his girth past Cora and walked over to the desk, leaning against it. Cora didn't mind the close quarters because she was confident in her ability to overpower the shmuck, if it came down to it, but he reeked of cigarettes and body odor, which was one thing her self-defense skills couldn't fight against.

"Finn is not my man. He's just a friend," Cora said, crossing her arms. "And I'm glad to hear you were happy with whatever favor he provided." She wasn't about to let Eli know she was aware of his underground fighting operation.

Eli smirked. "Honey, if you had any idea what that man did, you'd realize he's more than just a friend."

"I have some information that may be useful to you," Cora said, changing the subject. The sooner they talked, the sooner she could get out of there and breathe fresh air again. "But first, I want to know when your money was stolen. How? Where? Anything you can tell me."

Eli's gaze slithered down her body. "What do I get in return for telling you club business?"

"You already got it from Finn," Cora snapped. "That's all you're getting. That was the deal."

"No, no, no," Eli said with a chuckle, inching closer. Cora had to fight to stand her ground. She knew backing away would be useless, since there was only about a foot of space between her and the door. "That's not how this works. It's a big, bad world, filly. Nobody gets something for nothing."

Cripes, was this man kidding right now? Did he honestly think she'd be game?

He licked his lips, his bowlful-of-jelly belly getting closer by the second.

Nope. He wasn't kidding. Street Thug Santa was creeping on her. Cora's stomach lurched with revulsion. "You have a *wife* right outside that door."

He made a dismissive sound, like it didn't matter. "Mabel knows me."

"How very unfortunate for her," Cora said through gritted teeth. She planted her feet and lifted both hands in an easy, open stance, ready for whatever he tried to pull. Then she gave him her cold, police-officer stare, the one she reserved for the more obtuse criminals who never failed to underestimate her. "Let me make myself very clear. If you try to lay even one fingertip on me right now, I will snap your wrist, break your nose and kick your carcass to the floor in under five seconds. I know it's hard for you to grasp the fact that a woman like me could move a mountain like you, but I promise you, I can. It comes with the job territory. So what's it going to be, Mr. Shelton? Do you want to cooperate, or do you want to spend the night at the hospital?"

Eli blinked, then let out a bark of laughter. "Hot damn, you are a feisty piece. No wonder Finn's so taken with you."

Cora pressed her mouth into a hard line. Enough of this idiocy. "I found your stolen money."

His lecherous gaze turned cold and calculating. Now she had his attention. "The hell you talking about, girl?"

"I recovered what I believe to be stolen Booze Dog money," Cora said. "But I'm going to need you to answer my questions first before I elaborate. When did you realize it was stolen?"

Eli cursed a blue streak, but he settled back on the edge of the narrow desk in defeat. "Last Wednesday night. We keep the petty cash—that's what we call it—in three lockboxes in my office. One for June, July and August. Every summer we have some lucrative…business ventures. Each box holds our earnings for each month."

Oh, she knew exactly what business venture he was talking about. The cage fights were the draw, and Eli's illegal gambling operation meant vast amounts of cash exchanged hands. As long as he kept the fights going, the money would continue flowing straight into his pockets.

"How was the money stolen?" Cora asked. "The Doghouse doesn't exactly have a soft perimeter. I can't imagine someone just waltzed up to the front gates and convinced Bear to let them mosey on in."

"That's the thing," Eli said, scratching his head. His leather jacket parted, and a strong whiff of unwashed male hit Cora like a two-by-four to the face. She struggled not to breathe through her nose. "The gates are always watched, and there's always someone at the house. My office is locked, too. Whoever took the money must've done it when we were all out at—" He paused and checked himself. "Sometimes we attend gatherings away from the compound. On Tuesdays or Wednesdays during the summer, a lot of us are busy, and the compound has very few people who stay behind."

"So you think that's when your money was stolen?" Cora asked.

Eli grimaced. "The hell of it is, we can guess how it was done, but we can't pinpoint *when*. Last week I went to my office to deposit the money into the July lockbox like I always do. While I was doing that, I bumped the June box, and it felt lighter than it should. That was a red flag. When those lockboxes are filled with money, they're heavy. So I picked it up and saw the lock had been cut. The box was empty. All the money from June was missing."

"What about cameras?"

Eli grimaced. "We've got two, and they were both spray-painted over. Completely useless. None of it makes sense. Break-ins have never been an issue before at The Doghouse. We're a brotherhood, and we have our squabbles and infighting, but we don't bite the hand that feeds us. Whoever did this planned it out and knew when and where to strike."

"Twenty-five thousand dollars. That's a lot of petty cash," Cora said.

Eli gave an angry sneer. "Try two hundred thousand."

Cora's mouth fell open in shock. "You keep *two hundred thousand dollars* in petty cash lying around your office?" She knew the club was making money, but she'd had no idea they were raking in that much.

"Never been a problem until now," Eli muttered. "And we don't usually keep that much for long. I was planning to deposit the earnings from June's lockbox the day I realized it was stolen. What I don't get is how come they only stole the June money?"

"What do you mean?" Cora asked.

"The July lockbox was on the shelf right next to it. I'd already deposited some cash in it. The thief didn't even mess with July. They went straight for June, took all the money and took off. Left everything else. Like I said, it makes no sense. If I went through all the trouble of spray painting security cameras and breaking into an empty office full of cash, you can bet your ass I'd be taking all of it."

"I think I might know the answer to that," Cora said. If Lindsey was involved in the robbery somehow, if she actually took the money, she'd have only taken what was there before July third when she died. "But first, tell me something. The money we discovered yesterday at the gym was wrapped in paper sleeves. Can you tell me what kind of stamp—"

"Paw print with claws. Red ink."

"That's the one," Cora said with a sigh.

"That money's mine, and I want it back," he seethed. "Where'd you find it?"

"Kick Start Fitness. In Lindsey Albright's gym locker."

Eli's face grew red and mottled with anger. "That tiny piece of fluff stole my money?"

"That's the theory. She could've taken it shortly before she was killed. That would be why only the June money was taken. We only found twenty-five thousand. That leaves a lot unaccounted for."

"Where's the rest?" he demanded, pushing off the desk to stand. His body was taut with suppressed anger. "There was two hundred grand in that box."

Cora kept her feet braced wide, just in case he tried to get physical. "We don't know yet, but there's got to be a connection between the money and her murder. Someone must've found out she stole it and killed her for it."

"It wasn't the kid Slice," Eli said irritably. He was glaring hard at the wall, as if it was a puzzle he couldn't piece together.

"I know where he was that night. You already got proof he's in the clear."

Cora knew where they all were that night—at the barn watching Meat beat someone to a pulp—but she had to pretend she had no clue. For now, anyway. Later, she'd take down his whole operation, but the murder had to take priority. "Where were you the night of July third?"

Eli's bushy eyebrows snapped together, and he turned his glare on her. "You think I'd kill that girl for stealing my money? I didn't even know it was missing until last weekend. Ask anyone at The Doghouse. I raised holy hell. Ain't done raising it, either."

"You didn't answer my question."

"I was with some of my buddies," he said in dismissal. "They'll vouch for me."

Yeah, she knew they would. They'd all lie for each other, and that was the problem. "I want a list of the members' names on Monday," she said calmly. "We'll be checking everyone's alibis. I know you want to get your money back, and I can help. Since both crimes appear to be related, you're in luck." She gave him a saccharine-sweet smile. "You and I get to share information from here on out."

Eli turned his head to the side and spat. At least she could be grateful he'd turned his head first. "I don't take kindly to partnering up with cops."

"Yeah, well, I don't take kindly to partnering up with creeps. But sometimes we don't get a choice. Life's tough like that." She was so done with this guy.

"I want my money back," Eli growled.

Cora shrugged and reached for the doorknob. "It's evidence. Can't do anything about it right now. But you know what they say about patience being a virtue."

The scowl he gave her was borderline murderous. "I'm not too big on virtues, McLeod."

"Tell me something I don't already know. Send me a list of those names by Monday morning, first thing." She yanked open the door and got the hell out of there.

21

LIAM WAS SLUMPED ON A BAR STOOL WITH A smeary glass of untouched beer in front of him. The bartender had insisted if he took up space, he'd have to pay for it. But he was too focused on Magnus to drink anything. The idiot was trying to hustle some of the bikers at pool.

Jesus, did the man just fall off a turnip wagon? He had to know it wasn't worth the risk. Liam's opinion of Magnus had been steadily falling over the past few weeks, and now this was a record low. Magnus was swaggering around the pool table, smiling and talking to the bikers as if they were friends. What he didn't catch were the dirty looks the men exchanged whenever his back was turned. The snide comments. The crafty glances at the pool table. But Liam saw it all, and he feared Magnus was in over his head.

Cora's phone buzzed on the bar in front of him. He'd pulled it from his back pocket when he sat down and was using it to track the time. The name "Finn" flashed on the screen, and Liam felt the usual stab of jealousy, followed by frustration. He hadn't realized Finn and Cora were on such familiar terms, but he should be glad of it. Getting them together was the ultimate plan, after all. Letting the phone ring, he considered his options. If he ignored the call, which he dearly wanted to do, then it would just go to voice mail, and she'd have to call Finn back. Liam didn't like the idea. But if he answered the call now, then he'd have to actually speak to the man, and he didn't like that, either.

Staring at the buzzing phone, a thought suddenly occurred to him, and he perked right up. Liam would get immense satisfaction out of showing Finn how close Cora was with *him*. They were roommates, after all, and she entrusted him with her phone. In this society that seemed tantamount to exchanging wedding vows. Some people even seemed more attached to their phones than their spouses. Would it be a petty move on his part? Sure, but it wouldn't jeopardize his task to get them together.

Before he could change his mind, Liam answered Cora's phone. "Hello."

There was a pause, and then Finn said, "I'm sorry. I think I dialed the wrong number."

"Not if you're calling Cora. This is Liam. Cora's having me hold her phone for a bit. We do that sometimes." It was petty of him to say it, but it sure felt good.

"Oh." There was a brief pause. "Hi, Liam. Is Cora around?"

"She's in a meeting at the moment."

"With Eli? That's what I was calling about, actually. I just wanted to check to see how the meeting went."

"It's still going on, but—*damn*. Hold on." Liam strained to hear what was happening at the pool table near the wall. Magnus looked to be in a heated discussion with a couple of the bikers. They were arguing over the game. "Idiot man," Liam whispered.

"What's that?" Finn asked.

"Magnus is with us," Liam said, annoyed. Magnus and one of the bikers had resumed the game. The biker, a large man with a beer gut and a bushy red beard, was staring daggers at Magnus as he rounded the table. Magnus, on the other hand, looked arrogant and cocky as ever.

"What's he doing there?" Finn sounded unhappy. He wasn't the only one.

"He weaseled his way into driving us tonight. Cora's talking to Eli in the back room, and Magnus is trying to hustle someone at pool. I knew it was a mistake to let him come."

Finn whispered something under his breath that sounded a lot like a swear word.

Now it was Liam's turn to be surprised. "What?" Did Finn just show some less-than-perfect emotions? Did he perhaps have a personality, after all?

"Nothing. Can you tell Cora—"

"*God's teeth,*" Liam muttered as Magnus's opponent suddenly threw his pool cue to the floor and shouted in Magnus's face. "Looks like our idiot ride is in trouble. I've got to go." He hung up on Finn, who'd been in the middle of asking another question. Cora could call him back later when they were out of this mess. *If* they got out of this mess.

Now Red Beard and two of his unsavory friends had rounded on Magnus. With every step they took, Magnus backpedaled, holding his hands out and talking fast. Liam couldn't hear what he was saying, but it didn't seem to be having a good effect on the men. Suddenly, Magnus spun and walked briskly toward Liam. He looked grim and uneasy.

"The boys and I had a little misunderstanding," Magnus said in a low voice, so the men wouldn't overhear. "I bet them money on a game, and it seems they were a lot better than they looked. I don't suppose you have two hundred dollars in cash I could borrow?"

"No," Liam said, trying not to stare at the growing group of bikers closing in on Magnus's back. They looked like wild animals cornering prey. If his opinion of Magnus was low before, then this moment had to be rock bottom. Every good hustler knows how to read the room. Magnus should've known not to test these men. One of the men grabbed a rickety bar stool and flung it aside. On its own, it wasn't a huge gesture, but the statement it made was alarming. These men were ready to fight.

"Right," Magnus said, eyes darting around nervously. He forced an easy smile that was almost convincing. Liam had to hand it to the man; he was a good actor. Magnus turned to the angry men surrounding them.

"I've got it handled," he told them. "No worries."

"You play, you pay," said Red Beard in a voice like a rusty crowbar. "We made a bet, and I won."

"Yes, you did." Magnus shifted his weight, his shoes scraping on the sticky floor. The bartender backed away as if he expected things to get ugly. "And I'm good for it, as I told you. My friend here can vouch for me."

They all looked at Liam, and he could feel the violent energy pulsing around them. The dimly lit bar just added to the dark sense of foreboding in Liam's gut. This was bad. Liam dipped his head. It wasn't quite a nod, but it was the best he could do, because he didn't want to back Magnus up on anything. The man was a swindler and a cad. Instead, Liam closed his hand around his beer glass and took a long drink to buy some time. It was a bad move. Not because the beer tasted terrible—which it did—but because it gave Magnus time, too. When Liam put the glass down, Magnus had moved to the mouth of the hallway.

"Bathroom," he said, jerking a thumb over his shoulder. "Be right back."

He left Liam surrounded by the pack of dogs. Long minutes passed. They growled among themselves, growing angrier when Magnus didn't appear. Soon, their attention turned to Liam. He tried to look as unassuming as possible by focusing on Cora's phone. He'd just watched a documentary where these genius little rodent creatures played dead when threatened by predators. If only it was that simple. He checked the time. Cora had been gone long enough. Liam was just standing to get her when a skinny biker in a denim vest came rushing from the hall.

"That scumbag took off through the back door," he snarled, heading out the front to catch him.

Red Beard glared at Liam. "Your friend's a lying, cheating coward."

At this moment Liam couldn't agree with the man more. "Yes. I'm sor—"

"But I don't care," Red Beard said, moving in on Liam. The hyenas fell into formation behind him. "You want to know why?"

No, he didn't. He had a feeling whatever the bearded man was going to say, it would be bad news.

"Because the two hundred he owed? I'll just shake it out of you. Seeing as you're such good friends."

Liam scanned the room, considering all the angles. Hustling or talking his way out of this mess didn't seem to be an option. He supposed he could fight his way out, if he had to, but many against one was never good odds. Also, he had Cora to protect. Damn Magnus Blackwell for this.

The biker in the denim vest came in through the front door. "He's gone. Took off in his car."

Liam swore. No, *this* was rock bottom. Now Magnus Blackwell was officially scum of the earth. He'd gone and abandoned both him and Cora to deal with this fallout.

Cora appeared from the hall looking tired but composed. Liam could tell from the firm set of her jaw that her talk with Eli hadn't been pleasant.

"What's going on here?" she asked, coming up behind Liam.

"Magnus shoved a stick in the hornet's nest," Liam said in a low voice. "He bet the red-bearded man on a game of pool, lost and couldn't pay up."

Cora frowned. "Magnus?"

"Aye, it's as I've been telling you. He's a lowlife swindler. Suf-

fers from a double dose of original sin, that one." Liam kept one
eye on the angry bikers. "And now he's escaped out the back
door, abandoning us to these jackals. I don't suppose you've got
two hundred dollars on you?"

Cora shook her head slowly. "Magnus…left us." It was clear
she was having a hard time processing it.

Eli Shelton came up beside them, clicking his tongue in mock
dismay. "*Tsk. Tsk.* Looks like your friend owes us money."

Cora shot him a look of disgust. "It's not our fault."

"And he's not our friend," Liam added.

"You came in together," Red Beard said. "And you vouched
for him, so you're going to need to pay up before we let you go."

"We don't have the money on us, and you can't squeeze blood
from a turnip," Liam said, annoyed. "So we'll be taking our
leave now, and if we see that lying, cheating coward again, we'll
be sure to let him know you'd like a word." He placed his hand
on Cora's lower back to escort her toward the door.

He sensed the swing coming before it made contact. Liam
quickly pushed Cora to safety, spun around and ducked to avoid
Red Beard's punch.

Red Beard let out a grunt of anger, hauled off and swung
again, and this time Liam dodged the punch, threw himself sideways and delivered a sharp kick into the man's back.

Red Beard went careening into a table. He roared and came
hurling back at Liam with fists flying. Liam dodged him easily,
sending Red Beard tumbling to the floor from his own momentum. It wasn't that hard to deal with one angry man. A lifetime
growing up with Boyd and the Bricks, getting into scrapes and
brawls at the tavern, had trained him well. This was like sipping
tea from a china cup compared to that.

Everyone started yelling at once. Red Beard sprang from the
floor and rushed at Liam again.

"Stop!" Eli shouted, holding out his hand. Red Beard froze,
and the bikers quieted as Eli's calculating gaze roamed over

Liam, assessing him. "Not bad, son. A natural fighter. Where'd you learn?"

Liam lifted a brow in amusement. "Someplace that makes you lot look soft as plum pudding."

"Liam," Cora said in warning.

"No, girl." Eli raised a hand. "Let the man talk." He was looking at Liam the same way a man sizes up a racehorse. "Perhaps he can do me a favor instead of paying off the debt."

"Don't even think about it," Cora said through gritted teeth. She surprised Liam by getting in Eli's face. "We are with the Providence Falls *Police* Department in case you've forgotten. We don't do you favors."

"You'd be surprised," Eli said with a sneer. A few of the bikers chuckled.

"You really want him to do you a favor?" Cora continued. "Tricky business, those. You learn a lot about a person from the favors they ask. Lots of information that could be useful later."

Eli glared daggers at Cora, but he backed down. Whatever she'd just said must've hit home.

The front door opened, and the mood in the room suddenly shifted from hostile aggression to something much lighter.

Finn Walsh entered the bar as somber and expressionless as he'd been when he represented Slice in the interrogation room. Boring as ever. That was Finn for you.

"Jack," someone at a back table rumbled. A few others joined in, smiling. What the devil was there to smile about? The mongrels should be tearing Finn apart by now. Perhaps they mistook him for a better, livelier person named Jack.

"Finn," a woman said, pushing through the bikers. Eli's wife, Mabel, was all grins and happiness to see the man. To Liam's shock, she threw herself at Finn, giving him an enthusiastic hug.

Finn smiled weakly and patted her on the back. "Mabel, how are you?"

"Better, now that I've seen your handsome face," Mabel answered, giving Finn's cheek a pinch.

Liam felt as if he'd gone away with the fairies. Maybe someone had spiked his beer with poison and sent him to the great beyond. To see a hard-as-concrete woman like Mabel go all soft and gooey over *Finn*, of all people. This night was getting stranger by the minute.

Finn spoke quietly to Mabel as most of the bikers dispersed. Eli joined Mabel and Finn, and just like that, the tension in the room evaporated.

"What the devil just happened?" Liam whispered to Cora.

"Finn happened." She looked just as bothered as he felt.

Like outsiders, they watched as Finn charmed a giggle out of Mabel and received a slap on the back from Eli. Then Finn did something that shocked Liam further. He walked over to Red Beard, covertly pulled money from his wallet and handed it to him. Liam looked to see if Cora was paying attention, but she was staring at her phone. When Liam glanced back at Finn, Red Beard was trying to give the money back, but Finn wouldn't take it. Instead, he said something that made the man laugh.

By the time Finn approached Liam and Cora, the patrons in the bar weren't even paying attention anymore. Finn gave them a crooked smile. "You guys want to get out of here?"

"Hell, yes," Liam said, following Cora to the door. She said nothing, but he didn't think much of it as they climbed into Finn's car.

When they were on the highway heading home, Liam glanced to Cora in the backseat. "You all right? That old man better not have given you a hard time."

She was staring out the window. "I handled him just fine."

Liam turned to Finn. "How did you know to come for us?"

"On the phone you mentioned Magnus drove you there, and you said he was stirring up trouble. I was already on the road, so I thought I'd drop by just in case. I've seen Magnus get caught in some nasty bar fights in the past, so I wanted to make sure that didn't happen."

"Because you're so against fighting," Cora said. She almost sounded bitter, but maybe she was just tired.

"Magnus can be…a wild card," Finn said. "He doesn't always consider how his actions affect other people before he charges into something. Anyway, aside from his involvement, how did the meeting with Eli go?" He peered at Cora through the rearview mirror.

"Just great," she said flatly. "Eli was his usual, charming self."

"I'm sorry to hear that." Finn smiled, but it was lost on Cora.

She was so deep in her own thoughts, and visibly weary from the day, she ignored both of them for the rest of the ride home.

Liam tried to rack his brains to come up with a reason to invite Finn over for the weekend, but he was too tired to scheme. He'd play matchmaker tomorrow. If nothing else, the day ended on a high note for him because Magnus had just ruined any chance he'd had with Cora. She was visibly disturbed right now, and Liam could just imagine the fiery conversation she was going to have with Magnus—if she decided to speak to him again, that is. The very thought of her ripping into Magnus Blackwell put a spring in Liam's step for the rest of the night.

22

ON TUESDAY CORA RUBBED HER BLEARY EYES
and slapped the list of suspects on her desk. First thing yesterday morning Eli Shelton had surprised her by providing all the
names and alibis of his club members. Some of the other de-
tectives had spent the majority of the day verifying their stories
and now they were once again at a standstill. Everyone had alibis that checked out.

She stared at Lindsey's report for what felt like the hundred-
thousandth time, willing the evidence to reveal itself. So far all
they had was her dead body and a pile of Booze Dog money
found in her locker. The fact that Eli had been so forthcoming with the information was a relief, even though she wished
she could forget the man entirely. Just the thought of what he'd
tried to pull in that back room made her want to pop him in
the face. Friday night had proven useful for work, but it had
been emotionally draining. She still couldn't believe Finn had
shown up to save them. Once again, he'd surprised her. She'd
been uncomfortable seeing him again so soon. It wasn't that she
was mad at him anymore; she was just...unsettled. It was still
hard to believe Finn was the same man the Booze Dogs called

The Jackrabbit. When he surprised them at The Rolling Log, he was back to his usual designer clothes and pressed, crisp, collared shirts. How had he gotten involved in cage fighting, of all things? There was a story there, but he hadn't been willing to talk about it. She shook her head, trying her best to put Finn out of her mind. He'd been nothing but kind and helpful on Friday night, just like he always was, but she saw him differently now. Not bad, but...not quite the same.

"Cora, Brady's widow is on line one. She wants to know if there's anything new on her husband's case," Rob Hopper called from across the room. "You want to take it, or should I?"

"Rob, if you handle her today, I'll owe you huge," Cora said wearily. Rob waved her away and took the call, reminding Cora how lucky she was to have her team. They were a motley crew, but they looked out for each other.

"Anything new?" Liam asked, rolling a chair up to her desk and straddling it backward.

"Not unless you count over fifty bikers vouching for each other in obviously contrived alibis for the night of her murder." The problem was, she knew exactly where the bikers were that night—the fight at the barn. But before she brought that bit of information into the light, she needed a few more days to gather stronger evidence against the Booze Dogs regarding Lindsey. A gambling ring was one thing; a murder was another. As bothered as she was by Finn's involvement in the fight ring, she wasn't going to reveal to the Booze Dogs that she knew about their illegal operation. They might make a connection between her and Finn, and the last thing she wanted was Eli's crowd thinking Finn was a snitch. There was no telling what they would do.

"Boyd thinks Eli's behind Lindsey's death," Liam said. "All we have to do is find a way to prove it."

"That's the problem. My gut instinct tells me Eli Shelton had nothing to do with it. Why else would he admit how much money was really stolen? It would only give us reason to suspect him more. And I don't believe he's trying to cover for someone else, because he's just as driven to find out who stole his money. He's even stooping to work with the police."

"It could all just be an act," Liam suggested. "Maybe Eli wants you to believe he's angry in order to deflect scrutiny."

Cora sighed again, lowering her head to her desk. "Maybe. I'm just exhausted from all the subterfuge. I feel like everyone has things to hide." She turned her head to peek up at him. "Not you, though. That's why I'm grateful to have you on my side, Liam. I know we got off to a rocky start in the beginning, but I trust you to back me up now. Besides, you always tell me how you feel. Even when you know I'll hate it."

Liam's smile was bittersweet, and she didn't know why. Sometimes she felt like she knew him better than anyone else, and in other moments, like this one, he seemed a mystery to her.

"Like when you kept telling me Magnus was no good," Cora said, knowing it would snap him back to her. He had very strong feelings about Magnus, and never missed a chance to tell her. "I didn't want to hear it, but you were right."

Liam raised a dark brow. "So you believe me now?"

"At first, I was so angry he took off and left us, I refused to take his phone calls all weekend. I was just so shocked he'd do that. It seemed so out of character for him."

"Not at all," Liam said flatly. "Abandoning us to the wolves last Friday was well in line with the type of man he is. He rolls the dice, plays the game and runs when things don't go his way. And then it's on to the next game without looking back."

"Actually, he did," Cora said, arranging the mess of pens and markers on her desk. "Look back, that is." She knew this wasn't going to go well, but it was time to rip off the Band-Aid. "I know you can't stand him, and I agree that stunt he pulled was beyond the pale. He left yet another message last night, begging for a chance to explain."

"Magnus doesn't deserve to breathe the same air as you, let alone speak to you."

"Well, this morning when he called again…" She focused on arranging the blue and black pens in a cup on her desk. Then she gathered the highlighters for the top drawer. It was easier than having to face the look of condemnation on Liam's face.

"Cora," Liam said in a warning tone. "Tell me you didn't talk to him."

"I had to," she said in exasperation, slamming her desk drawer. "He'd left so many voice mails, I decided to give him a chance to explain his side of it, that's all. He said he ran to the nearest ATM and came right back. But we were gone by then, and when he tried to call me, I refused to answer—"

"God save us!" Liam threw his hands up. "He's doing it again. He's reeling you in like a mermaid caught in a net."

Cora straightened her spine but wouldn't make eye contact. "Nothing could be further from the truth. I'm in no danger of getting tangled up with him again. But I did agree to see him for dinner tonight."

Liam looked like he was about to explode.

"Don't." Cora held up a hand. "Don't say a word. I thought about hiding it from you, and pretending I was going off to see Suzette, but I decided to be open and honest about it, instead."

"Aye, well, your honesty is killing me," he said sardonically.

"I know what you're thinking—that I'm going to let Magnus back into my life—but that's not what this is about. I've already told him it wasn't going to work out between us, and he understands how I feel. I'm going to let him explain his side of things, then we are going to part ways with no animosity between us."

Liam eyed her like she was trying to sell him some oceanfront property down the road.

"It's just one last dinner, Liam. I'm not signing my life away. Enough, already. I'm going to put this whole thing to rest. Now, come on. Let's take over for Otto and Happy. They've been interrogating the last of the Booze Dogs this morning, and if Happy hasn't made one of them cry with his sunny disposition yet, I'll be very surprised."

Magnus Blackwell looked downright contrite when he picked her up for dinner. It was a new look for him, and Cora found it surprising that he seemed so…genuine. It made her realize just how much he may have been acting before.

"I'm sorry for the way we left things last Friday night," Magnus said once they were on the freeway heading south. He still looked handsome in his custom-tailored designer clothes, but there was an almost desperate edge to his demeanor. "Truly, I hate that you thought I'd driven off and abandoned you there."

"You could've called or texted me that you were on your way back."

"I thought I could just rush out and be back within ten minutes. But by the time I returned, you were long gone. And then you didn't answer your phone."

"Did anyone at the bar give you a hard time when they saw you again?"

"No," Magnus said, switching the radio station to smooth jazz. "I didn't stay once I realized you weren't there."

"But you paid the guy you owed, right?" Cora asked.

His hesitation was so brief, she almost missed it. "Of course."

Cora wondered if he was lying. Maybe Liam's warnings were messing with her head, or maybe she was finally seeing past Magnus's handsome face and easy charm. Turning her attention to the window, she realized they'd passed the exit to the sushi restaurant.

"Where are we going?"

He grinned and said, "It's a surprise. We're about fifteen minutes away. Is that okay?"

She nodded reluctantly. It was strange, because she'd been so into Magnus just a week ago, willing to have a fling and enjoy the wild ride. But now the spark was gone. Even if he was telling the truth, she just didn't feel the same about him. With Magnus's questionable actions, Finn's mysterious secret relationship with the Booze Dogs—which she still didn't understand—and all the secrets and lies flying around with the murder cases, Cora was mentally and emotionally drained. She just wanted normalcy, and Liam was the only person in her life who represented that.

The more she thought about it, the more she realized how much she depended on Liam. He was annoying sometimes with his overprotective attitude, but he was always there for her. They'd settled into a comfortable routine at home, and when she needed to talk, he was there to listen. When she needed to discuss the case, he was the man for that job, too. It was comforting to know he was in her corner, no matter how confusing things became in other areas of her life. Liam was really all she needed right now.

Magnus took a freeway exit with a sign that read Cedar Lakei. He drove down a paved winding road that led to a beautiful lake house right on the waterfront. It was a pale gray Cape Cod-style home with white pillars in front, sparkling bay windows and a large porch with Adirondack chairs. To Cora, it looked like something out of an upscale real estate magazine.

"This is my summer getaway," Magnus said. "I come here on weekends to fish or just unwind from a long week. Normally, I live downtown, but when things get hectic, there's nothing like this place. Anyway, it's such a nice evening, I thought I'd cook us dinner. The weather's too good to stay indoors, and there's a perfect spot on the dock to watch the sunset. I hope you don't mind?"

Cora felt torn. A sunset dinner by the lake was a lovely idea, but a little too romantic for her current mood, especially with all her conflicting emotions. The truth was, she *did* mind. She felt suddenly annoyed that Magnus would draw their dinner date out like this. She'd made it clear she didn't feel like getting to know him any further. This whole evening was supposed to be about giving him a chance to explain, then ending on a lighter note so things wouldn't be awkward if they ran into each other later.

"If you don't want to stay, it's okay," he said earnestly. "I can turn around, and we can head back into town."

She hesitated, then said, "No, it's fine." They were already there, so she may as well eat. It wasn't going to change the way she felt.

Magnus smiled and parked alongside the house. "Come inside, and I'll show you around."

Cora wasn't surprised to find that the place was model-home lovely on the inside. With exposed wood beams, a stonework fireplace and windows overlooking the shore, it had an open, airy vibe. Sisal carpets covered the wide-plank hardwood floors, and the soft furniture in earth tones invited conversation and relaxation. It smelled like pine and something masculine and earthy. If this was Magnus's man cave, the guy really knew how to live.

"It's beautiful," Cora said, meaning it. As annoyed as she was for being coerced into coming, no one could argue the place wasn't gorgeous. Maybe Magnus knew that, and he hoped to soften her up. The thought made the place lose some of its luster.

"Why don't you relax, and I'll get dinner started," he said, heading toward the kitchen. "Wine?"

Cora nodded, because why the hell not? She was here; she might as well lean in. Down the hall was a guest bathroom, and through an open door, she caught site of a large sunken tub that appeared to be *in* the master bedroom. Yeah, if Magnus had sprung this place on her under any other circumstances, she'd have been a goner. A mermaid caught in his net, just like Liam had said.

The sound of Magnus working in the kitchen gave her the nerve to wander into the master bedroom. She only wanted to take a quick peek, and there was a gorgeous view of the lake.

"I am in the wrong profession," Cora muttered, taking in the sleek, upscale furniture and luxurious bed linens. She knew some attorneys did very well, and Magnus was obviously one of them. He must've paid interior designers a small fortune to help with the decor.

A cobalt ceramic pot of orchids sat on one of the nightstands, and Cora wandered over, admiring the profusion of white tropical flowers. She reached out to touch one of the blooms, rubbing the decadent, waxy petals between her fingers. Of course they were real. He wasn't the type to mess around with fake plants.

Suddenly, the orchid stalk snapped off and fell to the floor. Cora bent to grab it when something caught her attention. Under the bed, a duffel bag was pushed against the back wall. She almost overlooked it, but a familiar symbol was visible through the partially open zipper.

Cora froze.

She would never have noticed it, but for the flash of white paper and red ink. A prickling sensation of unease radiated through her body. Unable to stop herself, she scooted to her stomach, hooked a finger around one of the straps and pulled the duffel toward her. When she slid the zipper open a bit more, all the color drained from her face.

23

STACKS OF CASH WERE TOSSED INSIDE THE DUF-fel, bundled in narrow white sleeves with the red Booze Dog stamp.

Cora's hands began to shake. For a moment all she could do was stare at what must've amounted to over a hundred thousand dollars. This had to be the missing money Eli was searching for. But why would Magnus have it?

With frantic, jerky movements, Cora zipped the bag and shoved it back against the wall. She pulled herself from under the bed and rose to her knees to stand.

"Everything okay?" Magnus asked from the doorway.

Startled, she jumped to her feet, holding up the stalk of orchids. "Yes! I'm so sorry. I was admiring your plant because I love orchids. They're one of my favorite flowers of all time, so I wanted to see if these were real, which they are. So that's really great that you keep real orchids, because I know they're not easy to take care of. But I broke it by accident. I'm sorry," she repeated, giving him her best fake smile with a sinking feeling in her stomach. He was smart, and wily and there was no way he'd buy this act. Even to her own ears, she sounded guilty and flustered.

"They're real," he said smoothly, holding out a glass of wine. "Drink?"

Cora walked over on shaky legs, pretending everything was normal. Just a normal drink with a normal dinner date who had not recently committed larceny and maybe homicide. No big deal. She accepted the glass and took a tiny sip, eyeing him over the rim of her glass. He seemed calm and amiable. Maybe he hadn't caught on, after all.

"The salad's done," he said. "I need to throw the steaks on the grill. Ready to head outside?"

"Sure. I'm just going to run to the restroom." She eased around him and made a beeline for the guest bathroom she'd seen on her way down the hall. Once inside she locked the door and yanked her phone from her pocket, relieved she hadn't left her phone in her purse in the living room. With shaking hands, she quickly texted Liam.

At Magnus's house on Cedar Lake. Found stolen money! Come get me. Call station. Am dialing 911 but can't talk.

She waited, praying Liam would respond immediately. When a couple of minutes went by without a response, she pretended to wash her hands. Then she dialed 911.

The dispatcher picked up, and Cora began to whisper, but Magnus interrupted when he called out, "Cora? Everything okay?"

"Yes, I'll be right out." She heard the dispatcher asking questions but had no way of responding without being overheard. Staying silent, she slid the phone into her pocket, knowing it was protocol for the dispatcher to report the call and send someone out to investigate. Cora hoped it would be fast enough. Once

Magnus started grilling, she could make an excuse to get away and try calling again.

She left the bathroom to find him leaning against the wall near the master bedroom door. He was staring at the floor and appeared to be deep in thought.

She pasted a bright smile on her face. "Ready."

He glanced up, and for one heart-stopping moment she saw something cold and calculating in his gaze, but then he snapped back to his charming self and led her down to the shore.

There was a beautiful entertainment area with an outdoor gas grill and a low fire pit surrounded by decorative rocks. Across the lake, she could see a few other houses nestled in the trees. The gardens around Magnus's house were well maintained, but the surrounding wooded area gave one the feeling of seclusion and peace. Even though they were less than thirty minutes outside Providence Falls, they could've been anywhere. It was like being on a movie set. Unfortunately, the movie wasn't going to be a happy one.

Magnus wrapped an arm around her shoulder as they stared out at the water lapping along the shore. The weight of his arm, his nearness, felt like a blanket of prickly thorns, but she pretended everything was fine.

He smiled down at her and said, "I'm really glad you came out with me tonight. Thanks for giving me the chance to see you." Then he pulled her in for a quick hug. All her senses were screaming at her to jerk away, but she eased from his hold and took a seat on one of the chairs like nothing was amiss.

Magnus fired up the grill and made small talk. She answered when appropriate, but she got the feeling neither of them were paying attention. He seemed distracted, which only heightened her alarm. Was he trying to manipulate her into a false sense of security right now? To what end?

His movements were smooth and easy as he seasoned the steaks and told her about his last trip to Hawaii, but there was a slight lack of tone inflection in his voice that she hadn't noticed before. "Have you?"

Cora realized he'd just asked her a question. "I'm sorry, what?"

"Have you been to the Hawaiian islands?"

"Not yet, but it's definitely on my bucket list," she managed. "I've heard the beaches are gorgeous."

"Paradise on earth," he agreed, launching into the pros and cons of visiting Maui during the height of tourist season.

Cora tried to feign interest, but her mind was busy calculating how long it would take for the police to arrive, and whether or not Liam got her text message. She hoped he was already on his way. All she really needed to do was stall Magnus long enough until someone arrived, but her self-preservation instincts had kicked in to high gear. For all she knew, Magnus was a stone-cold killer. Maybe he and Lindsey stole the money and had a falling out, and then he killed her. She began cataloging her surroundings, automatically scoping out escape routes out of habit. There was a small rowboat down by the dock. The road out wove through the trees, but she could run if she had to. She was dying to check her phone to see if Liam had responded, but she didn't want to draw attention to it.

Magnus finished at the grill and took a chair beside hers to watch the sunset.

"It's really beautiful," Cora offered, pretending to sip her wine. If she needed to make a run for it, she didn't want a foggy head to slow her down. "A person could get used to this."

"Could you?" he asked suddenly, studying her face like she was a coded message he was trying to decipher. "Would you want to live like this? Summer houses, fancy cars, easy living."

"I can't think of many people who wouldn't," she said.

"Not everyone's willing to do what it takes to get what they want."

Cora kept her eyes on the last sliver of sunlight as it disappeared beyond the tree line. "My father always said if you work hard and you have a goal, you can achieve anything."

"That's the fairy tale we're told when we're children," Magnus said with a condescending huff. "But the reality is a little more nuanced."

The detective in her wanted to fire off a hundred questions in rapid succession, but she forced herself to appear casual. "What do you mean?"

There was a smug twist to his lips. "Life's a game, Cora. You have to learn the rules, so you can break them. It's how all the people in power get to the top. Oh, they'll tell you it's hard work and perseverance and all those things—and it is. Part of it. But mostly, it's about finding opportunities to get a leg up, and knowing when to take them."

She tried to keep her tone light, but it wasn't easy. "No matter the cost?"

"Sometimes you've got to make sacrifices," he said. "But once you figure out how to game the system, nine times out of ten you're not the one doing the sacrificing. It's easy, but not for everyone."

Cora was afraid to look at him because she was almost certain he was talking about theft and maybe even Lindsey's death. And if he was steering the conversation in this direction, then he must know—

"I saw you in my room. I know you found the money under my bed." He pierced her with a dark, almost menacing look, then grinned. "It's okay, Cora. You don't have to pretend."

The hairs on the backs of her forearms stood on end. "All right. Yes. I did find the money. Why is it in your house, Magnus?"

"I didn't think you were the type to go snooping like that," he said calmly, ignoring her question. "I'd have thought it was beneath you. But I suppose it's refreshing that some people can still surprise me. Most of them are too easy to read. Finn, for example. Such a do-gooder. Still plays by the book and believes justice will prevail. The man should wear a cape." He sneered. "Your roommate, Liam, now there's an enigma. I thought we were knit from the same cloth when we first met, but he changed once I showed an interest in you."

"He's my partner. We look out for each other," Cora said, gauging how far it was to the edge of the woods. She could reach it, then hide if she had to. Magnus's false charm had gone down with the setting sun, because this man beside her seemed cold and calculating. Ruthless. Cora stood and walked toward the shore to put some space between them.

"Do you tell yourself that in order to deny your own feelings for him, or his for you?" Magnus said, joining her near the water's edge.

Cora's body tensed, but she faced him and said, "Why'd you take the money, Magnus?"

He smirked and dug his hands into his pockets. "Because it was there."

"How did you know where to find it?"

He shook his head. "You've already discovered more than I planned to share. I'm afraid it wouldn't be wise to give all my secrets away. A wise man is a rich man."

"And in your case, a criminal," Cora said.

Annoyance flashed across his face. "You're so naive, Cora. I was hoping you'd understand the game and want to play it with me now that you've found me out. We could share the money. Surely, there's something you want?"

An image of Cora's dream house —the lovely cottage that was going up for sale at the end of the summer— flashed in Cora's mind, but she quickly dismissed it. She did not need Magnus's dirty money, and she'd be damned if she took the criminal route to make her dreams come true. Nothing was worth that.

"There's a lot we could accomplish if we teamed up." He

gave her his charming smile, but this time Cora recognized it for what it was—a mask.

"You seem to be forgetting I'm a police officer."

"And why should a position of authority matter when it comes to going after what you want in life?" He stepped closer, looking down his nose at her in a condescending way that grated on her nerves. "If you knew how many people in power think like I do, you might reconsider your stance." He reached for her hand.

Cora jerked away, backing up to put more distance between them. She had to ask, even though she was afraid of the answer. "Did you kill Lindsey Albright?"

"No." Magnus looked offended, but he was a good actor, so she had no way of telling if he was being genuine. "I'm no murderer, Cora."

"Then why was some of the Booze Dog money found in her locker?" Cora asked. "Was she your partner?"

Magnus laughed. "Of course not. I didn't even know the girl." But he knew something. She was certain of it. A sudden thought occurred to her.

"You planted that money in her locker," Cora said. "To throw suspicion on the Booze Dogs." Magnus didn't respond, which was answer enough. "But why would you bother? Are you covering for someone? Do you know who killed Lindsey?"

He tipped his face to the sky. "So many questions. You're a very smart girl, Cora, but there's a lot going on you wouldn't understand. It's that unshakeable belief in justice that gets in your way. You and Finn are very similar that way." He shook his head in disappointment. "It's too bad. I was hoping you'd be more reasonable than this."

Cora had heard enough. Any moment now Liam or the police could arrive. They had to. But doubt crept in on her. What if her message didn't get through? Not caring anymore if Magnus saw, she reached for her phone in her back pocket.

It was *gone.*

"Looking for this?" Magnus asked. Her phone dangled from his fingertips. He must've slid it from her pocket when he gave her that awkward hug. He hauled back and sent it sailing into the lake.

Cora watched it hit the water and disappear beneath the surface. Now she was well and truly screwed. She had to find another way to call for help. The nearest house looked at least a quarter of a mile away on the other side of the lake. It would be an easy run on any other day, but the woods were sure to slow her down, and she was wearing flimsy sandals. If she could get to the small rowboat, she might have a chance, but she'd have to divert his attention first.

"I'm sorry, Cora. I can't have you calling anyone until we discuss what happens next," Magnus said with an unhappy sigh.

"And what would that be?"

"To be honest, I have no idea. I never thought we'd be in this position." He shook his head, grimacing. "If you could just see reason, then we could put this behind us and enjoy our evening."

"And by *reason*, you mean I should throw away my integrity, my better judgment and all my years of training to become your partner in crime? No, thanks. I'd rather see you behind bars where you belong."

"Why must you be so stubborn?" He was getting angry now. Bright spots of color bloomed across his cheekbones. He ran his hands through his hair and glared at her. "If I'd known you were going to be this tiresome, I wouldn't have bothered with you. This moral rigidity of yours holds no interest for me."

"I'm crying buckets on the inside about that," Cora assured him.

Magnus's lip curled into a sneer. "At least this saves me from discovering what a disappointment you'd have been in the bedroom. Let's not waste any more of each other's time, shall we?"

"Finally, something we can agree on. What do you propose?"

He took another step closer, nodding to himself as if he'd just come to a decision. "I can't let you leave." The words hung in the air like the blade of a guillotine. She had no idea what he meant, but she knew she wouldn't like it.

"So what's your plan? Kill me and leave me for dead in the woods like Lindsey?" Cora calculated the distance between them, bracing her feet. She'd have to make her move quickly. If she could incapacitate him for a few moments, it would buy her time to get to the boat at the end of the dock.

"I told you, I'm not a killer," Magnus said furiously, then muttered, "though you do tempt a man." He closed the distance between them so fast, Cora sprang into action.

When he was just an arm's length away, she tightened her fingers into a rigid spear hand, retracted her arm and made a lightning-quick jab to his throat.

Magnus jerked in shock, then fell to his knees. He reached for his throat, gagging.

With no time to spare, Cora bolted toward the dock.

24

LIAM SLUNG AN ARM OVER THE BACK OF THE booth at Danté's, waiting for Finn to hurry up with the beer. He still couldn't believe he'd called the man and asked him to go for drinks. Of all the otherworldly, unbelievable things that had happened to him since he'd cannonballed through the mist and dropped into Cora's life, this moment was the strangest.

Finley Walsh had always been a nemesis, as far as Liam was concerned. In his previous life the dullard had been engaged to Cora, and he'd been the biggest hurdle standing in Liam's way. In this life Finn and Cora were mere acquaintances, and while Liam enjoyed watching Finn bumble about in Cora's presence, he knew it was time to make changes.

Magnus Blackwell was the anvil to the skull Liam needed to finally realize this. The man was a conniving weasel, and he'd somehow managed to turn Cora's head. Every time Liam thought about Magnus and Cora together, he wanted to kick something. If he was being completely honest with himself, and he needed to be, the reason he was so against Magnus was because Magnus was just like him. He was capable of manip- ulating situations to get what he wanted, and Liam hated that

Cora could fall prey to that. For the first time in his wretched existence, he was beginning to understand what Finn must've felt when Liam had stolen Cora from him a hundred and seventy-six years ago. It was not a comfortable feeling. In fact, he rather hated it.

The angels had been so cryptic about why Finn and Cora were destined to be together. Liam couldn't understand it, but what if there was a reason that far surpassed his own personal desires? What if the necessity of their union was for a cause greater than himself? Liam tilted his face to the ceiling and groaned in frustration. He used to be so sure of what he wanted, but now he was starting to question everything.

Finn set two glasses of beer on the table and slid into the booth. He'd just come from a long day at the office, so he looked like a stuffed shirt, as always. Pressed, collared shirt. Charcoal suit. Blasted necktie. It irked Liam to see Finn looking so staid and proper. If the man was going to be worthy of Cora, he needed to climb out of his shell once in a while.

"How can you wear those bloody ties around your neck every day?" Liam asked irritably, taking a drink of beer. "Cora tried to get me to wear one once, and I almost suffocated just thinking about it."

Smiling, Finn set his car keys and wallet on the table. Then he loosened the blue tie around his neck. "You get used to it, after a while."

"I wouldn't," Liam said with a snort. "The only time you'll ever catch me in one of those is when I'm laid out in a coffin, because I'd have to be dead first. They're the devil's own creation, neckties. Hands down, the worst article of clothing ever to grace the face of the earth. I'd rather eat glass than wear one."

"But tell me how you really feel," Finn said with a chuckle. "Maybe that's why so many attorneys wear them. It's part of our demonic uniform." So he did have a sense of humor. Except Liam hadn't been joking. Just the thought of having something cinched around his neck gave him chills. He rubbed his throat reflexively.

Finn took a drink of beer, his gaze traveling around the bar. It was Tuesday night, so Danté's wasn't as packed as usual. "Is Cora coming?"

And there it was. The reason Finn agreed to meet for drinks. Liam's first inclination was to make the man squirm a bit, but then he remembered he was trying to change for the better, damn it all. "Unfortunately, she's not. She's chosen to waste her time on a deceitful, skirt-chasing jackass. A friend of yours, I believe." Okay, that was a dig, but a small one. Rome wasn't built in a day.

"Who do you mean?" Finn asked, confused.

"Magnus Blackwell." Liam tossed the name out like garbage.

All the good humor faded from Finn's face. "Magnus and I are not friends."

Liam shrugged, just to goad him. "If you say so."

"We work at the same law firm, but he and I don't see eye to eye." A muscle ticked in Finn's jaw, and he looked almost... angry. This was getting interesting.

"In what ways?" Liam asked.

Finn frowned. "Magnus performs his job effectively, but I've seen him cut corners and take risks that challenge moral and ethical boundaries, and I disagree with his flippant attitude when people's lives are on the line."

"I thought all lawyers stretched the truth to fit their agenda." Liam knew he shouldn't egg Finn on, but he made it so damned easy.

"Only the bad ones," Finn said moodily. "Magnus and I have always clashed and probably always will. He has a god complex and tends to look down on those who don't play by the same rules. His blatant disregard for differing viewpoints and the feelings of others makes him, frankly, abhorrent to be around, and I'm very sorry he ever met Cora."

"But tell me how you really feel." Liam almost smiled. He'd never heard Finn say anything so bluntly negative about anyone. Seeing him so visibly annoyed at Magnus was refreshing. Perhaps Finn had an interesting side, after all.

Finn toyed with his car keys on the table, his brow creased in frustration. "Magnus is, for lack of a better word, a womanizer. I've watched him go through many of the single women in our office, and some who weren't single. It's become almost a joke among some of the colleagues at the firm. They lay bets on how long a new receptionist will last before Magnus swoops in. While I know this isn't my business, I take it personally when he goes after friends." He paused, then said more quietly, "When he goes after Cora."

"Agreed." Once again, Liam was on Finn's side. This was getting downright spooky.

"Anyway, Magnus abandoned you both at The Rolling Log last weekend. I'm surprised Cora wasn't upset about that," Finn said.

"She was, but the scheming weasel called and left messages for her all weekend, full of excuses. He whittled away at her defenses, and she finally agreed to see him tonight so he could explain himself."

"That was a bad idea," Finn said darkly. "Magnus isn't good for her."

Liam eyed Finn thoughtfully. "What kind of a man would be good enough for her?"

"Someone with integrity and honor, like her. Someone who appreciates her for who she is, not what she can do for them. Cora's brilliant at her job. It's her calling. She works hard to protect the people and ensure peace in Providence Falls, and she's got a kind heart. Her compassion hasn't wavered over the years, even though she's seen the darkest side of humanity. I think that's just…" Finn trailed off and shook his head, smiling slightly. "It's special. She's special, and she deserves someone who's going to respect who she is. She deserves someone who wants to stand beside her in life, not try to control her. Someone who will give her the room to experience life on her terms."

"And do you know anyone like this?"

Finn looked surprised. "No, I just think—"

"*You*, perhaps?" Liam pushed. His phone vibrated in his pocket, but he ignored it. He was trying to see if Finn would be honest with him, because it was painfully clear Finn was in love with Cora. All the things he'd just said made Liam's gut churn with a bitter sense of loss. Finn understood exactly what Cora needed. Had Liam ever thought much beyond what he'd wanted? He'd fallen for Cora the moment they'd met. He'd wanted her with that driving passion and exuberance of youth that eclipsed all logic. But had he ever truly understood what she needed most? Had he ever seen her as clearly as Finn saw her now? Liam thought he had, but their lives had been different back then. The entire world had been different.

An uncomfortable feeling settled over Liam, scratching at his ego. He'd known the shy, sweet, impressionable girl Cora had been back in eighteen forty-four. They'd been young and impetuous and filled with dreams of a future together that was never realized. Had Liam ever truly stopped to think about Cora in the wise, understanding way Finn had just described? If Liam had never met her, she could have lived a happy life.

She could have *lived*.

He swallowed hard, refusing to think about the tragedy that had befallen them. Instead, he focused on the man across from him, who now looked extremely uncomfortable.

A blush crept across Finn's cheekbones. "That's not what I meant, at all. I was only saying what Cora deserved, not implying that *I'm* that man who's worthy of her. I think very few are. All I know is she deserves to be happy however, and with whomever, she chooses."

Liam's mind was in turmoil, because Finn Walsh sounded like

a hero, and it hurt like an arrow through the heart. If the angels were right, and Finn was the best man for Cora, could Liam love her enough to do the right thing? Could he truly let her go?

His phone vibrated again, and he pulled it out of his pocket. Glancing down at the text message, his heart dropped into his stomach.

At Magnus's house on Cedar Lake. Found stolen money! Come get me. Call station. Am dialing 911 but can't talk.

"What's wrong?" Finn said in alarm.

Liam didn't think; he reacted. Reaching across the table, he grabbed the one thing that could ensure he made it to Cora as fast as humanly possible: Finn's car keys. Without even pausing to explain, he bolted for the door. Finn called after him, but Liam raced into the parking lot, pressing the key fob to find Finn's Porsche. In the far corner the car beeped in response, headlights flashing.

Rushing for the driver's side, Liam jumped in and started the engine, pulling out of the parking space and barely missing Finn.

"What are you doing?" Finn slammed a hand on the trunk, which had only missed him by a hair's width.

"Cora's in trouble," Liam yelled, not bothering to roll down the window. "Get in or get out of my way before I roll right over you."

Finn rushed to the passenger side and was still pulling his leg in when Liam peeled out of the parking lot and sped toward the freeway.

"Tell me," Finn said grimly.

Liam wove through traffic like the devil himself was after them. He tossed his phone at Finn. "Read it. I'm heading south, but you'll need to give me directions."

Finn read Cora's frantic text message and swore under his breath. Then he pulled his own phone out and said, "I have the address in my contacts. Magnus hosted a company party there last year." He punched the location into his phone and gave rapid directions.

When Liam made it to the freeway entrance, he stomped on the gas and bypassed two cars in front of them by driving on the shoulder. One of the drivers honked and flipped him off, but he barely noticed. Not wasting a moment, Liam made high-speed lane changes on the freeway just like he'd learned in the driving class. Within moments he'd maneuvered successfully past three other cars, and they were speeding down the freeway headed south.

The next ten minutes felt like an eternity. Liam's hands ached from their tight grip on the steering wheel. Cora needed him, and he'd ignored her text! Guilt stabbed at him as his mind spun up all the dangerous situations she could be in right now. He tried to tell himself he knew Magnus, and as conniving as the man was, he'd never hurt Cora. But deep down Liam couldn't be certain.

Finn called 911 and explained what they knew. Liam concentrated on weaving through traffic at breakneck speeds, pushing the car as far and fast as he could. Never once did Finn complain. They were both hell-bent on getting to Cora as fast as possible, and once again, Liam found himself and Finn on the same side. He was glad of it.

The GPS on Finn's phone announced the upcoming exit just as he pointed and said, "There. Take the hard right at the bottom."

Liam took the off-ramp without slowing down. He saw the turn, shifted gears and flew around the corner. The wheels screeched, skipping across the asphalt, but he kept his gaze on the winding road ahead until the car gained traction again.

"Jesus." Finn had a white-knuckled grip on the roof handle, his other hand braced against the dashboard. "Where'd you learn to drive like this?"

Liam gritted his teeth. "You don't want to know."

"There it is." Finn pointed to a narrow trail through the trees. "His house is just down that road."

They came out of the woods so fast, Liam had to slam on the brakes or risk crashing into the house itself. The tires skidded across the driveway, sending gravel flying in all directions. A flock of birds in the nearby trees took to the sky in startled protest.

"Cora," Finn choked out, his horrified gaze on the waterfront.

Liam whipped his head toward the lake. His heart slammed into his throat. He threw the car into Park, jumped out and started running.

Cora sprinted to the end of the dock and attacked the rope tethering the boat. The twilight sky cast a cold, eerie glow over the lake, but she was grateful it wasn't too dark to see. She unwound the rope with shaking hands. Every second counted.

He was getting closer. She could hear his stilted footsteps on the wooden planks as he lumbered toward her, swearing hoarsely. But she refused to look up from her task.

Almost there. The rope came loose, and she jumped to her feet. The small boat bobbed in the water. She yanked the rope to bring it closer.

"You're going—" Magnus rasped, coughed "—to be sorry for that."

Not in a million years, buddy. She lifted her leg to swing into the boat, but Magnus's steely arm snaked around her throat, yanking her back against his chest.

Cora's reflexes kicked in. She couldn't allow him to get her in a headlock. If he cut off the blood circulation to her brain, no amount of martial arts training would help her. She twisted her hips, then used the momentum to slam her elbow into his stomach. He let out a guttural curse and loosened his hold for a split second.

Wasting no time, she spun to face him, striking upward with the heel of her palm. It met his nose with a loud *crack*.

Magnus roared, one hand flying to his now-bloody nose. He fisted his other hand in her shirt and shook her so hard, her teeth clacked together. Cora lifted her foot and slammed her heel onto his instep.

He let out another painful grunt. She shoved him. He coiled, and before she could react, he backhanded her across the face.

Pain blossomed on her eye and cheekbone. She staggered backward, jerking on Magnus's sleeve for balance.

He stumbled into her, and then they were falling.

Icy water closed over Cora's head. Magnus landed on top of her, his weight pushing her under until she saw nothing but murky darkness. She shoved at him, trying to break free, but his fist was tangled in her hair. She yanked at his fingers, but his grip was too tight. Panic seized her. *I'm no murderer, Cora.* Had he lied?

Magnus suddenly let go and kicked toward the surface. She tried to follow, but his heel lashed out, connecting with her temple.

Cora's head exploded in pain. She gripped her skull and began to sink. Feebly, she tried to kick toward the surface, but her legs were sluggish. *Move!* She tried again, but her lungs were burning, and she felt disoriented and slow. Darkness was everywhere, and she was suddenly so tired.

25

Kinsley, Ireland
1844

CORA SLID OFF HER BED TO LIGHT A CANDLE, then slowly limped through the shadowy room to her window near the rose trellis.

She'd turned her ankle on the stairs earlier that day, but she wasn't going to allow such a slight injury to ruin her plans. Too much was riding on tonight, and she needed everything to go off without a hitch. It was still raining, which was poor luck for her and Liam, but the weather couldn't dampen her excitement. Nothing could.

Tonight they were running away together.

A thrill shot through her as she leaned on the windowsill and stared out at the midnight sky. At least there was a full moon to help light their way. In a few minutes the clock would strike twelve, and then it would all begin. She, the squire's sheltered daughter who'd never been anywhere, was going on an adventure that would change her life forever.

On a small table near the window, she'd left two letters. The first one was for Finley Walsh, asking for his forgiveness and ex-

·plaining that she couldn't marry him because she'd fallen in love with someone else. She told him how grateful she was that he'd singled her out and hoped that someday he would find someone worthy of his regard. When she thought about the quiet man with the soulful brown eyes, she was gripped with guilt. He deserved better than a letter; he deserved a conversation in person, but she couldn't risk it. She didn't know Finley well enough to predict what he would do if she told him her plan to run away. He'd likely go straight to her father, and they would try to stop her. So this was the best she could do. In her heart she believed Finley was a good man. Someday, heaven would see fit to send him a woman who would love him like he deserved.

The second letter had been harder to write. Just holding the folded parchment in her hands made her breath hitch and tears spring to her eyes. Saying goodbye to her father, the man who'd raised her and loved her above all else, was impossible. How could she put into words the gratitude and adoration she felt when she knew it could never be enough? Yes, he'd been overbearing and overprotective, but Cora understood it all came from a place of love. Her mother had died years ago, and Cora was all he had left. This letter was going to break his heart, and the guilt was almost too much to bear. In the end, she'd told him how she'd never forget him and begged him to understand that she had to follow her heart. She'd also promised to write to him as soon as she and Liam were settled in America.

Setting the letters aside, she stooped to gather the bag she'd hidden under the bed. It had been easy enough to pack, since her nanny had been too old and distracted to notice the missing items of clothing, the silver hairbrush and the small purse of coins. Cora had said good-night to her nanny, giving her an extra hard hug, which caused the old woman to pinch her lips together and reprimand Cora for such an outward display of emotion. "A lady must appear serene and dignified at all times," her nanny had said reprovingly. Cora had just smiled and hugged the old woman harder.

The clock on the mantel chimed midnight, and she shivered with excitement, taking one last look around her bedroom. The fireplace glowed with banked embers, casting shadows along the walls. She'd spent so much time in here, dreaming about the great big world, that for the rest of her life if she closed her eyes, she'd be able to see every detail. The blue-and-white porcelain wash basin on the wall by the door. The painted silk screen in the corner by the armoire. The vanity table with a bottle of French perfume, a bowl of hairpins and a small box of ribbons. Her bed was a very feminine, frilly affair with lacy pillows and ruffles, and it struck her that she had no idea where she'd be sleeping next. A roadside inn, most likely. The only thing she knew for certain was that Liam would be with her.

The very idea of sleeping beside Liam caused her cheeks to flush with heat. She'd be a married woman soon, but she knew almost nothing about relations between a husband and wife. Once, after she'd become engaged to Finley, Cora's nanny gave her a strange lecture about suffering a man's baser nature and a woman's duty to remain still and quiet and endure for God and country. She had no idea what any of it meant, but she figured Liam would know. He knew everything about the world. And she couldn't wait to experience everything with him.

Cora buttoned her wool traveling coat and picked up her bag. With a final look back, she shed her old bedroom like a butterfly emerging from a cocoon. Making her way silently toward freedom, she was careful not to put too much weight on her sore ankle as she crept down the stairs. She'd bound her ankle with strips of cloth, which helped, and she'd already vowed that no matter what, she wouldn't tell Liam about her mishap. He was so protective of her, she was afraid he'd cancel their plans, and he'd already spent so much time and money arranging everything.

Slinking past the drawing room, she took the side door into

the garden and made her way toward the stables, doing her best to shield her head from the rain. The moon cast deep shadows on the path, and the wet mud slowed her pace, but excitement and determination urged her on until she saw the faint glow of a lantern through the stable window. The comforting smell of horses, leather and warm hay enveloped her the moment she stepped inside. A horse snuffled in the far stall, and another horse perked its head up when she drew closer.

"Cora," Liam whispered from the shadows. "You walked here alone? I was just coming to get you."

She grinned as he swept her into his arms. "I couldn't wait. Are the horses ready?"

"Aye, are you?" He held her face gently in his hands, rubbing a thumb over her cheek.

Cora swallowed past the lump in her throat. As excited as she was to go, she was suddenly overwhelmed with the reality that she'd never see her home or father again. "I am."

"You're sad," he murmured, looking deep into her eyes. "Are you certain you want to do this?"

"Yes, of course." Overcome with nerves, she searched his face. "You haven't changed your mind, have you?"

A low, rumbling chuckle vibrated through Liam's chest. "Wild horses couldn't drag me away from this adventure with you." He dropped a kiss on top of her head. "I want to go very much, but if you changed your mind right now, I'd say to hell with the plans. I only want to be wherever you are, *macushla*."

In the glow of lamplight, Cora drank in the sight of him. All her sadness about leaving fell away, because all that mattered was their being together. From now on they'd always have each other. Liam was her future. "I love you, Liam."

He brushed her nose with his. "And I, you."

They quietly led the horses from the stable. Cora's was a dappled gray mare named Merry, who nickered softly in the moonlight. The sweet horse was getting on in years, but she was a gentle soul, and Cora loved her. Liam took her father's black horse, Vulcan. He was a gorgeous creature in his prime, and could be a bit temperamental, but he was perfect for Liam. Once they arrived at the next village to take the coach to the coast, they'd leave the horses with a stable boy at the inn. Liam had arranged for the boy to bring the horses back to her father, which comforted Cora. She knew her father would never come after her for horse thievery, no matter how upset he was, but Liam was a different matter. More important, she truly cared for the horses and would've hated to abandon them so far from home.

"Wait, you're limping," Liam said sharply behind her. "Are you not well?"

Cora squeezed her eyes shut. She couldn't lie to him, even if she wanted to. He always saw right through her. "I only turned it on the stairs this morning. It's already feeling better than it did earlier."

"Cora, it's not safe to ride if you're injured." He bent to study her wrapped ankle. Then he looked up at her quizzically. "When were you planning to tell me?"

She chewed her bottom lip for a moment. "Never?"

Liam gave her a look that was so stern, he reminded her of her father. A frustrated prickle of annoyance overtook her. "Cora—"

"I am perfectly fine, Liam O'Connor, and I'm not stopping now. If you try to hold me back, I will go on ahead without you. Just watch me." Cora's hand flew to her mouth. Good Lord, where had that come from? She looked almost as surprised at her outburst as he did. Blinking rapidly, she was unsure of what to say next. Should she apologize? *No.* She wasn't sorry. She meant what she said, and it felt...*good* to stretch her wings. She was free of the rules and trappings of her old life. She began to smile with the realization.

Suddenly, Liam surprised her more when he threw his head back and laughed. He stifled the sound of it, since they were aiming for stealth, but his shoulders shook, and his eyes sparkled with deep admiration. "Captain Cora, you are a vision when you're like this. Adventure suits you. I'm afraid I'll be at your mercy for the rest of my days, and I'll be a luckier devil for it."

Still chuckling, he gripped her by the waist and lifted her into the sidesaddle. "You'd have far more control if you rode astride, you know."

"I've never ridden anything but sidesaddle," she said in surprise. "I once pondered aloud what it would be like to ride astride with trousers, and my poor nanny almost keeled over from apoplexy. She said only women of ill repute would consider such a thing."

"Polite society is filled with silly rules, and that is one of them," Liam said wryly. "Your nanny won't be telling you what to do anymore, so from this day forth, you shall do as you please." Liam smiled up at her as he gently helped place her injured foot, taking extra care with her ankle. Then he swung onto Vulcan, and they left her old life behind.

Cora cast a last look over her shoulder as they left the edge of her father's land. The large house was a deep smudge of shadow against the night sky, with only the single candle shining from her bedroom window. It was a bleak reminder of how dark her life had become. When her mother was still alive, the place had been full of music and laughter and friends. But over the years everything had fallen into neglect, including Cora. She'd often felt like a lone candle, flickering hopelessly within all that gloom. The night Liam first climbed through her bedroom window, he'd shone like the sun, with his roguish smile and sparkling, expressive eyes. He was the one glowing light in her otherwise dreary existence, and now they were headed toward a brighter future. With a final, silent goodbye, Cora turned her back on her old life and faced the future.

"When we get to the main road, we'll need to pick up our pace," Liam said as they rode across the open field toward the highway. The rain had slowed to a steady drizzle, and the horses' hooves made squelching sounds in the wet mud. "They'll discover you gone by morning, so we've only the night hours to make it to the next village before they send out a search party."

"What about your family?" Cora asked. "Will they be looking for you, too?"

"No." Liam's face looked bleak in the moonlight. "I've always come and gone at odd hours. They'll think nothing of my absence for at least a day or two."

They reached the main road, and soon they were moving at a fast clip along the highway. It was darker now, with the forest trees looming on either side, but the horses seemed to know the way.

Suddenly, two huge shadows on horseback appeared on the road ahead of them.

"Halt," one of them shouted.

Liam jerked his horse to a stop, and Cora did the same. Her horse danced nervously underneath her, and she struggled to remain steady.

"We've no time for this. Stand aside and let us pass." Liam motioned for Cora to stay behind him as he maneuvered his horse forward.

"Not until you pay the toll," one of them growled.

The shadows came closer and Cora saw two hulking men in ragged clothes atop sturdy farm horses. The men were identical, with wide shoulders, thick arms and menacing faces.

"Well, well," one of them said in a raspy voice. "Fancy meeting his highness at this hour."

"With such a pretty companion," the other one said, eyeing Cora. She cringed and drew her horse closer to Liam. The rain was cold, but it was nothing compared to the stranger's expression. It chilled her to the bone.

"Stay back, both of you," Liam said in a voice she'd never heard before. He sounded as frightening as they looked. Cora was suddenly glad to have Liam on her side.

"Still feeling uppity, eh, O'Connor?" the man said. "We've always shared the spoils before."

"And plenty spoiled she looks, too." The other one leered. "A fancy bit of skirt."

"Touch one hair on her head, and you'll regret it," Liam said icily.

One of them scoffed. "You think you're better than us now, but you're nothing." They looked dangerous enough to kill, and it was clear they had a history with Liam. Cora knew Liam was a thief who stole from the rich to give to the poor, but she'd never stopped to think if he was part of a band of thieves, like Robin Hood. In her mind what he did was noble and just, but these two men appeared to be the exact opposite.

"Get out of the way," Liam demanded. His horse sidestepped nervously as the men came closer. "This is none of your concern."

"Wait, what's this?" One of the men squinted at Cora like he was trying to bring her into focus.

She instinctively drew her hood down over her face, but it was too late.

"That's the squire's daughter," the man said in astonishment.

His twin shoved a wet clump of hair from his face, trying to get a better look at her. To Liam, he said, "And where might you be headed with such a pretty piece in the dead of night?"

"I'm escorting her to a relative's house." Liam paused, then reached into his pocket and tossed two gold coins into the dirt at their horses' feet. "Go buy yourselves some ale and be on your way."

The man shook his head, and Cora had a sinking feeling in the pit of her stomach. "Going to cost you more gold than that, O'Connor. Seeing as we're not *friends* anymore."

Liam leaned closer to Cora and whispered, "We're taking to the trees. Follow me when I give the signal and stay close. Can you do that for me?"

Cora blinked rapidly, her heart pounding in her chest as she stared into the dark forest. She'd never gone off the path before. The idea of what could be lurking in the darkness was almost as terrifying as the two men blocking them now.

"Cora." Liam whispered her name, and she dragged her gaze back to him. "You're stronger and braver than you know. You can do this." Liam gave her an encouraging half smile, and that was all she needed to fortify her resolve. This was the man she loved. She'd follow him to the ends of the earth.

One of the men hurled a string of curse words at them.

Liam's voice grew low and urgent. "Promise me you'll stay right behind me, no matter what. *Promise.*"

"Yes." She gripped her reins. "I'm ready when you are."

In the next heartbeat Liam dug his heels into Vulcan's sides and yelled. The horse bolted forward with Cora's poor mare doing her best to follow. Instead of racing forward to bypass the two men on the road, Liam charged straight into the woods.

Wet branches slapped at Cora from all sides. She gripped the saddle and stayed low over Merry's neck as she followed him through the thick foliage.

Angry shouts came from behind them, and Cora could hear the two men giving chase.

The forest was dense, and it was difficult to keep a fast pace, but somehow her horse managed to stay close behind Liam. He called over his shoulder, urging her on and shouting encouragement.

She gripped the reins and flattened herself against Merry's neck, praying her horse could keep up with Vulcan as they crossed a shallow stream.

A shot rang out behind them, and suddenly Liam yelled, *"Faster now!"*

Cora dug her heel, ignoring the sharp twinge of pain in her ankle. She closed her eyes and tried to shield her face with one arm. The scent of rain, wet earth and leaf mold filled every breath as she clung to Merry's back.

The sound of the angry men's shouts grew fainter once they crossed the stream.

Hope surged in Cora's chest. "I think we're losing them!" The forest floor was rife with fallen logs and damp foliage, and the two men's larger farm horses weren't nimble enough to navigate in the dark. She was just grateful Liam knew his way, and she prayed her old horse could hang on a bit longer.

"Keep going!" Liam shouted. "We're almost to the field on the other side." He called to Vulcan, urging him onward.

The path dipped at a sharp angle, and Merry stumbled.

Cora gripped her horse's mane with both hands. She tried to steady herself in the saddle, reflexively bearing down on her left foot. Her ankle wrenched sideways, and she cried out.

"Cora!" Liam jerked on Vulcan's reins, pulling his horse around.

Merry lurched to an abrupt stop before a fallen log.

Cora lost her grip and flew over the horse's neck. She was suddenly airborne, with no way to break her fall. There was no time to think, or even scream. She hit the ground in a tangle of skirts and limbs and rocky earth. A sharp, hot pain cracked across the back of her head, and then she lay still.

"No!" Liam cried. "Oh, God, *macushla*. Open your eyes. Cora, can you hear me?" Liam was on the ground beside her, shaking her and calling her name.

She couldn't seem to open her eyes, but she saw their future stretched before them—traveling the ocean, the home, the babies, the golden years. She wanted to tell him she loved him, and not to worry because everything was going to be okay.

He was holding her close now, whispering words she couldn't hear anymore, but she could still feel his warm breath on her cheek, and the pressure of his strong arms around her.

It was dark, and so very cold, but they were together, and that was all that mattered. The pain in her head faded away, and Cora exhaled a soft sigh.

26

Providence Falls,
Present Day

IT WAS DARK. CORA WAS ONLY VAGUELY AWARE
of a loud splash above her. Then another. Suddenly, strong arms
gripped her, yanking her up and hauling her onto the dock.

Liam was holding her in his arms. She was unable to open
her eyes, but she'd recognize that Irish accent anywhere. Relief
flooded her because it meant she was safe. But he was angry.
He was yelling something at her. She just wanted to close her
eyes and rest, but he kept shaking her. Suddenly, he rolled her
to her side and thumped her hard on the back. Once. Twice.

Cora's lungs heaved and then she was coughing, gasping and
choking on slimy water. Strands of wet hair clung to her face,
obscuring her vision. She cracked her eyes open and could just
make out Liam's broad shoulders as he loomed over her.

"Cora!" he shouted. "Holy mother of God, *macushla*. Are you
okay? Speak to me!"

When she'd stopped coughing, she weakly rasped, "Liam."

"Yes! Yes, I'm right here, love. You're going to be okay now.
I'm here." He leaned closer until she could feel the warmth

from his body through her wet clothes. They were almost nose to nose, and his breath was coming in sharp gasps. Liam was cradling her head, gripping it almost too tightly in his haste to assure himself she was okay. The look on his face was that of a broken, haunted man. A man who was terrified to lose her.

Cora reached up weakly, cupping his cheeks in her hands. "Liam, I was wrong."

"Shh, don't talk," he said hoarsely, pressing her hands hard into his face, as if trying to assure himself she was there with him.

"I was wrong before," she said in a voice barely above a whisper. "You're nothing like him. You're a good man." Then she pulled his head down and pressed her freezing lips to his.

Liam's entire body jerked in surprise. Cora didn't care if she'd shocked him. All she cared about was driving out all the wrong things that had happened tonight with something that felt so effortlessly *right*.

He pulled back on a hitched breath, staring down at her with glittering eyes. He opened his mouth to say something, but she didn't want to hear words. She didn't care if this was unreasonable. Cora drew him closer and kissed him again. This time he melted into her and kissed her back, wrapping one powerful arm under her shoulders and pulling her closer. His lips were soft and warm and so familiar, like a favorite song she'd forgotten how to sing until exactly this moment. Something sparked in the back of her mind, a fragment of a memory or a dream. They'd kissed like this before, with the wind in their hair and the full moon shining above them. The image was so vivid, yet so fleeting. She wanted to grab fistfuls of the dream and yank it back to her. Hold it close. Instead, she grabbed fistfuls of Liam's shirt, and reveled in the feel of his hard chest pressing into hers. The warmth of his hand gently cradling the back of her head. The featherlight brush of his mouth over her lips, her eyelids, her forehead.

Liam slowly pulled back, his face racked with sadness and regret. He gripped her hand tightly. "Cora, lie still. You need to rest. I'm here now. Everything's going to be okay."

"I'm not sorry," she whispered.

"For what?"

She closed her eyes. "The kiss. Thank you for saving me."

He started to speak, but a loud shout and more splashing came from the water.

Cora turned her head and saw two dark shadows break the surface—Magnus and someone else. The lake house's outdoor lighting system automatically switched on, and suddenly there was enough ambient light for her to recognize the other man clearly. Finn's face was granite hard as he struggled with Magnus. He started to drag him toward the dock, but Magnus caught him in a chokehold and they both went under again.

"Finn," she gasped, trying to rise.

"Don't move," Liam commanded, gripping her shoulders. "Finn's got him."

Suddenly, Finn burst through the surface and swam toward the dock, dragging the struggling Magnus behind him. Hooking a leg over the edge, Finn pulled himself up with one arm, still holding Magnus with the other. Liam helped haul Finn out of the water. Together, they dragged Magnus onto the dock.

Magnus coughed and sputtered, then jumped to his feet and started to run, but Finn leaped in front of him with a surprising burst of speed. Or, it might've been surprising to anyone else, but Cora had seen him do it before.

Magnus wound his arm back to punch Finn.

Finn dodged his swing, pivoted and punched Magnus so fast, she almost missed it.

Magnus crumpled to the dock.

"Game's over." Finn's shoulders and chest heaved with exertion, and his wet clothes molded to his body. With his stark, cold expression, he looked more like The Jackrabbit than ever.

"*Jesus, Mary and Joseph*, man," Liam said in shock and admiration. "Where'd you learn to hit like that?"

Finn pressed his lips into a grim line. "You don't want to know."

Sirens in the distance snapped Cora out of her daze. She tried to sit up, but Liam kept his large hand firmly on her shoulder.

Finn knelt beside her, his expression tight with worry and fear. "Are you okay?"

"Yes," she whispered. "I'd be a lot better if I weren't lying here soaking wet, freezing my butt off." The two men exchanged an amused look. An ambulance and three police cars broke through the trees and parked around Finn's car.

"Stay with her while I go talk to them," Liam said to Finn.

Cora bristled. She wasn't going to just lie around when there were things to do. She struggled to rise again, but they each kept a hand on her shoulders. Annoyed they were treating her like an invalid, she scowled. "I am perfectly—"

"Aye, we know you're capable of handling yourself and every situation that comes your way," Liam said in irritation. "You're a corker, and everyone knows it. But for the love of God, woman. Just this once, can you let other people take care of you?" Liam didn't wait for a reply. He rose to his feet and strode toward the police.

Cora looked to Finn, but he was no help. It was obvious he and Liam were together on this. She gave up and lowered her head to the dock. "Fine, but just this once." She'd never admit it, but she did feel a bit woozy.

Finn smiled softly. "You're safe now."

She swallowed hard, suddenly wanting to cry. It was ridiculous, and it made no sense. She was a police officer, for heaven's sake. Tough situations came with the territory. But the night had taken a toll, and she'd been so scared when the water closed over her head. She turned away from Finn's understanding gaze, wishing she could blink out of existence and reappear in her bedroom with Angel and her favorite quilt and a cup of cinnamon orange herbal tea.

She struggled to get her emotions under control and said, "Is Magnus still out?"

"Yes. Liam cuffed him, so even if he wakes up, he won't go far." Finn surprised her by gently stroking the wet hair from her eyes. "You did really well tonight, Cora. There's no telling how far he'd have gone."

"I tried to get away on the boat, but he—"

"I saw." He looked livid, like he wanted to punch Magnus all over again.

"You can take another swing at him even though he's knocked out," Cora said with a weak smile. "I won't tell if you don't."

"Don't tempt me," Finn said angrily. "Only a true bastard would hit someone smaller and weaker than himself."

"Who are you calling weak?" she asked halfheartedly.

"Not you," he assured her. "Never you." With a featherlike stroke, he brushed his fingertips over the spot Magnus hit. Cora suspected she was going to have a black eye in the morning. "You're brave and stronger than most people I know. I saw you hand it to him right before you both fell in the water. You really know how to pack a punch."

"Not as good as The Jackrabbit," she whispered.

Finn smiled down at her. "Oh, I don't know. I think you could give him a run for his money."

"As long as he doesn't piss me off, he'll never have to find out." Cora tried to look tough, but she knew it was futile.

"He's very sorry if he made you angry," Finn said in earnest.

"When are you going to tell me how you got tangled up with the Booze—"

"Out of the way, sir." A man strode toward them with a paramedic kit. Behind him were two other paramedics wheeling a stretcher.

"Looks like your chariot has arrived," Finn said.

Cora wanted to protest, but she knew it would be useless. Between Finn's solid presence and Liam's fierce persistence, there was no getting out of this. She was cold, wet, hungry and so tired, she could barely keep her eyes open. The paramedics took over, with Liam and Finn standing shoulder to shoulder, watching over her. They were like two sentinels guarding her, ready for battle. *Her warriors.* The thought almost made her smile. Liam and Finn were as different as night and day, but she felt safe knowing they were there.

Maybe just this once it was okay to be the damsel who needed rescuing. Cora entertained the thought for exactly three seconds. Nah, who was she kidding? The only reason she hadn't given Magnus's unconscious body a good kick was because she barely had the strength to lift her head. But soon, that would change. For now the guys could take care of her, but when she got back to normal, Magnus was going to pay.

═══════════════════════════

27

ON THURSDAY LIAM SAT IN THE INTERROGATION room and watched Cora rake Magnus Blackwell across the coals. Even though Magnus was a high-powered attorney and had no problem deflecting her accusations with his sullen arrogance, Cora never faltered. It was a thing of beauty to witness.

Magnus's clothes were wrinkled, he hadn't shaved and with dark circles under his eyes and a swollen nose, he looked like the worst kind of vagabond. For once, his sheep's clothing had slipped to reveal the wolf underneath. Liam wanted to crow at the top of his lungs with satisfaction, but this was Cora's moment, so he watched her go for it. Magnus hadn't admitted to anything yet, but it was just a matter of time.

"You can play the innocent all day long, Mr. Blackwell," Cora said calmly. There was a dark bruise on her cheekbone and around her eye, but she still managed to look cool and unruffled. Liam couldn't have been more impressed than he was in that moment. She was magnificent. "But we know you took the money. You even offered to share it with me."

"I don't recall that."

Cora gave him a scathing look. "That money was part of

the same stash we found in Lindsey Albright's locker, after she was murdered. As far as I can see, you're the missing link to her death."

Magnus scoffed. "That's a pretty big jump to a conclusion with no evidence to back it up."

"A smarter man would just get on with it, and tell us what we need to know, so we can all stop wasting each other's time." She pushed the notepad and pen toward him. "Could be the difference between life and death."

"You think you know so much, but you're clueless," Magnus said with a sneer. "I'm embarrassed on your behalf."

Liam wanted to drag the man out to the parking lot and settle things with his fists. Cora broke his nose. Finn knocked him out. It was only fair he got a turn. "The game is over, Magnus, and you've lost. You're in no position of power, so I'd advise you to watch your tongue," he said.

"Keep your advice for someone stupid enough to value it," Magnus said with exaggerated boredom. He leaned back in his chair and checked the clock on the wall. "In fact, I'm done wasting my breath. My legal counsel will be arriving soon. I've nothing further to say to you." He flicked his fingers at both of them. "Run along."

Someone rapped on the two-way mirror. Boyd. It had surprised Liam that the captain didn't want to lead the interrogation, but he knew Boyd was up to his neck dealing with the press and the mayor's office. Every day that passed he looked more exhausted and anxious.

Liam and Cora joined Boyd out in the hallway. He looked as gruff as he always did, but this time there was a weariness etched into the fine lines of his face that made it seem as though he hadn't slept in days. "That was a waste of time."

"I know he hasn't admitted to it, Captain," Cora began. "But we feel there's a strong possibility Magnus killed Lindsey. We'll get it out of him."

"How many times do I have to tell you, McLeod? I'm not interested in what you *feel*. I'm interested in the facts."

"The man has it in him," Liam said flatly. He kept envisioning the scene at the lake as if he was watching everything play out in slow motion all over again. Magnus hauling his arm back and hitting Cora. Both of them falling into the water. Magnus breaking the surface for air. Cora lost in the murky depths. Every image was like a snapshot in his mind he'd never be able to forget. Just thinking about it made his heart race and his limbs feel shaky. Though Cora said she didn't believe attempted murder was Magnus's goal that night, Liam had no problem believing it. Perhaps Magnus hadn't planned it, but he'd been visibly furious. There was no telling what he could've done to Cora in the heat of the moment. Magnus could've very easily killed Lindsey Albright, especially if she'd attempted to blow his cover and shatter the carefully concocted illusion he'd built around himself.

The door to the interrogation room opened, and the guard began escorting Magnus back to his holding cell.

Magnus smirked at Cora. "You had a chance to run with the big dogs, and you chose this?" He gestured to the bare hallway and cramped room, then gave a mirthless chuckle.

Liam stepped into his personal space and said, "You may think this is all very amusing, but I doubt you'll be laughing when they haul you off to prison."

Magnus looked unruffled. His gaze darted between Liam and Cora, then settled on Boyd. "I won't go down for this." The guard led him around the corner until all they could hear was Magnus shouting, "I didn't kill anyone, and you know it. You even try to pin this on me, you won't like what happens."

"Recap in my office after lunch," Boyd told them before striding away.

Cora blew out a breath. "Well, that was an exercise in futility."

"Magnus is a piece of work, but you did well in there," Liam told her as they headed back to the pen. "I enjoyed watching him squirm."

"I did, too," she admitted. "But I'll enjoy everything a lot more once he's behind bars for good."

It wasn't hard for Liam to convince Cora to have lunch with him at The Rusty Spoon. They both needed a break, and the restaurant's lively atmosphere was a much-appreciated reprieve after dealing with Magnus.

They were sitting outside enjoying the sunshine, and Liam was thoroughly savoring his barbecue burger, when Cora suddenly put her fork down and said, "Are we going to talk about the elephant in the room?"

Burger halfway to his mouth, Liam stopped and stared uneasily at his sandwich. "Elephant?"

"The kiss," Cora said.

Liam's eyes flew wide, and he fumbled with his napkin. "Ah. That." What was he going to say? That it didn't matter, and it was an accident? That he felt nothing for her? All of that would be a lie. He knew he should never have done it, but *she* had kissed *him*. Only a saint could've resisted, and heaven knew he was no saint. "What about it?"

She looked down at her hands folded on the table. "I just wanted to say I'm sorry if I made you uncomfortable."

Uncomfortable? God, yes, but not in a bad way. If she only knew how many times he'd replayed that moment, wanting to feel her lips on his again. And again. "I didn't mind," he managed. "Emotions were high, and you'd almost drowned."

Cora looked troubled. "Yes, I suppose it's common to resort to physical affirmations after one suffers through a potentially life-threatening ordeal." If she was trying to convince herself this was the reason she'd kissed him, she didn't appear to be doing a very good job of it.

"Yes to all that," Liam said, though he knew it wasn't that simple.

"But Liam…" A deep blush crept over her cheeks. She wasn't at ease with this topic, but she soldiered on, because that was the type of woman she was. Fearless. "I can't explain it, but sometimes when we're together, it just seems like… Like we belong together. It just feels so comfortable and easy." She shook her head and gave a nervous laugh. "I must sound crazy to you."

"No." He swallowed hard. "No, I understand what you mean."

"Do you?" The hopeful, shy smile she gave him tore at his heart. "Do you feel the same way?"

This was the part where he could reel her in. Play the game and secure her affections for himself. This was everything he'd ever wanted with her, and for the first time since he came to Providence Falls, she finally wanted him back. But the angels' warning came back to haunt him. Cora's lives always ended in tragedy, and the only way to fix that was if Cora and Finn ended up together. Even if Liam didn't understand why, he still recognized their union was part of a divine plan much bigger than himself. How did he compete with something of that magnitude?

The answer was simple. *He couldn't.* He was sent here to do the right thing. Liam's heart felt as if it were ripping at the edges. His stomach sank, and he braced himself for what he needed to do. He was suddenly so very angry. His conscience had never troubled him before. When the hell had he decided to become a bloody good person?

"Are you mad?" Cora asked uncertainly. "I'm sorry if I—"

"I'm not mad at you, *macushla*," he said gruffly. "Only at myself."

Cora's smooth brow wrinkled in confusion. "What is that word? You've called me that before. It's so familiar to me, yet I have no idea what it means."

If his heart was ripped before, then this was going to tear it clean in half. He cleared his throat. "It's a term of fondness."

Understatement. "Like, *my dear.* That sort of thing." *Lie, lie, lie.* Maybe he wasn't such a good man after all, if he could still lie so easily to the only woman he'd ever loved. But he couldn't admit to her that she was the "pulse of his heart." Not if he was going to reject her right afterward.

"My dear," she repeated. "Good to know."

Liam took a deep breath, pushing his plate away. The knot in his stomach killed his appetite. He gathered himself together, looked her straight in the eyes—because she deserved his full attention, especially at a time like this—and told her what she needed to hear. "Cora, that night after I pulled you from the water and you kissed me, you said you weren't sorry. It's important that you know I wasn't, either. Both of us were high on adrenaline and fear, and it *did* feel like the right thing to do."

She smiled, and he tried to commit that to memory. Because what he was about to do was going to crush her almost as much as it crushed him. "But I don't think it's the right thing for us, going forward."

The light dimmed in her eyes, and she glanced away self-consciously. "You don't."

"What I mean is I'm not the right man for you." God, why did that hurt so much to say? Because it was a truth he could no longer escape? He pushed through the pain and continued. "I think you're the most wonderful, special person I've ever—"

"Liam…" Cora held a hand up, and tried to laugh. "Please don't give me the whole 'It's not you, it's me' speech. If you aren't interested, it's fine."

"It's not that," he said in frustration. "If I could, I'd sweep you up right now and carry you off to a place no one could ever find us. I'd shower you with cottages and riches and every seashell on the face of this earth."

She tilted her head in confusion. "Seashells?"

"Whatever would make you happy," he said fiercely. "Whatever you've always wanted… I'd give it to you if I could."

"What if I didn't need any of that, and I just wanted to see where this could lead?" she asked in a small voice.

Liam briefly squeezed his eyes shut. "Even if all you wanted was something as insignificant and undeserving as me, I'd do everything in my power... I'd wait lifetimes, just to be with you. But it isn't that simple."

"Why not?" she challenged, folding her arms.

He almost smiled, because he dearly loved this feisty side of her. If only he could reach across the table, drag her into his lap and hold on and never let her go. "Because we all have a path to follow, and ours doesn't run side by side. It only intersects for a very short time. Do you understand?"

Cora frowned. "Are you planning on leaving?"

God, there was the question for the ages. "I wish to never leave Providence Falls." *And you.* But he didn't get to have what he wanted. "Cora, I love living with you and working with you. It's been the highlight of my life here. But I think it would complicate things too much if we took it further." At least that was the truth, though the complications were far more dire than she'd ever know.

"So you don't feel this thing...between us?" she asked hesitantly, searching his face.

"That's not what I said." He felt everything for her. That was the problem.

She chewed on her lower lip for a moment. "You're afraid if we got together and things didn't work out, it would make our living situation difficult and ruin what we have now."

"Yes." Because in a roundabout way, it was the truth.

"You do realize our living situation will change at the end of the summer?"

He nodded, because she wasn't wrong. He had one more month to save his immortal soul. If he didn't succeed, his living situation would go from peace, love and a comfortable home to flames, pitchforks and rivers of fire.

"My dream cottage—the one I've loved since I was a little girl—is going on the market next month," Cora continued. "I'm putting an offer on it, and if all goes well, I'll be moving out. We won't live together anymore. We'll only work together, and partners get shifted around at the station all the time. Now that you've settled into the job, the captain will probably pair you up with another officer in the next month or so."

"It's possible," Liam said. But it wouldn't matter, because he'd be long gone by then.

Cora sighed. "These past two months at work have been incredibly hard on everyone. And then of course, I've had my own personal dating disasters, Magnus being the worst." She rubbed a hand over her eyes. "God, I can't understand what I ever saw in him. I meant what I said on the dock the other night. I was wrong about you. The two of you are nothing alike. He's selfish and manipulative, and possibly even a murderer. You're a far better man than he could ever be."

Liam glanced away because it was too hard to look at her. She was being so sincere, and he didn't deserve such high regard. Magnus and he were cut from the same cloth. If Cora only knew how he'd manipulated and schemed and stolen in his past life, she'd never say these things now. But this world had changed him, and he didn't want to be that person anymore. Unfortunately, it was too little, too late.

"I've begun to realize how much I trust and rely on you," she continued. "Someone once told me whenever you experience things in your life, whether it's joy or sorrow, consider who the first person is you want to tell. That's the person who means the most to you. And for me, that person seems to be you. If I hear something funny, I want to share it with you right away. If something bad happens, I seek you out first because you're always there to listen and offer solutions. I… I care for you, Liam. That's all."

"And I, you." He had no other declarations to give her. If he opened his mouth to say how much he loved her, he'd never stop, and he'd probably scare her with the intensity of his feelings. "But right now I don't want to risk what we have. I might seem like the right man for you, but there could be someone out there who's much better than me. The odds are extremely good, considering it's me we're talking about."

Cora didn't look amused, or convinced, but she let it slide. "I guess we'll have to see what happens in a month if I get my cottage. Who knows? Maybe you'll miss me desperately when I'm gone."

"I'm certain I will." Hell, he missed her already. A hundred thousand years could pass, and he'd still feel this deep, yearning ache for her. It had taken up a permanent residence in his heart, right alongside the sweet sound of her laughter.

―――――――――――――――

28

THE ATMOSPHERE AT THE PROVIDENCE FALLS PO-
lice station felt much lighter than it had for the past few weeks,
and Liam was glad of it. Mavis was chirpier than usual, and she'd
even added a second candy bowl to the reception desk. Finding
the Booze Dogs' stolen money and capturing Magnus seemed
to be just the pick-me-up everyone needed. While they still
had the unsolved murders of John Brady and Lindsey Albright
hanging over them, it was encouraging to know they'd made
some forward progress.

Rob Hopper waved at Liam and Cora when they walked
into the pen. He was holding the phone away from his ear. *Mrs.
Wilson*, he mouthed, rolling his eyes and lowering his head to
his desk.

"Poppy seed muffin?" Otto gestured to a pink-and-white-
striped box in front of him, his doughy face cheerful as always.
"Freshly baked from Sugar Pie's."

Still unsettled from his conversation with Cora, Liam couldn't
bring himself to accept. "Any news from forensics?"

"Inconclusive," Happy said sourly. He checked his watch and

gathered a gym bag under his desk. "There's speculation some- one placed it under Blackwell's bed to frame him."

Cora let out a derisive huff. "Please tell me that's not the angle he's taking."

"It's looking that way," Happy said. "He claims he had no idea where the money came from. He's also hinted he may have information to trade for a deal."

"Magnus offered to share the money with me," Cora said in exasperation. "If that's not enough information that he was in- volved in the theft, then I don't know what is."

"No, he may have information about the *murders*," Otto ex- plained, lifting a muffin and peeling back the paper lining. "But we don't know for sure. He's mostly keeping his mouth shut, and his attorney is being very vague."

"If that snake thinks he can slither his way out of serving jail time, he can think again," Cora said heatedly.

"The problem is he's got friends in high places, and a pow- erful law firm on his side." Happy grabbed his car keys off his desk. "He's going to make this as difficult for us as he can. Any- way, I'm off to lunch."

"At two o'clock?" Otto asked.

"Some of us prefer to prioritize work over food, Otto. Late lunches are the result of that." Happy checked his watch again and hurried out of the pen.

"Where do you suppose he goes?" Otto chewed thoughtfully as he watched his partner leave.

Cora took a seat at her desk. "Probably Munchie's Drive- Thru."

"That's not what I meant," Otto said. "At least once or twice a week, ever since the summer started, Happy leaves at exactly two o'clock with that bag from under his desk."

"Maybe it's a change of clothes for the gym." Liam grimaced at the memory of Kick Start Fitness. "Not that I'd ever be caught dead in a place like that, but I saw many people there with similar bags."

"I wouldn't know," Otto said around another mouthful of muffin. "But I suppose you could be right."

"Or maybe he has a standing date with a lady friend," Liam offered. Though he couldn't imagine many women being drawn to Happy. He was the grumpiest man at the station, not including Boyd.

"But then, why take a change of clothes?"

"I can think of a few reasons," Rob said, wiggling his eyebrows. He'd just hung up the phone with Mrs. Wilson, and already he looked happier.

"No one wants to hear your reasons, Hopper," Cora said, her attention on her computer screen. "Keep them to yourself."

"You sure? I've got some pretty good ones," Rob said with a laugh.

"Spare me. I just had lunch."

Boyd's office door opened, then slammed shut again. Liam looked to the windows, but Boyd had closed the blinds. The sound of a woman's angry voice came from within.

"His wife, Alice," Otto stage whispered. "She came in right before you two did, looking like she was on the warpath. Poor Captain Thompson. Seems like he's got trouble from all sides. I heard him saying something about credit card bills, and then she went nuclear on him."

Liam raised his brows. Poor Boyd, indeed. This modern-day version of Alice may look more polished now, but she was still the same woman who'd heckled her husband back in Liam's old life. Alice had been a pretty woman who'd been very affectionate with the men. For a short time Boyd had secured her full attention. He'd promised her the world, and she'd fallen for it. They'd wed young, but Alice quickly became disenchanted with Boyd's boastful attitude and lack of fortune. Though Boyd hadn't often talked about his marriage, Liam knew they'd had problems. Unfortunately for Boyd, he was no luckier in this life than the last.

Liam could hear Alice's shrill voice rising over Boyd's angry, clipped tones.

The office door swung open again, and Alice came *click-clacking* out on patent leather stilettos. In a fitted dress, dark sunglasses, with a red clutch tucked under one arm, she was as eye-catching as a shiny red fire engine. Otto waved to her, but she ignored him, bypassing everyone in the pen, including—thank goodness—Liam. Within seconds she was down the hall and out the door, but the spicy perfume she'd been wearing still lingered in the air.

Boyd opened the blinds to his office again, and everyone pretended to be hard at work. Even Liam didn't want to look at the man, knowing from experience that Boyd would be in a devil of a mood.

Unfortunately, he shouted, "McLeod! O'Connor!"

Liam and Cora exchanged a look before heading into Boyd's office.

"Sit," Boyd said angrily. His face was red, and his hair stuck up in tufts from running his fingers through it. "The forensics report came back, and Magnus Blackwell's prints were nowhere on that bag or the money."

"So maybe he wore gloves," Cora said. "That doesn't mean he didn't do it. He offered to share it with me if I agreed to look the other way."

"Other than the appearance of the bag under his bed, there's no concrete evidence he stole it," Boyd said. "It's your word against his, and he's denying it."

"Captain," Cora said, shocked. "You don't believe me?"

"It doesn't matter what I believe. My point is this doesn't look good on paper. You were dating him. You two had a lover's quarrel—"

"They were not lovers," Liam interrupted.

Boyd glared at him. "O'Connor, your track record in this department isn't squeaky clean, so forgive me if I don't take your word on this." It was true; Liam had lied about his affair with Margaret Brady. It had been a blow to everyone working on her husband's murder case when they found out he'd kept it from them. Even though Cora had forgiven him for withholding information, Liam was certain Boyd still held a grudge.

"Take my word, then," Cora said in a tone Liam had never seen her use on Boyd. "I was not in a romantic relationship with Magnus Blackwell. We went on a couple of dates, but before things went further, I decided to break things off with him."

"They were mere acquaintances, at best," Liam insisted.

"Be that as it may, Cora was dating him. Then she found money on his premises, as evidenced by her fingerprints on the bag. They argued and got into a scuffle."

"The bastard *hit* her," Liam growled. "She almost drowned."

"He's claiming self-defense," Boyd said. "She's a police officer, yes, but her word against his won't hold as much weight in court because they were in a relationship. It will call her credibility into question. Magnus says he was set up, and someone framed him. He's got the power of Johnston & Knight behind him because, whether or not they believe him, their reputation is at stake. Since Magnus has never had a record before this, I don't like him for the theft, or Lindsey's murder. I'd say there's a good chance someone at that motorcycle club is behind it."

"Captain, Magnus is in on it," Cora said. "You should've seen his face. He wasn't even shocked or surprised when I found it under his bed. He tried to pay me off!"

Boyd appeared unmoved. "I've already heard your report. There's no need to keep repeating yourself. It's your word against his, and right now I want you to stop focusing on Magnus and start focusing in the *right* direction."

"The Booze Dogs?" Cora scoffed and rose stiffly from her

chair. "Forgive me, Captain, but I think you're wrong about this."

Liam was impressed at all the attitude she was throwing right now. Once again, he was filled with pride for this beautiful, brilliant, headstrong woman. Cora was convinced Magnus was the criminal, and she wasn't going to stand down without a fight, even if her captain didn't agree. Liam loved it. And, more important, he was one hundred percent on her side.

"You're walking a fine line with me, McLeod," Boyd said testily. "But I'm going to overlook it this time since I know you've been through a lot this week. Now, get out there and bring me the evidence I need, or I'll let someone else take over, and you'll find yourself appointed as Mrs. Wilson's personal contact for all her future complaints."

Cora stormed straight down the hall to the kitchen, and Liam followed. She was so visibly angry, her hands shook as she tried to scoop coffee into the machine.

"Here, let me do it," Liam said, gently taking the bag from her.

"Make it extra strong," she said. "I mean it. Strong enough to knock some sense into me before I march right back into Thompson's office and show him the meaning of the word *scuffle*."

Liam raised a brow, but wisely said nothing. He tossed a few extra scoops into the filter, with Cora watching him like a hawk. She signaled for another scoop, and then she was satisfied.

When the bitter sludge from hell was finally brewing, she turned away and began to pace. "What is wrong with Captain Thompson? He's been under so much pressure, it's like he can't see reason."

"I believe you about Magnus," Liam said. "It's baffling that Boyd doesn't see it, too."

"He's a hardheaded man." Cora slumped into a chair near the vending machine. "Always has been. But until this moment,

I've always respected his judgment. Now I'm just floored that he could be so obtuse."

Liam agreed. He'd known Boyd his whole life, and even though it wasn't the same world, Boyd was essentially the same person. He was shrewd, enterprising and a bit hotheaded and boastful, but he wasn't stupid. In fact, he was usually quite good at seeing through a person's ruse. "We'll find a way to prove Magnus's guilt. Don't worry."

"How can I not?" She dropped her head into her hands. "We've just been ordered to take the investigation in a different direction, even though my gut instinct says it's wrong."

"Take heart, Officer McLeod. You've got me on your side." Liam hooked a chair leg with his foot and dragged it to sit beside Cora. "If there's one thing I've a lot of experience with, it's bending the rules."

"There's an irrefutable fact," she said through her fingers.

"Aye, well, it's true. I propose we follow Boyd's orders *on paper* but do a side investigation on our own. Between the two of us, we'll find the proof we need to convict Magnus in no time. It will be a pie walk."

She smiled. "Cakewalk."

"That, too. And did you see Boyd just now? The state of him! He looks five minutes away from falling flat on his face from exhaustion. If we're careful, he'll be none the wiser. Then, when we uncover the evidence needed to convict Magnus without a doubt, there will be nothing Boyd can say except, 'Excellent work, McLeod, O'Connor. I was so very wrong. Thank you for proving it. Here, have a raise. And please, take a month's vacation for all your hard work. Now, get out of my office before I change my mind.'"

This time Cora laughed, and Liam felt it all the way to the tips of his fingers and toes. He was going to do whatever it took to make her happy, and if he got to throw a degenerate scumbag like Magnus behind bars in the process, even better.

29

CORA STEPPED OFF THE ELEVATOR TO FINN'S penthouse on Saturday evening with Suzette and Liam right behind her. The first thing she noticed was the floor-to-ceiling window with a panoramic view of downtown Providence Falls at the end of the hallway.

"Wow," Suzette said for the third time since they'd entered the upscale building. She balanced a dessert platter on one hand, using her other to photograph the view with her phone. The hall to his penthouse was decorated the same as the lobby, with rich, monochromatic hues and silver accents. To the left of the elevators, a narrow table lined the wall with a vase of fresh flowers and greenery. "I didn't expect Finn Walsh to live in a place like this."

Cora was equally surprised, though it wouldn't be the first time Finn threw her for a loop. Yesterday he'd called Liam— another surprise, because she hadn't realized they'd become friends—to invite them all to his sister's going away party. Liam had accepted on behalf of all of them, and Cora didn't have the heart to refuse. Ever since Finn had helped rescue her, she'd felt a nagging sense of guilt about the way she'd treated him.

Granted, he'd been engaging in a dangerous, illegal activity the night of the cage fight, but he'd never meant for her to be involved. And now that her anger had dissipated, she had to admit it was nice to have him in her corner. He was a lot like the wickedly handsome Irishman standing beside her, except without the brash mannerisms and cocky attitude. Strange how Liam and Finn seemed so different, yet in essentials they had undeniable similarities.

"Where did you expect him to live, a barn?" Liam asked.

Suzette laughed. "I guess I just imagined him someplace like a basement apartment surrounded by video game monitors. Either that, or in a secret underground lair with bubbling test tubes. The latter being far cooler, of course."

"Because you have a thing for comic book villains?" Cora asked as Liam rang Finn's doorbell.

"I've always gravitated toward the bad boys," Suzette said with a sigh. "Which is why I'm never going to try sinking my hooks into Finn, even though he has a hot car, and this building makes my heart beat fast. I have zero interest in good guys, and he is good to the bone. I bet he doesn't even jaywalk for fear of breaking the law."

"You might be surprised," Cora said under her breath.

Liam shot her a curious glance just as the door opened.

"Cora, you made it! And you brought friends. Awesome." Finn's sister Genevieve stood in the entry, beaming at all of them. Her hair was pulled into a high ponytail, and she wore denim capris and a white tank top. With her vivacious smile and the sprinkling of freckles across her cheeks, she looked young and fresh faced and ready to conquer the world. In a way, Cora supposed that was exactly what Genevieve was setting out to do. She was heading off to New York City soon, excited to start her new life.

Genevieve gave Cora a quick hug, and Cora introduced her friends.

"I hope you're okay with Rice Krispies treats," Suzette said, pushing the tray of dessert into Genevieve's hands. "If not, blame Liam. He insisted."

"No, I love these," Genevieve said with a laugh. "They're a classic."

"We brought wine, too, just in case." Liam held up two bottles of Merlot.

"Even better. Come and have a drink. Finn's outside on the patio doing some magic on the grill." Genevieve led them through the foyer and into a spacious kitchen where a lively group of her friends was playing cards.

"Everyone, these are Finn's buddies," Genevieve announced over the music. She made introductions while a girl in a black sundress set a plate of hot artichoke dip on the table.

"Hey, I know you," she said, pointing at Suzette. "You work at the spa downtown." Suzette struck up a conversation with her while Liam followed Genevieve into the kitchen with the wine.

Cora wandered farther into Finn's home, admiring the gorgeous dark wood floors, the expansive open floor plan and the sleek, modern decor. It wasn't quite the old English library scene where she'd once imagined a stuffy version of Finn sitting by the fire sipping cognac, but then he'd already blown that image to smithereens. No, this place suited him much better. It was inviting, but also a little mysterious. The walls were a muted grayish blue with crisp white trim, and there was a deep gray accent wall in the kitchen. The sunken living room had dark leather furniture and a plush area rug in front of a giant flat-screen TV. Even though the place was distinctly masculine, Genevieve's decorative touch was noticeable. There were a few sparkly throw pillows on the sectional sofa, a fluffy pink blanket laid over an armchair and a pair of bunny slippers on the floor. A large, potted tree sat in the corner near a glass sliding door.

Cora caught sight of Finn outside at the grill, surrounded by a few men with pressed slacks and designer golf shirts who appeared to be his colleagues from work. Sunlight turned Finn's hair deep bronze, and it struck her how handsome and relaxed he looked with them. Then again, he'd seemed just as comfortable in a fight cage surrounded by a dangerous motorcycle gang, so what did she know? Not much. Though, if she was being perfectly honest with herself, she was deeply curious.

Cora wandered past the patio doors to a narrow hallway filled with beautifully framed photographs. Some were brilliant images of wildlife. A blue jay in flight. A deer silhouetted against the backdrop of the setting sun. A close-up of a fox staring through tall grass. Other frames held photos of landscapes and natural elements like tide pools and meadows speckled with wildflowers. Cora stopped in front of a few close-up images of seashells. They were so crisp and clear, with such attention to detail capturing the different textures and striations, she felt as if she were holding each shell in her hand.

"Beautiful," she breathed.

"Finn took them." Genevieve came up beside her and handed her a glass of wine, peering up at the photos. "He's always loved photography. When we were kids, he said he wanted to work for *National Geographic* and take pictures all around the world."

Cora smiled. "That sounds like a fun adventure."

"Yes, he always did love to travel. I think he might have done more of it, too, if he hadn't decided to go into law."

Cora remembered Finn's story about his father being unjustly accused. If that had never happened, what a different life he might have had. Her gaze roamed over the photos of lush mountain ranges and barren desert canyons, until she landed on an image of a man and woman at the beach. The pretty woman's head was thrown back, midlaugh, and the man looked awestruck. They were so clearly in love.

"My mom and dad," Genevieve said wistfully. Then she pointed to another photo of two little kids. "And that's me and Finn. As you can see, I was the bane of his existence."

Cora looked at the photo of the mischievous little girl in a polka dot swimsuit, grinning as she held a bucket of water over her older brother's head. He was busy building a sandcastle, oblivious to the deluge that was coming.

"What the picture doesn't show," Finn said from behind them, "is how I chased my sister down the beach with a hermit crab in retaliation. She was a tiny terror back then."

Cora turned to smile up at Finn. He'd just come in from the patio, and his windblown hair was a glorious mess. She had the ridiculous urge to reach out and ruffle her fingers through it.

Genevieve gasped in mock outrage. "I was perfect."

"Perfectly terrible, yes," Finn said, his eyes sparkling with amusement.

Genevieve nudged him with her shoulder, and Cora suddenly felt like an intruder. This was one of those sibling relationships she'd always wished for but never had.

Genevieve's phone chimed. "That's the timer for the baked brie. I have to go pull it from the oven." She was gone before Cora could respond.

Someone in the living room switched the music, and the crooning lyrics to "How Long Will I Love You?" floated in the air around them.

An awkward silence followed, where Cora was very aware of Finn standing beside her in the narrow hall. She hadn't seen him since the night he'd arrived with Liam at Magnus's lake house, and before that she'd only seen him at The Rolling Log. That was twice he'd rescued her, three if she counted the time he'd hauled her over his shoulder during the barn fight. She suddenly felt sheepish and a little shy.

"How've you been?" he asked softly.

"Oh, I'm fine." Cora waved a hand like the fiasco with Magnus at the lake had been no big deal. "All in a day's work, you know?"

Finn wasn't amused. "I hope Magnus gets the book thrown at him."

"Me, too," Cora said with a sigh. "But he's not going to go down without a fight."

A muscle clenched in Finn's jaw, and for a second Cora remembered how he'd looked as the undefeated Jackrabbit. She had so many things she wanted to ask him. It was strange how long she'd known Finn, but never really *known* him. Now that she'd seen a secret piece of his past, there was an intimacy between them she hadn't expected. Maybe this is what happened when you each witnessed the other's potential downfall. His in the cage fight, and hers in the lake.

"Finn." Even though she was uncomfortable, Cora forced the words out because he deserved an apology. "I'm sorry I was so hard on you back at the barn that night. I was just really scared for you, and it made me so angry to think you could've gotten hurt because of me."

"Don't apologize." He looked pained. "You did nothing wrong, Cora. All of that was my own doing. Let's just put it behind us, okay?"

She nodded. "Thank you for the other night at the lake. You helped Liam find me, and I'll never forget that."

"He really cares for you," Finn said quietly.

She looked up in surprise. "Liam? Yes, he's a good friend."

Finn leaned a shoulder against the wall, staring into his wineglass. "I saw you both on the dock."

"Hmm?" Heat flooded her face, and she pretended to examine one of the photographs. Please don't let this go where she thought it was going to go.

"Together."

Crappity crap crap. He was talking about that frantic kiss she'd given Liam after he pulled her from the water. What was she supposed to say to that? "Oh, right. I was feeling a little crazy from adrenaline. It was a weird night."

"Understatement of the year," Finn said with an attempt at levity.

She didn't know how else to respond. There wasn't anything going on between her and Liam. Not yet, anyway. "Can you please forget what you saw?"

"Of course." Finn's expression became unreadable. He was so good at that. "I only meant you deserve to be happy, Cora. And if he gives you that, then I'm glad for you both."

"What are you glad about?" Liam sauntered up and slapped Finn on the back. Again, it struck her that Liam was acting so friendly with Finn. It seems they must've bonded when they saved her that night.

"He's glad that I'm happy," Cora said quickly.

Rowdy laughter erupted from the kitchen table. Suzette and Genevieve's friends were slapping cards down and hollering over each other.

"Did you tell them the news?" Genevieve called to Finn from the kitchen.

Finn shot her the type of familiar, reproving look that only a sibling could. "It's not official, yet."

"What is it?" Cora asked, lifting her glass to her lips.

Finn lowered his voice. "I've been offered a job in New York City. I'll be going at the end of the summer."

Liam choked on his beer.

Cora lowered her wineglass, feeling a hollow, twisty sensation in the pit of her stomach. Finn couldn't leave. He was a part of this place. He'd grown up here and belonged here. "You would leave Providence Falls?"

"It's the same firm that offered my sister the internship. They've actually been trying to recruit me for a while." Finn's expression grew pensive. "I never thought I'd go, but it's been a strange year. And after this whole thing with Magnus, Johnston & Knight's going to have a hell of a time rebuilding its reputation. Seems like a good time to move in a new direction."

"It's a terrible time," Liam sputtered. "You have to stay here." He looked so upset, Cora was shocked. She hadn't realized he cared so much.

"Liam's right," she told Finn. "You're *from* here. If you left, it would be like…" She tried to find words that wouldn't sound melodramatic. Cora didn't have a huge family growing up. It was probably why the people of Providence Falls—especially her friends—were so important to her. Somewhere along the way, Finn had become one of the people she didn't want to lose. "It would be like losing a piece of what makes this city truly *good*. You belong here with us."

Finn looked surprised. So did Liam.

So much for not sounding melodramatic. She needed to lighten up. "Just don't make any rash decisions, that's all. You're a great lawyer, and we'd be very sorry to see you go." There, that was more logical.

Finn dipped his head. "I've already discussed it with the partners at the firm, so everything's pretty much set."

Don't go! a tiny voice inside her cried, but she smothered it. She had no right to demand anything of Finn. It was ultimately his choice. So why did she feel like something monumental hung in the balance? People switched jobs and moved away all the time. This shouldn't be any different.

"Don't be an idiot, man." Liam glowered at Finn as though he'd just said he was going skydiving without a parachute. "Cora's right. You need to stay here, and that's the end of it."

Finn chuckled, which only made Liam angrier. Cursing under his breath, Liam stormed outside to the terrace.

"Wow," Finn said, watching Liam march to the balcony and stare out at the horizon. "I didn't know he cared so much."

Cora could only shake her head, because neither did she. It seemed Liam had formed some kind of attachment to Finn, but it didn't make any sense. They'd only just become friends.

"I should go check on the dinner," Finn said. "Do you want another drink?"

"No, thank you." She forced a smile, but it fell the moment he walked away. Liam was throwing a silent fit outside, and Cora wanted to join him. He was leaning against the balcony railing and appeared to be talking to himself. Whatever he was saying, he looked as frustrated as she felt.

"My brother told you the news?" Genevieve walked up in an apron, holding an oven mitt.

"Yes. I wasn't expecting it."

"Neither was I. They'd been headhunting him for years, but he always turned them down. I just figured there was something very important keeping him here." She paused, then added, "Or someone."

"Family does make it hard to leave," Cora said, keeping her eye on Liam outside.

"I was talking about—"

"Cora," Suzette called from the kitchen table. She was in a laughing argument with one of the guys. "Come and play this terrible card game. I need backup because these people are animals."

Cora looked back at Liam, who was still on the patio. He was talking and gesturing with his hands, but there was no one out there. Maybe he was using one of those Bluetooth headsets. He was clearly in a heated conversation. But with whom?

Liam suddenly looked her way. With a fake, plastic smile that didn't fool her for a second, he lifted his hand and waved.

Cora waved back. *What are you up to out there?*

"Ah," Genevieve said as if she understood the answer to a puzzle. "That makes sense."

"What?" Cora dragged her gaze back to Finn's sister.

"I'm biased, of course. But that guy?" She nodded to Liam. "I get it." With a knowing smile, Genevieve went back to the kitchen.

Cora was too focused on Liam's odd behavior to respond. His gaze kept darting to the railing, and he'd toned down his hand gestures. She once caught a kid leaving a grocery store with his pockets full of stolen candy. Liam had that same guilty look on his face. He glanced back at her once more, then turned away sharply. She felt as if she'd just been dismissed. Whatever was going on with him, he didn't want to share it with her. That hurt. Maybe he was talking to another woman. That possibility hurt even more. She had no right to feel possessive, but she couldn't help it.

Suzette let out a squeal, and the group at the kitchen table hollered like a pack of banshees. A man with a goatee sitting across from Suzette fanned out his cards and pumped his fist in triumph.

"That's it," Suzette said. "You're all going down because I'm bringing out my secret weapon. Cora!"

With a final glance at Liam on the balcony, Cora made her way to the kitchen.

Suzette took one look at her face and told the people at the table, "I need a minute." To the man with the goatee, she added, "No peeking at my cards while I'm gone, or I'll sic my friend on you, and she fights dirty."

Suzette led her down the hall and into the bathroom. Once the door was shut, she spun around and crossed her arms. "What's wrong? You have that look you always get right before you cry."

"I do not," Cora said, doing her best to gather herself together.

"Do, too. Your face is doing that sad, lost-puppy-in-the-rain thing."

"I'm fine." Cora rolled her eyes.

"Cool, cool." Suzette studied her hair in the mirror and began smoothing it. "Now, tell me what's really going on."

"I don't know," Cora said with a heavy sigh. "Finn just told us he's moving to New York City at the end of the summer."

"Wow." Suzette stopped fixing her hair. "That really sucks."

"It does," Cora said. "But it's not just that. I don't know what's wrong with me. I'm all mixed-up inside."

"Just tell Finn you like him, and you don't want him to go," Suzette said. "Anyone can see you guys would make a great couple. He'd be a fool to leave you."

"That's not the problem."

"Look, if you're worried, don't be. I'm a zillion percent sure he's into you."

"Suze, I'm sorry Finn's leaving, but this isn't about him." Cora took a deep breath and exhaled in a rush. "I think I'm falling in love with Liam."

Suzette raised a russet brow and slowly leaned against the counter. "Whoa."

"Yeah, and he doesn't feel the same," Cora said miserably. "I casually brought up the fact that I had feelings for him at lunch the other day, and he said he didn't want to do anything to jeopardize our friendship."

"Oh, I hate that excuse." Suzette looked disgusted. "If a guy really wants you, then he's not going to let anything stand in the way."

"I think he might still have feelings for his ex, or maybe he's seeing someone else. I have no idea." Cora rubbed her temples. "It's so weird because I swear a part of him feels the way I do. He even agreed that when we kissed the other night, it felt right."

"Hold up." Suzette lifted her hand. "You *kissed* him?"

Cora nodded. "Briefly."

"Okay, first of all, you're in trouble for not telling me sooner. But that can wait. More important, he kissed you back and agreed it felt right?"

"Yeah, but then he said something about our paths not running parallel." Cora shook her head in frustration. "All I know is for whatever reason, he isn't interested in starting something with me."

"Then *make* him interested," Suzette said with a wicked gleam in her eye.

Cora stared warily at her friend. Whenever Suzette got that look on her face, wild things ensued. "How?"

"Oh, honey. You're brilliant, you're beautiful and more important, you *live* with the guy. The opportunities are endless. For starters, we need to go shopping." Suzette began laying out all the ways Cora could lure Liam over to "the dark side," and by the time they rejoined the people at the kitchen table, Cora's head was spinning with possibilities.

Suzette's grand scheme was way over-the-top, but Cora was in a much lighter mood because, if nothing else, it gave her hope. Liam had feelings for her; she was certain. They'd only kissed the one time, but there was no way he could deny the spark between them. She was determined to make him realize it. If it didn't work, then at least she'd know she'd tried. He was an enigma; one moment familiar, the next moment a mystery. But Cora was good at solving mysteries. Whatever was really going on with Liam, she felt certain she could help him overcome it. They were meant to be more than just friends; the connection they shared was undeniable. She just needed to find a way to show him. From now on, no matter what obstacles came their way, Cora was bound and determined to make it happen.

EPILOGUE

LIAM BRACED HIS ELBOWS ON THE RAILING OF Finn's penthouse terrace. It was late evening, and the setting sun washed the downtown view of Providence Falls in glorious shades of crimson and fuchsia and gold. The people below looked tiny, like insects going about their business, and Liam wondered if this is what mere mortals looked like to the angels. Maybe to them, human lives were just as small and insignificant.

The music on the terrace stereo began playing a slow song about falling into a ring of fire. A single white dove swooped from overhead, floating on the wind in front of him for a moment before flying off toward the setting sun. Liam closed his eyes, and when he opened them, Samael and Agon were sitting on the railing on either side of him.

"I wondered when you were going to show up," Liam said, still watching the horizon.

"The dove was adequate notification?" Agon asked.

"It was your best hint yet."

Agon looked pleased, but he was always upbeat, even when Liam's life was falling apart. Samael, on the other hand, looked subdued and maybe even a little sad. This was new to Liam, and therefore, alarming. If Samael looked depressed, then Liam's chances must truly be abysmal.

He pushed away from the balcony railing. "Just tell me now if I've no hope to succeed. Cora is falling for me. And now Finn says he's moving up north to New York. Nothing is going right, and before you say it, I know. I *know* I've only a few weeks left. And things are worse now than they were in the beginning."

"All is not lost, rogue," Samael said. "There's still a bit of time."

Liam flung his hands in the air. "All I've managed to do is make a mess of things, time and again."

"Let us reflect on what has gone right," Agon said kindly. "But first, what is this lovely device?" He floated to the stone fire pit in the center of Finn's terrace.

"For ambience," Liam said distractedly.

Agon studied it, his dark eyes gleaming with interest.

"Absolutely not," Samael said to Agon. "The Chamber of Judgment is cluttered enough as it is. Don't think I haven't noticed the new floor blanket."

"Rug," Agon corrected.

Liam caught sight of Cora watching him through the glass doors. He pasted a smile on his face. "Can Cora see the two of you?" he asked the angels through his teeth.

"No," Agon said. "She only sees you right now."

"Talking to myself? Great." Liam gave her a nervous wave, then tried to tone down his expressions. From the look on her face, she wasn't convinced everything was fine. If he wasn't careful, she'd be out here to investigate. Liam turned his back on the glass doors.

"Cora has had an interesting adventure with Finn recently," Samael said. "It counts as progress."

"Yes," Agon agreed. "There's still a glimmer of hope on the horizon."

"You mean the adventure where Finn helped me rescue her from Magnus? That backfired in a spectacular fashion. She *kissed* me."

"And you kissed her back, ruffian," Samael said reprovingly. "But we were speaking of a different night she shared with Finn."

Before Liam had a moment to reflect on this, Samael continued. "She now sees Finley Walsh in a much more favorable light."

A night she shared with Finn. Liam knew he should be glad, but he couldn't quite dredge up the feeling. When the hell had they shared a night together? There were too many emotions warring inside him right now, jealousy being one of them. He knew it was wrong, but he just couldn't help it. "Well, that's all fine and good, but Cora fancies me now. She told me so."

"Yes, but how did you respond when she told you?" Samael asked. "Think."

Liam ran his hands through his hair in frustration, then leaned on the railing and watched the last sliver of the setting sun just as it disappeared. "I said what I had to in order for her to see the truth." The painful truth.

"Which is?" Samael floated over the railing and faced him, blocking his view of the horizon. Agon joined him. Their snowy wings unfurled in the wind as they hovered in the air. Their gazes bored into his soul with infinite wisdom, and if Liam had known the truth before, now he felt the epiphany like a lance through the heart. It seared him from the inside out.

"I'm not right for her," he whispered. The razor-sharp truth of it sliced into him from all sides. "I love her, but... She deserves a better man." He knew once he spoke the words into the wind, he couldn't take them back. He almost hated the angels in that moment, for making him rise above his old ways and see farther than himself. "She told me I wasn't like Magnus, but she has no idea how wrong she is. I've been selfish and uncaring of consequences my whole life, just like him."

Agon and Samael were silent, for once.

"That's why you arranged for Magnus to cross paths with me, isn't it?" Liam asked, not expecting an answer. He already knew. "He's a reflection of my own flaws."

Again, they were silent, which was answer enough.

Liam swallowed hard and dropped his head into his hands. "What should I do?"

"Love her enough to let her go," Samael said.

"I have complete faith in you, ruffian," Agon added kindly. "You and Magnus may share some similarities, but at his core, he's missing something that you have in abundance."

"What's that?"

The dark-haired angel smiled softly. "I'll tell you another time."

"Of course," Liam mumbled. Always with the secrets, these two. "Can you at least tell me why it's so important for them to be together? *Why* must she be with Finn?"

Samael and Agon exchanged a long look, in which Liam was certain they were having a private discussion.

He didn't expect an answer, so when they stood on either side of him, enveloped him in their snowy wings and rose into the sky, Liam almost jumped out of his skin. With growing alarm, he watched Finn's terrace become smaller and smaller as they rose through the atmosphere toward someplace far beyond.

And then they showed him.

Later, Liam wished he'd never asked for answers, but it was too late for him to go back to blissful ignorance now. All his desires were nothing compared to what hung in the balance. Cora *had* to embrace her true destiny with Finn. This time, no matter what obstacles came their way, Liam was bound and determined to make it happen.

★ ★ ★ ★ ★